About the author

Blair Wylie is a retired Canadian oil and gas engineer and manager. He worked thirty-five years in a number of interesting places, including the Arctic, Western Siberia, the North Sea, Newfoundland, and Trinidad and Tobago. In his second career as a writer, he prefers to stay in the plausible world with respect to science, and character studies. His stories place everyday people in awkward if not outright terrifying situations, then have them discover hidden strengths while they rescue themselves. He hopes readers will come away feeling better about themselves, and about the future in general.

WOLF SLAYER

Blair Wylie

WOLF SLAYER

Vanguard Press

VANGUARD PAPERBACK

© Copyright 2019
Blair Wylie

The right of Blair Wylie to be identified as author of
this work has been asserted by him in accordance with the
Copyright, Designs and Patents Act 1988.

All Rights Reserved

No reproduction, copy or transmission of this publication
may be made without written permission.
No paragraph of this publication may be reproduced,
copied or transmitted save with the written permission of the
publisher, or in accordance with the provisions
of the Copyright Act 1956 (as amended).

Any person who commits any unauthorised act in relation to
this publication may be liable to criminal
prosecution and civil claims for damages.

A CIP catalogue record for this title is
available from the British Library.

ISBN: 978 1 784657 2 46

*Vanguard Press is an imprint of
Pegasus Elliot MacKenzie Publishers Ltd.*
www.pegasuspublishers.com

First Published in 2019

**Vanguard Press
Sheraton House Castle Park
Cambridge England**

Printed & Bound in Great Britain

Also by the author

The *Master Defiance* Series:

Wolf Slayer

Master Defiance

Tube Dwellers

Tube Survivors

Covert Alliance

The Perils of Isolation

1

Earth History, Second Chance Archive, Reference 2483.000:

The year 2483 was marked by increasing worldwide civil unrest. As always, the people of Earth were divided. There were secular divisions based upon the concept of Nationhood. There were also religious, political, racial, cultural and economic schisms within nations themselves.

A cynic might argue that the history of humanity is essentially the history of terrible conflicts. The more recent conflicts were struggles over the remaining and vastly diminished 'turf'. The resources of the world were mostly depleted. The devastating effects of over-population, climate change and pollution had impoverished most of the planet.

However, to save the human species, there was worldwide support for establishing a colony on a planet that looked to be Earth-like, using the best technology then available. The task was monumental, but many people living on Earth, and within a subsurface Moon base, were passionately engaged with the construction of the massive Second Chance generation spaceship.

The partially completed vessel was now maintaining itself in a stable orbit around the Moon. In spite of the myriad of problems on Earth, the project was still on track for completion in 2514.

The Second Chance had been designed to run virtually by itself for thousands of years. By exploiting centripetal acceleration, the inside surface of its massive, spinning, cylindrical hull would provide the equivalent of Earth's surface gravity. The interior living spaces of the spaceship would also provide carefully-selected flora and fauna with a self-sustaining ecosystem approaching the complexity of Earth's.

After a globe-spanning and highly convoluted, partially political process, it was eventually agreed that 'Tube World', or the interior living space of the Second Chance, would start out with six thousand people that met or exceeded very exacting standards. This initial population would be above every scientist's theoretical 'Minimum Viable Population' for the maintenance of a healthy gene pool. But the selection of the original 'Tube Dwellers' was still many years away.

The Moon is basically a small planet that orbits the Earth instead of the Sun. The Moon has one-sixth the gravity of the Earth and it has no appreciable atmosphere. So, it is a lot easier to launch things into space from the Moon than from the Earth.

The international Moon Base had been greatly expanded by the nation-states that had agreed to work together to build the Second Chance. The expansion of the base took advantage of lava tubes discovered on the Moon. Lava tubes provide natural radiation shielding, and engineers devised ways to effectively seal them to make them airtight.

The Second Chance was being assembled in orbit around the Moon, mostly using modules built inside the Moon Base. Some things just had to be built on Earth, however, and sent at great cost to the orbital construction site. But most of the mass of the ship would be Moon mass.

The predominant construction material was high compressive strength concrete made from Moon rock. The composite material was reinforced by high tensile strength synthetic fibres. The concrete, or 'mooncrete', could also be made completely airtight by adding layers of an epoxy-fibre fabric. Mooncrete could also withstand the vacuum and extreme temperature variations of space quite well, and it also functioned as an efficient gamma ray shield.

Air would be manufactured on the Moon for the Second Chance by exploiting the deposits of frozen water on the Moon, and the enormous energy generated by fusion reactors. The air manufacturing sub-project had not yet begun.

The people living and working in the Moon Base had managed to largely ignore a major war that occurred on Earth during the Second Chance construction activity. It greatly helped that some of the world's wealthiest people, known collectively as the 'benevolent oligarchs', took a personal interest in seeing the project completed.

The emergence of a demented, fascist and malevolent American president threatened to destroy the Second Chance at an advanced stage of construction. But a covert organization was forming with the intent of stopping the president from destroying the Second Chance, and starting another war…

2

Mathieu 'Matt' Adams took the last seat in the very cramped waiting area of the Veterans Affairs Centre in El Paso, Texas. There were already eleven other honourably-discharged US Army veterans tightly jammed together in the tiny room.

The room was decrepit, and badly in need of a thorough cleaning, and a new paint job. It also smelled heavily of body odor. Flies were buzzing around everywhere, and there was a creaky, wobbly and obviously very old fan spinning overhead. The fan was feebly circulating the very warm air in the room. Like everywhere else in Texas, an air conditioner was a long-forgotten luxury of the past.

It was Monday, August 9, 2483, and the peak of the especially hot and dry season. It was also early morning. Matt cringed to think what the VA Centre would be like later in the day.

These days, the winters in El Paso were not much better than the summers. But then again, west Texas had always been desert-like.

For many years now, people living in the rest of the United States had thought of winter as the cool and stormy season. And summers were viewed as the hot and thunder-stormy season. And all storms were now very violent, and usually damaging events.

Things were tough everywhere in the US, and the rundown, malodorous condition of the El Paso VA Centre was not unusual.

Like the other veterans in the waiting room, Matt was proudly wearing his last dress uniform, even though it made the intensifying heat even more oppressive. Matt's uniform, however, was by far the one that attracted the most interest.

No one said anything to Matt, of course. The military tradition was to casually observe, and then demonstrate proper respect by showing complete disinterest.

But the outrageous display of medals precisely arrayed on Matt's massive chest was *way* beyond the conceivable.

Matt had a jagged, inflamed-looking scar on his forehead, and he wore an eyepatch over his left eye socket. The VA doctors were going to try to fit a fully-functional artificial eye in that socket, but they said some more restorative surgery would be needed first. Matt's next scheduled preparatory surgery had just been pushed out again by another year.

The United States was essentially bankrupt, and the miniscule VA budget had just been trimmed yet again.

Like most veterans, Matt had been struggling to find work. There had been a fully-fledged worldwide economic depression for over three decades now. But the VA had just sent him an impressive-looking letter that asked him to book a time in the El Paso VA Centre for a 'special job interview'. Matt had jumped at the opportunity.

Surprisingly, Matt did not have to wait long to hear his name called. No one said anything as he made his way to the reception desk, but he could tell the other veterans were really pissed that he seemed to have jumped the queue somehow.

The receptionist was young and pretty, and surprisingly cheerful. She smiled at Matt, and with a Hispanic accent, she said pleasantly, "Please follow me, Mister Staff Sergeant Adams. Colonel Boudreaux, he is ready for you now."

The receptionist led Matt to the open door of Colonel Boudreaux's rear-section, poorly-lit and dusty office. Then she left him on his own. Matt knocked on the door frame, took one pace inside the room and came to full attention. He waited almost a full minute for the colonel to finish reading something on his cluttered desk. When the colonel finally looked up, Matt saluted him, and held the salute. The colonel grunted, rose from his seat and quickly snapped off a smart salute of his own. Then the colonel said gruffly, "At ease, retired Staff Sergeant, and take a seat."

Colonel Boudreaux sat down again, and started reading something else on his massive, cluttered desk. Matt figured the colonel must also be a retired veteran, in his late sixties probably. His working uniform showed he had mostly been with US Army artillery units, and had seen some sort of action in the Eurasian theatre. He was a stocky, rather short man, with thick, wavy grey hair, black-rimmed glasses and a tanned, wrinkly but handsome face.

After another couple of minutes, Colonel Boudreaux sighed, crumpled up the single-sheet document he had been reading, and then threw the wadded-up ball at a large overflowing trash can that was placed against the wall on Matt's left.

Colonel Boudreaux stared at Matt's face for a long moment. Then he growled hoarsely, "Let's see, I have your service record here, Staff Sergeant, somewhere in this heap of bureaucratic nonsense. Oh yes, here it is.

"Staff Sergeant Mathieu Adams, honourably discharged on the third of March in the year 2483. That was about six months' ago.

"Mathieu is French, isn't it? Are you Louisiana Cajun, like me?"

"My mother was Quebecois-Cree Metis," Matt replied proudly. "Louisiana Cajuns were once Acadians, French-speaking people kicked out of Nova Scotia by the British well before Canada became a country. So, I suppose we may have some common roots, sir."

"I know my damn history too, Staff Sergeant," Colonel Boudreaux snapped off in reply.

Matt reacted by simply saying, "Sorry, sir."

Matt's tone of voice and body language did not betray his anger stemming from the rebuke. He had many encounters over his very active military career with officers who figured enlisted soldiers were all idiotic poor people who could never get into a proper high school, let alone a good university. Matt was saddened by the thought that Boudreaux might fit the stereotype of an elitist, probably racist officer. They were common in the Army now, with the rise of American fascism.

"And you should completely forget about *Canada*, Staff Sergeant. It was absorbed by the US over a century ago. You are an *American* citizen, now and forever, and a civilian again. At least as an American citizen *veteran* you will now be allowed to vote, unlike the 'great unwashed' out there."

Colonel Boudreaux chuckled at his own crude joke, and went back to studying the piece of paper he was still holding in his right hand. Then he said, "Born and raised in Baie-Comeau, Quebec, wherever the hell that is. You told the Army you have English, Irish, French and indigenous heritage. Well, none of us could pick our parents, but your genes don't look too bad. Age thirty-four. That's still quite young, Staff Sergeant. But I suppose you're really lucky to be alive at all.

"Fourteen years with the 75th Ranger Airborne Light Infantry Division. Central America Service Medal. A sniper for almost three years. Sharpshooter with the MK49 semi-automatic rifle, and the M209 extreme long-range, fifty-calibre, bolt-action rifle.

"How many men did you kill as a sniper, Staff Sergeant?"

Matt was shocked by the question. He was not proud of that part of his military record. But after hesitating for only a few seconds, Matt replied, "Two hundred and four, sir. All enemy soldiers and officers."

"Then, you were right up there with the World War Two Russian commie, Vasily Zaitsev. See, I really do know my history, Adams. But I for one won't denigrate your accomplishments. You *should* be a famous guy. But the press never talked about you, for some reason. I guess we should have done better in the war for them, or something like that.

"Medals for Good Conduct, Meritorious Service, Purple Heart, twice, no three times. Also Bronze Star, Soldier's Medal, Legion of Merit, Silver Star, Distinguished Service Cross and the holiest-of-holies, the Medal of Honor. You were a regular Audie Murphy hero, Staff Sergeant, only you are obviously not the old-fashioned Hollywood type. Not any more, anyway, with that eye missing and that ugly scar on your forehead."

Matt wondered why Colonel Boudreaux was being so crude and disrespectful. In a flash he concluded the colonel was probably jealous, and a bit of a bully. Matt figured the colonel's military career must have been a whole lot less exciting than his own had been.

Colonel Boudreaux used his right index finger to trace down to the very bottom of the piece of paper he was still holding on to, and then he growled, "Finished your career as First Sergeant, First Ranger Battalion. Seriously injured by the improvised explosive device that killed your commanding officer, Lieutenant Colonel Herbert Barrymore. That earned you your third Purple Heart, and an honourable discharge.

"And now you are struggling to live on a puny veteran's disability pension. And you are probably actively looking for work, and not doing very well at that. Millions of lesser and greater people than you are struggling the same way, of course.

"Your situation is not your fault in any way, and I'll admit, it's a tough break.

"So, would you like a job, retired Staff Sergeant, perhaps doing something that would really help out your country, too?"

"Yes, Colonel Boudreaux," replied Matt immediately. "What have you got in mind for me, sir?"

Colonel Boudreaux abruptly stood up, spun around on his right heel and marched over to the grimy, half-open window behind his desk. The screen in the lower part of the window was rusty and full of holes. While staring out of the filthy glass part of the window, Boudreaux said quietly, "Close the door behind you, Staff Sergeant."

Matt jumped up to obey the command, then he stood at ease in front of the closed door. Colonel

Boudreaux turned around, and then stood at ease with his back to the window. Then he said sternly, "What you hear now inside this room, Staff Sergeant, must always be treated as *top secret*, no matter what you decide to do next.

"Army Intelligence thinks there may be some kind of trouble brewing in Akron, Ohio, of all places. We know there have been a few clandestine meetings by a group that calls itself the 'Workers Social Club', or something like that. All of their communication is by word of mouth, so we don't know much about them.

"There is only one political party allowed in the United States, and that is the Veterans Party. When you vote now in the federal election, for the first time in your life, you will only be voting for congressmen and senators. They pick the president and vice-president of course, by some means or another.

"So, when the Army, as an integral part of the government, thinks a revolutionary movement might be starting up, we immediately investigate, *discreetly*, and then we stamp it out, *completely and ruthlessly*. That's just the way of it.

"If you love your country, and your fellow veterans, you can help us out by looking into this suspected bunch of pinko, long-haired rebels in Akron. You will file informal, hand-written reports by regular mail to, ah, *Mister Cranston P. Snord*, your assigned pseudonym for Army Intelligence. They'll know a letter is from you just by that name written on the envelope, and your handwriting.

"They don't want you to date your letters for some reason. The postmark will provide that to them I guess, as well as the point of origin.

"You know, the more I think about it, the envelopes probably will get stapled to the back of your letters for filing purposes. That part is all a bit bureaucratic, and probably nonsensical. But we're not to question those things.

"Keep your letters brief, and write them like you're updating a friend. And provide information *indirectly*, you know, by alluding to things, and skirting around the edges. Mail doesn't work very well these days. Letters could be intercepted, and we have to be careful. Still, it's safer than making a cell phone call. The mailing address you will use will be somewhere pretty close to Akron. You'll get that later, before you leave today.

"If you want to proceed, also before you leave today, I'll get you to write out a copy of your military record so Army Intelligence can have an example of your handwriting on file.

"Your disability pension payments will be suspended until you re-register after this assignment. Your pay will be room and board, and you can also work as a road repair labourer and flagman for a patriotic government contractor, at minimum wage of course. All you'll mostly have to do is turn a 'stop-and-go' sign around to control traffic, which isn't very heavy these days, anywhere. So, no big deal really.

"Your flat won't be very nice, but that's part of your cover story. You're supposed to be just another starving, oppressed worker. Use your cover alias to get invited to a Social Club meeting. Work your way up the organization ladder to get access to more information, you know, the good stuff. Then tell us what they're up to, that's all. We'll handle the rest. And when the Military Police or the FBI make their move, well, they'll know who you are, and they'll let you go.

"I can't promise you anything more than that. If you do a good job, and don't get found out and killed by these traitorous bastards, maybe there'll be some other job you can do for your country. But who can know for sure? We live in uncertain times in a very harsh world.

"So, do you want this job or not, retired Staff Sergeant Adams?"

"Yes, Colonel Boudreaux, I'll take the job!" Matt barked immediately. "And thank you, sir!"

"Okay, great," Colonel Boudreaux said with just a hint of a smile. "So, you'll need a new identity. Hmmm, let's see. Your new name will be, ah, ah… *Audie Zaitsev*! Yes, that's good! You were injured as a flagman when a hit-and-run truck driver knocked you into a ditch in Cleveland, Ohio. And you are a native Buckeye, born and raised in Cleveland. You have a fairly nondescript accent, so that will work okay.

"We'll fill in more of your new life history before you leave today. You will memorize that history *perfectly*, and an intelligence officer will grill you hard to make sure you don't mess it up. Sign all of your letters to Army Intelligence, or rather Mister Cranston P. Snord, as *Audie Zaitsev*.

"You've now got one week to get ready. We won't pay for storage, so you might want to sell everything you own except for your favourite civilian clothes. You can put that dress uniform complete with your many medals in a secure locker in this VA Centre. It'll be okay there until you come back to claim it, if you ever do.

"You'll be travelling by train in lower class, so it will be a long, rough and dangerous journey. But you're a tough guy, and you'll figure out how to survive it.

"We'll give you a two month rail pass. That should be more than enough to get you there all right. The best route to take will be El Paso, San Antonio, Dallas, St. Louis, Chicago then Cleveland. All trains are milk runs now, and they break down *a lot*. And lots of people make a living selling food and drink to travellers when trains stop. So you probably won't starve or die of thirst. We'll also give you a bit of travel money, but if you get robbed, well, you'll be completely on your own.

"You'll have to take a bus to get to Akron from Cleveland. Bus service is even less reliable than train service, so the more I think about it, you might have to improvise a bit to complete your journey. But you'll figure something out, I'm sure.

"Now, go sit in the next room, the empty one. Look out the window, or something. An intelligence guy will visit you in an hour or so to take this induction process the rest of the way. He'll be dressed like a civilian. Don't ask him for his name. He won't tell you anyway. And when he's done with you, forget what his face looks like, for your own good.

"Okay, that's it, *Audie*. Don't bother saluting before you leave. Get into your new identity, starting *right now*!"

3

Ernie Wolf was President of the United States. His unmarried mother had been an illegal German immigrant. She was also a less-than-successful stripper, who dreamed of being a porn actress. She had named her unwanted baby Ernst, because the name had sounded sexy to her. She had only used her stage name, Candy Fitzwilly, so the surname Wolff might not have been her own either.

When Ernie was just three years old, Candy drove off with a truck driver, and was never seen again by her slum tenement neighbours. Ernie was found wandering the dangerous and filthy hallways of the twice-condemned tenement building by an elderly, kind-hearted lady. She took him into her modest flat, and then tried to raise him as best she could.

Not surprisingly, Ernie was very troubled, and he developed into a really bad kid. He spent very little time at home or at school. He basically grew up with a street gang. Then he joined the US Army to dodge a prison sentence for theft.

His military career was less than stellar. In fact, he spent most of his three-year term of service working kitchen-duty in a logistical-supply outfit. But military service was military service, and it opened a few doors for him.

A major armed conflict initially went very badly for the United States, especially in Central America. Six months into the war, the 'Conservative Family Party' won the presidency, and a slight House and Senate majority. During their campaign, the Conservatives blamed the 'Liberal Labour Party' for completely mismanaging the war. And they were touting a mysterious, unsubstantiated conspiracy as the only way the Liberals had managed to win *any* seats in the previous election. The Conservatives also shamelessly admitted that their prolonged gerrymandering of Electoral College districts had not been enough to keep the socialist-leaning 'non-patriots' out of office.

Right after the election, and very unusually, the Conservative Family Party held another convention. After many heated and protracted discussions, they eventually agreed it would be best to rename and re-brand themselves as the 'Veterans Party'. They decided that point-forward, only honourably-discharged veterans could become new party members. And to 'ensure national security' they wanted only American-born citizens, who were at least second-generation, to serve in the armed forces. And furthermore, if re-elected with a clear majority, they promised that only military people on active service, and honourably-discharged veterans, would be allowed to vote in future elections, 'because their loyalty to the nation was unquestionable.'

The war started to go slightly better for the United States, but frustratingly, three years later it ended in a humiliating stalemate. After the brutal war, and decades of economic depression, the US was no longer a world power, and it did not command a military advantage over its rivals.

The possession and testing of nuclear weapons had been banned for centuries by a multi-national treaty. The treaty signatories had feared that wartime escalation would likely result in complete world destruction. But some countries, like the United States, did not sign on to the treaty. The US argued that it needed, 'a strong deterrent against retaliation and aggression,' since it had made a lot of enemies over its war-filled, turbulent history.

The state of the US nuclear arsenal was uncertain, but because of lack of funding over many years, the arsenal was suspected by both allies and foes alike to be decrepit, and possibly unsafe.

Most of the world was *de facto* run by wealthy dictators, who openly and proudly called themselves 'oligarchs'. In their minds, the occasional war was good for business, but a *world war* was something to be avoided at all costs. And the network of oligarchs blamed the United States for starting the last major conflict that almost became a world war.

The only thing to show for the last war from the US perspective was a re-defined border with Mexico. The new southern border averaged about one hundred fifty miles further south than the previous border. Right after the truce treaty was signed, the US extensively mined a ten-mile-wide 'de-militarized buffer zone' on the US side of the new border.

Thanks to a thoroughly disgruntled electorate, the Veterans Party won the next Presidential, House and Senate elections by a landslide. Then the Veterans Party banned all other political parties, unanimously passed the necessary constitutional amendments, and fulfilled all of their campaign promises.

When Private Ernst Wolff was unceremoniously but honourably discharged from the US Army, he joined the Veterans Party. He was immediately encouraged by his new friends in the party to change his name, 'because people might suspect he was a neo-Nazi, or something.' The newly-named Ernie Wolf had agreed without hesitation, because he had high political ambitions. And of course his mother was long gone from his life, and would not have cared about the name change anyway.

The irony was that Ernie Wolf was *very much* a neo-Nazi. And he almost certainly would have been recruited by the SS in Hitler's Germany. He was tall, blond, handsome, blue-eyed, white-skinned, atheistic and very Nordic-looking. In other words, Ernie was perfectly 'Aryan', according to the misguided German Nazi criteria for classifying that fictitious super-race. Ernie could never have proven, of course, that he did not have any so-called 'Jewish blood'. But that might have been overlooked in Hitler's Germany, because there was no proof either that he was genetically Hebrew to some degree.

The only books Ernie read were about the American Ku Klux Klan, German Nazism and Italian Fascism. His knowledge about how those nefarious organizations with their warped ideologies had functioned was impressive, and he incessantly talked about what he knew. His seemingly profound and highly relevant political knowledge was eventually made known to senior members of the Veterans Party, and Ernie's star began to shine.

Ernie's presidential predecessor, Samuel Portifoy, had leaned towards fascism without actively trying to change the fundamental nature of American society. Before being elected president by the innermost members of the Veterans Party, Portifoy had been an American oligarch, and therefore a member of an exclusive, white, secretive, elitist, very rich-guy, old-boys club that *de facto* ran the impoverished nation.

Surprisingly, Portifoy had picked the relatively young and impoverished Ernie Wolf, a virtual unknown at the time, to be his vice-presidential running mate. He did so because Ernie looked the part, was not very bright, was inexperienced and would do *exactly* what he was told to do.

Or so he had thought.

For centuries, presidential candidates did not have to publicly disclose the size and source of their wealth, or their tax returns. And they never had to provide proof of mental and physical health to run for office.

Portifoy had a massive, instantly fatal stroke in the middle of his second year in office. And to the surprise of everyone, Ernie Wolf was sworn in as interim president for what was left of Portifoy's four-year term of office.

Then all hell broke loose.

Ernie was probably about average with respect to intelligence. But he knew that the political base inside the Veterans Party was racist, ignorant and easily manipulated. They all wanted to be rich white guys rather than poor white guys.

Ernie had astutely cultivated personal relationships with the leading members of that political base, and he was immensely and fanatically popular with them. Ernie could do no wrong in their eyes, and was perceived as some sort of national savior. They believed Ernie would be the best man to protect the country from further immigration, and the perceived racial, religious and ethnic 'contamination' that immigration caused. And Ernie obviously loved the military and veterans, so losing wars was not conceivable if he was in charge. And with Ernie in control, there would still be lots of wars, and a continuous supply of veterans to replenish the party ranks.

Ernie always talked like he knew everything about everything, and people believed him, mostly because the country and the world were so messed up, and nothing else gave them hope.

As president, Ernie immediately started breaking the rules. He openly consorted with strippers and prostitutes. He told lies about everything, especially about the state of the economy, and about how bad other countries were, and how smart he was, and how bad free-trade was, and why fighting wars all of the time was a good thing. He did not name a vice-president because he said, 'the entire Veterans Party will now function in that capacity.'

Then Ernie established the equivalent of the German Nazi SA, or the infamous Brown Shirts. It was easy to recruit willing young thugs from his political base. The newly-formed organization of bullies was called the 'Loyal Order of Patriots'.

When Ernie took office, only veterans were allowed to vote in municipal and state elections, and in federal elections for members of the House of Representatives and the Senate. And only Veterans Party members could run for any political office.

But usually two or three Veterans Party members put themselves forward in each election. The candidates were almost exclusively heterosexual, white and middle-aged men.

It quickly became apparent that President Wolf did not take kindly to criticism of any kind. He had a few competent advisers, but he never listened to them. Ernie was also vindictive, selfish and cruel. If he had a conscience, he never revealed it.

Sometimes things were said about him in Congress and in the press that were not complimentary, especially about his impulsive irrationality, his lack of fundamental knowledge, his lack of experience and his inability to effectively run a nation.

So, five months into Ernie's interim term, he sent the Loyal Order of Patriots to work on Congress. About a thousand LOP thugs stormed the House of Representatives with clubs and torches during a night session. They drove the congressmen out of the building, and then set fire to it. Then they stormed the vacant neighbouring Senate chamber, and set fire to it as well. Then they surrounded the building, and with the help of another three thousand LOP brutes, they made sure that firefighters could not put out the flames.

The following morning, and three days after Matt Adams had started his long journey by train from El Paso, Texas to Akron, Ohio, a very grim-sounding President Ernie Wolf went on national radio and television.

Ernie said that what happened was an unfortunate event, but it was not his doing. Then he said Congress was useless anyway, and no taxpayer money would be wasted building a new capital building. Then he said, 'You know, to simplify everything, I have just decided that Congress will be completely disbanded, and that will certainly be no great loss to our nation.'

And Ernie said the only way for America to survive and be great again was to make the president all-powerful, and support him in every way, without criticism of any kind. So, the media companies would immediately be abolished as well. Furthermore, from now on, Ernie's newly-appointed 'Secretary of News' would tell people what they needed to know, using newly-commissioned, state-owned radio and television networks. And for national security reasons, the president would now be in power for life, and would name his own successor. And the judiciary would no longer be an independent wing of the government, rather it would become an integral part of the Veterans Party.

Then Ernie went into an off-script rant, and yelled that America was finally all-powerful again. And no American citizen could be outside of the newly invigorated and vastly improved nation. And every American must remain completely loyal to the nation, or else they would be sent to a 're-education camp', or worse. And the VPF or Veterans Police Force would replace the FBI and the other federal law enforcement agencies to make sure everyone stayed aligned with Party principles, and followed all of the many new rules that would soon be announced.

And Ernie said for national security reasons, everyone would have to apply for the use of a telephone, and the use of the internet. He said businesses could *probably* get a limited license, but most citizens should not even hope to qualify for a license. However, Veterans Party members, police officers and military officers would *of course* have a phone, and be able to fully make use of the internet. And from now on, only the police and the military could access the global positioning system. And a newly established VYO or Veterans Youth Organization would flush out all of the lingering, disloyal threats to American society within families and schools. And to keep their jobs, all police officers, active and reserve military personnel, and all federal government employees, must immediately swear an oath of allegiance to the Veterans Party, and directly to the president, who again, was now president for life.

Ernie seemed to suddenly calm down a bit, and closed by saying 'God Bless America'.

And incredibly, Ernie Wolf got away with it.

Americans just blinked as a form of fascist totalitarianism took hold of the nation.

4

Matt Adams was finding it very hard to stay awake. He had not slept well for days. His seat was in the last row of the rearmost car of a combination freight and passenger train. He was sitting beside a grimy, right-side window on a filthy, worn-out seat.

Matt's seat reclined a bit, which should have given him the opportunity for at least a few restful periods of sleep. But the train was continually stopping and starting, sometimes for no apparent reason, and usually well away from a station. And people were continually getting on and off the train. As far as Matt could tell, he was the only long distance traveller.

It was now about an hour after sunrise. The train had just started moving again in a jerky fashion, possibly at an average speed of twenty miles per hour or so. There was a lot of rolling noise, and sometimes there were violent, jarring vibrations, even at slow speeds. The track was obviously in terrible shape. That seemed to be the new norm in America.

Matt knew for certain that it was Thursday, September 2. His geographical location was a lot less certain. He guessed he was somewhere between Little

Rock, Arkansas and Poplar Bluff, Missouri. He was definitely not near a city or town.

Matt noted a man was slowly making his way down the centre aisle of the car towards him. The man was struggling with a tattered, old duffle bag, and he was pausing to quietly talk to people. He was a short, balding, black man, and probably middle-aged. Matt soon realized the man was asking permission to sit down on any vacant seat, and he was being rebuffed by everyone on the train.

When the man finally got to Matt's row, Matt could see that the man was on the verge of tears. The seats on the other side of the aisle were occupied by an older, white couple and their many paper-wrapped bundles. The older couple would not even look at the black man. But they had been consistently keeping to themselves, and they seemed a bit frightened, and overly suspicious of everyone else on the train.

Matt had his backpack on the seat beside him. But the two seats opposite him were unoccupied. Before the distressed little man could say anything, Matt smiled at him and said, "You can sit opposite me if you would like, sir. And can I help you with that bag? It looks pretty heavy."

The man just stood there with a surprised look on his face. So, Matt stood up and helped him set his large bag on the empty aisle seat. Then both men sat down on the window seats. Matt took his previous seat, facing forward.

The man still looked distressed, and a bit confused, so Matt leaned forward, extended his right hand, and said pleasantly, "Hi, I'm Audie Zaitsev."

The man attempted to smile, shook Matt's hand with a firm grip, and then stammered, "I'm Daquan... Daquan Jefferson. Ah, I'm very pleased to meet you, Audie. And thank you *so much* for letting me sit down. You were obviously my last hope."

Matt shook his head and said quietly, "I don't know what's got into people."

Daquan tried again to smile, but otherwise his body language clearly told Matt that he was still very upset. Then the man seemed to gather himself a bit, and he said a bit more steadily, "It's because I'm not white, Audie. It's suddenly like the bad old days again, you know, from the history books. President Ernie seems to be stirring it all up. And racism never completely disappeared I guess, especially in the south."

Matt nodded in sympathy. Then he asked, "So, are you travelling far, Daquan?"

"To be completely frank with you, I'm not sure where I'm going exactly, Audie," Daquan admitted, with a vacant look on his face. "I just lost my job, you see, working for a white shop owner that I thought was a decent fellow. And my wife died last year, after a loving marriage of thirty-five years. We had a beautiful daughter, but she was killed in the war. She was a medic.

"I figured somewhere in the north might be the best place to look for work. I'm a barber, and I guess I'll shine shoes now too if that's what it takes to get by… " He trailed off while lowering his head.

"I'm heading north myself," Matt replied cheerfully. "Got a job through my uncle in Akron, working road construction. Might just be a flagman for a while, until they recognize that I can do a lot more than just turn a simple stop-and-go sign. Anyway, it will be nice to have some friendly company on this train for a while.

"I've never been married. And I haven't had a real girl friend since I left my home town of Cleveland, ten years ago. I guess I'm sort of heading home now, close enough to home, anyway.

"I guess I look a bit rough. I've travelled all the way from El Paso, and you're the first person that's sat down across from me! As you can see, I haven't had a shave or a haircut for a very long while. And I lost my left eye when a truck almost ran over me. I must look a bit like a pirate, or maybe like an escaped convict? And I probably smell a bit ripe too. Sorry about that…" He trailed off with a questioning look.

Daquan laughed and said, "Well, I can't smell you from where I'm sitting, Audie, so you can't be *that* bad! Look, my specialty is sprucing guys up. When we stop at a station, I'll give you a shave and a good trim, if you'd like. I've got all of my tools of the trade with me. That's why my bag is a bit on the heavy side. And I've heard that some train stations have rain water barrels where you can give yourself a splash for free."

Matt smiled, and said, "Thanks, Daquan! And I'll treat you to a good lunch, from a vendor at the station. How does that sound?"

Daquan smiled in return, and said, "It's a deal!"

Matt and Daquan spent the next couple of hours quietly telling stories, and talking about what was happening in the country. Daquan was a wealth of information. He said that being a barber had been a great way to stay on top of the 'real' news. And he said that until recently, he could get a true sense of what people were thinking about, and what they were concerned about most in life.

But he said things were suddenly very different. People were becoming really frightened by what was happening in the country, and they were becoming more and more reluctant to speak openly about it. Everyone knew what the new 'official party line' was, and they all repeated the many new patriotic slogans as if they were true believers in all of them. And they were all now referring to the president in nothing but glowing terms, and even calling him 'Cousin Ernie'.

After a while, the train jolted to a stop again in the middle of nowhere, and Matt and Daquan both dozed off. Matt was jarred awake when the train started moving again. After a few minutes, he figured it was probably moving again in fits and starts at about twenty miles per hour.

The conductor was making his way down the aisle again, checking or rechecking people's tickets or rail passes. He was a tall, friendly, native-American man, probably in his thirties.

Two young, brutish-looking guys were following along a few paces behind the conductor. Matt had not seen them before. He figured they must have just climbed aboard the train. They were both wearing black tee-shirts, faded blue jeans and shiny, black, Army-style boots. And they had white arm bands that had been stamped with 'LOP' in large black letters. Matt figured they were probably members of the Loyal Order of Patriots that Daquan had just told him about.

The two thugs were looking very carefully at every passenger, but they were not saying anything to anyone. They each held a black, wooden club in their right hand, and they were definitely not trying to hide their simple weapons from sight.

The conductor quickly glanced at Matt's and then Daquan's rail pass. He smiled at them both, but said nothing. Then he brushed his way without hesitation or discussion past the two young men standing in the middle of the aisle. He walked all the way back up the aisle without stopping and left the rearmost rail car.

The two young men stood very still and stared hard at Daquan for an uncomfortably long moment. Then they stared at Matt for equally as long. Then one of the men growled, "A nigger, and obviously a nigger lover. Now ain't that nice. But you boys ain't welcome on this here train. So, you're both getting off, *right now*!"

Daquan suddenly looked very scared, and stood up. Matt just said calmly, "Sure, fellows, we'll leave by the back door. I'll handle our bags."

Matt motioned for Daquan to go first. Then he waited for the two thugs to follow Daquan. Then he grabbed the two bags and followed along behind.

When Matt passed through the door onto the small, open-air, metal platform at the back of the passenger car, one of the thugs grabbed Daquan's arms from behind, and held on to him forcefully. Matt instantly dropped the two bags. Then the other thug struck Daquan in his solar plexus with the butt end of his club. Daquan instantly gasped with pain, and doubled over.

The thug that had struck Daquan then swung his club hard at Matt's head. Matt deftly deflected the blow with his left forearm, and with the same practiced, fluid motion, punched the thug very hard in the throat with his right fist at full arm extension. The thug staggered back, gasped, and with his eyes bulging, put his hands to his throat. Matt then grabbed him by the back of his tee-shirt, turned him around and pushed him hard off the side of the little platform. The man landed very awkwardly on the hard barren ground beside the tracks, flopped to a stop in a cloud of dust and did not get up.

The other thug was still holding on to Daquan, and he now looked very frightened. This was obviously not how this was supposed to go down. Matt was bigger and stronger than he had looked while sitting down, and he could obviously handle himself in a scrap.

Matt said quietly, "Let him go."

The thug instantly complied.

Then Matt said quietly, "You have two choices. You can be pushed off this train like your buddy, or you can pick a safe enough looking place, and jump off."

The thug hesitated for a few seconds, and then he staggered over to the left side of the platform as the train continued to lurch down the rough tracks. They were still travelling through arid farmland. It was late summer, and it was hard to tell if the brown, stubble-filled fields had yielded any crops recently.

The thug waited for the train to pass a wooden pole of some kind at the side of the tracks, and then he jumped. Matt watched the guy tumble down the gravelly bank of the railroad bed, and into a dusty ditch. But the young guy staggered to his feet, and looked back at the departing train. So Matt figured he had come through his ordeal okay. How his buddy had fared was a lot less certain.

Then Matt went over to Daquan, who was still doubled over in pain. Matt gently placed the palm of his right hand on his back, and asked quietly, "Are you all right, Daquan?"

Daquan gasped, "I think so... just got the wind... the wind knocked out of me... I think."

Matt had a quick glance through the greasy glass in the door of the passenger car. Then he said quietly, "I don't think anyone saw any of that, Daquan. But we better get off this train ourselves at the next opportunity, maybe when it starts to slow down again. Those two guys might have a way to call ahead to their buddies. Who knows?

"I'm thinking out loud, but I think we should hoof it to the next station, and maybe let a train or two go by. Then watch to see who gets on the train we pick out. If we don't see any LOP guys or cops, we'll get on that train, and keep going north, together. How does that plan sound to you, Daquan?"

Daquan had finally managed to stand more upright, and he looked to be coming around a bit. He was breathing easier, anyway. After another long moment, Daquan managed a real smile, and he said, "Phew! Yea, okay Audie! Sounds like a good plan to me."

5

Daquan Jefferson ended up travelling all the way to Akron, Ohio with Matt Adams. They completed their long journey on Wednesday, September 29. Their relationship proved to be mutually beneficial. Daquan was intelligent, pragmatic and street-smart, and Matt was wise, discreet and wary. Matt was also a large, muscular, scarred, eye-patched, brutish-looking man who intimidated people just with his appearance.

Still, they had a few anxious moments on their journey.

Just before they reached St. Louis, another pair of Loyal Order of Patriots thugs came on to the train, presumably to harass non-white people. But when they loudly announced they were going to drag Daquan off the train, Matt simply stood up and said, "That's what you won't be doing." The thugs then demanded to see Matt's identity cards. Matt asked them if they were police officers. When they admitted they were not, Matt simply told them to, "Bugger off then, you jerks."

And they did just that.

Matt wondered for a while if he might be a marked man because of that encounter, and the previous, more serious altercation. Daquan and Matt had no way to know if the LOP organization had a way to record and relay physical appearances of targeted individuals, or an alert network of some sort with an accessible databank. But Matt stopped worrying about that when two VPF or Veterans Police Force officers came on to the train in Chicago.

The VPF officers were wearing very smart-looking, dark green, military-style uniforms, complete with old-style, state-trooper-like, broad-brimmed hats. They hesitated for a long moment while they took turns looking at Matt's identification cards, and at his face. But they eventually just nodded to each other as if they recognized him, and his pseudonym. One officer scrawled something hurriedly into a note pad. And then they just gave Matt back his cards, and said nothing more to him.

The VPF officers closely studied Daquan's identity cards as well, and asked him where he was headed. When he replied Akron, Ohio, they nodded at each other again, and handed Daquan back his cards. Then the officer with the note pad scrawled something else down in it.

Matt figured the VPF officers were actually on the look-out for him, and would report his travel progress to Army Intelligence. He figured that was not such a bad thing. But it was unfortunate that they now knew he was travelling with a man named Daquan Jefferson, and that he and Matt were both going to the same place. He had never wanted to get Daquan into any kind of trouble, quite the opposite actually.

There were a few stretches in the journey were edible food and safe, drinkable water were especially scarce. Matt and Daquan concluded some places were totally impoverished, and the people trying to live there could not spare *any* food or water to sell to travellers. So Matt and Daquan went hungry a few times, and they drank a *lot* of rain water from public barrels at train stations. Some of the water was full of what Daquan referred to as 'creeping uncertainties'. They were amazed it did not make them sick, although they figured they both must have acquired significant tolerance against infection through living in near-poverty most of their lives. Still, they both lost some weight during their long journey together.

When they finally got to Cleveland, Daquan really showed his value to Matt.

The city was almost a ghost town. There was no longer any means of public transportation. Daquan talked briefly with a black marketer, and found out that the VPF had a few electric cars and a couple of LNG-powered armoured personnel carriers. A few LNG-powered trucks were still operating, but otherwise there was very little traffic on the roads. A few people, presumably slightly wealthier people, had bicycles. But most people were getting around by walking. Some people pulled little baggage carts behind them.

Electrical power was mostly off in the city, and there were very few items on store shelves.

But the black market was flourishing. And there were chickens running around everywhere, even on city streets, and pigs and goats were being raised in backyard pens. Vegetable gardens were located everywhere, even along public roadways and railway tracks.

The once affluent and productive mid-west of America now resembled a third-world country. Urban areas had been significantly depopulated, and people lived wherever they could scratch out a living.

Daquan somehow managed to finagle a ride for himself and Matt on a rickety, old, LNG-powered truck making a black market delivery of salted and dried Lake Erie perch to Akron. It cost him one of his most prized electric razors, but he figured he might not be able to use an electric razor much any more the way things were looking.

When they got to Akron, they quickly decided they better split up. Segregation had obviously re-appeared. There were 'whites only' signs everywhere, and various ethnic ghettos had sprung up. LOP thugs patrolled the boundaries of the some of the ghettos, and beat up people that challenged the boundaries, or their alleged authority.

Daquan quickly found a job working in a blacks-only barber shop near the old downtown bus station on Broadway Avenue. Having his own tools really helped him get the job, and he really was a top-notch barber.

The owner let him sleep in the back of the shop until he could find his own place to live. And he gave Daquan the use of a bicycle to get around town until he could afford to buy one of his own.

Matt asked Daquan if he could keep his ears open about some kind of social club for workers. He told Daquan that he had heard about it from a road construction buddy in El Paso. Matt said it apparently was non-segregated, and all hush-hush for that reason. But he suggested that maybe they both could meet some interesting, decent people there, and even a few ladies.

Daquan looked a bit puzzled by the request, but he said he would do his best to discreetly find out about the club.

Matt had an address for the road repair company. It was on Morgan Avenue about a mile and a half from the old downtown bus station. It was located where a steel treating company had once operated in more prosperous times. Matt checked in to a hostel for white, single men a couple blocks away to the east on Morgan Avenue. It was a really rough, rundown and filthy place. There were a lot of illicit drug users living in the hostel. Matt figured they all must be hardened criminals to be able to fund their nasty, expensive addictions. But he also figured he would not have to live in the disgraceful dump very long if he really did have a secure job with a government-favoured contractor.

Since Matt by law could never have a cell phone, and phone booths did not exist any more, he would have to make a visit to the contractor's yard in person. He guessed that they probably started their operations at about eight o'clock every weekday morning. He planned to make his first visit to the yard early in the morning the day after he had checked into the hostel.

There was an old city park on Morgan Avenue that had returned to a wilderness area through centuries of neglect. Since Daquan had a bicycle, they promised each other they would keep in touch by meeting every Sunday morning at nine o'clock in a secluded, heavily-wooded area in the park beside a busted-up, fallen-down statue.

6

Ernie Wolf found he really liked being president. The highest position in the land gave him the attention he had always craved. And he really liked pushing people around.

He had started the job poor as dirt, but his wealth was quickly increasing. The oligarchs in the nation were trying very hard to contribute to that cause. They reasoned that by directly corrupting him, Ernie would become a *de facto* member of their elite network, and he would favour their interests above all others.

But Ernie had drastically changed the way things worked in the United States. He did not actually need the oligarchs to get wealthy. He surrounded himself with cunning and savvy 'yes men' who creatively skimmed hordes of money from the public coffers for Ernie, and to a lesser degree, for themselves.

And Ernie only trusted his own judgement, which was largely based on prejudice, and street-thug instinct. He really did not like to read long, boring reports, or to be briefed on fact-based, objective intelligence. His weekly, hour-long cabinet meetings were mostly for show. He would bring in the cameras for the first half-hour or so, and brag about how smart he was, and how great everything was in the country. He usually used the subsequent closed-door session to criticize his underlings. He liked it when they fought amongst themselves. He viewed the chaos and stress he maintained in his cabinet as a good way to prevent an organized rebellion, and to stay one step ahead of everyone else.

Not surprisingly, the turnover rate in his administration was historically high. Furthermore, Ernie did not seem to care if key positions went officially unfilled for long periods of time. He found that overworked and interim appointees were more willing to please, and make him look good.

Ernie was surprised to learn that the oligarch network actually spanned the entire world. At the end of his first month in office, he received an unsigned, hand-delivered letter. He found out later that a kid on a bicycle had delivered it to the Secret Service guard on duty at the front door of the White House. The laser-printed letter simply invited him to a secret meeting in Moscow where, 'matters of mutual interest would be discussed by the only people that matter in the world.'

Ernie did not reply to the invitation, or attend the meeting. But he did ask his key intelligence people to find out who might have sent the letter.

They immediately told him most countries in the world were autocracies or dictatorships. Over the last few centuries, some large nations had splintered into fiefdoms that were run by warlords or mafia bosses.

Something resembling communism still existed in a few Chinese splinter states. And a few nations were fascist totalitarian to some degree, like the United States. But their espoused political doctrines were mostly for show.

Most world leaders were openly corrupt, and motivated by personal greed. And they liked to decide together when wars should start and end. 'Controlled wars' were viewed as mutually good for business. And quite a few world leaders still believed the *Second Chance* project was good for business. The rockets that supplied the materials for the project were all built and launched by for-profit corporations that were owned collectively by dictators and non-governing oligarchs. And since the project was popular with the masses, most dictators and oligarchs talked it up, and urged the 'common folks' to work harder to ensure the project would be successful.

About a month after receiving the first letter, Ernie received another one. Once again, the letter was unsigned, and delivered to the White House by a local courier riding a bicycle. Once again, the letter was not in an envelope, and it was sealed shut with a nondescript blob of wax. The courier claimed he did not know the source of the letter, even while being tortured.

The second letter was much longer. In a condescending, lecturing manner, it basically reiterated what Ernie's intelligence people had told him about how things actually worked in the world. It closed by threatening Ernie on a personal level. It said that if he did not attend the next monthly meeting, this time in Singapore, the club of oligarchs would see to it that his remaining days on the planet would be very limited indeed.

The letter greatly angered Ernie. He personally crafted a response letter of his own, and asked his intelligence people to arrange for it to be hand-delivered to every oligarch in the world. It simply said that he was untouchable, and that he took orders from no one. Furthermore, it said Ernie would start and end wars, 'whenever the hell he wanted to, and the world better not mess with him.' And it said the *Second Chance* project was an incredible waste of money, and the United States would no longer contribute to funding it. And furthermore, it said Ernie would find a way to stop the project, and completely obliterate whatever had been built.

However, Ernie took the not-so-subtle oligarch death threat *very* seriously. He decided he would quadruple the size of the Secret Service, and model the re-vamped organization after Hitler's elite SS. They were still the 'men-in-black', but in addition to basic two-piece suits and skinny, boring ties, they were issued very smart-looking military uniforms, complete with expensive and sleek-looking body armour, and flat-black, lightweight helmets. The organization was still called the Secret Service, but some administration people jokingly referred to them as 'All the President's Men'. But no one called them that around Ernie.

The new Secret Service quickly became the only organization that Ernie consulted with before making critical decisions, and he always listened to their advice. They told him not to travel very much, not even to the Pentagon, and to stay behind bullet-proof glass whenever he gave a speech.

And the other thing Ernie did after receiving the second letter was to very quietly reinstate the Space Force. He gave it the ancient name of 'Strategic Air Command', or SAC. Its secret mission was straightforward but very difficult. He told the new organization to find a way to give him reliable ballistic missiles with functioning nuclear warheads that he could launch at a single-city target that he would name later.

After careful study, the top SAC general told Ernie he thought they *might* be able to cobble together, or more likely re-construct, three Minuteman VI ICBM's, and make them ready for launching from long abandoned underground silos in North Dakota. The general said each missile would probably have three 160 kiloton, W148 thermonuclear warheads mounted in MK-20A re-entry vehicles.

Ernie did not really go in for all of that technical stuff. He just told the SAC general to get on with it, keep it all top secret and give him weekly progress reports.

Ernie also told the top SAC general to start discreetly looking into, 'a good way to send a W148 or whatever nuclear weapon into lunar orbit.' He added that once in orbit, the weapon must be steerable from Earth. Furthermore, he insisted the weapon must be constructed in such a manner that it could be detonated in an exact location at an exact time upon receiving a signal from Earth.

7

Dear Cranston,

How are you? My, it's been over two months since we last talked. Where did the time go? I'm now settled in Akron, Ohio. I'm working for Devo Road Construction, mostly as a flagman, but I'm also a bit of a gopher (you know, go for this, and go for that). Have to start somewhere I guess! Part of my pay includes the use of a flat in a camp building located in their yard on Morgan Avenue. There's also a small cafeteria on site where I can pick up basic meals for free. So, not a bad deal.

My social life might improve shortly too. A friend of mine told me about a social club of sorts for workers like me and him. Yesterday we went to one of their Saturday noontime 'get-together sessions' at the old student centre on the university grounds. There's not much left of the university of course, but the student centre is still sort of functional. Alumni volunteers keep it operating I think, so it's actually more of an alumni centre now. Anyway, we met a lot of interesting people there, from all sorts of backgrounds. People played cards (mostly euchre), threw darts, and talked a lot, mostly about things happening in their lives. People also brought food and drink, and everyone put it on a big table where it was shared. Sort of a socialist thing I guess? Workers of Akron, Unite! Or at least share some grub together?

One older fellow asked me in a whisper what I thought about Cousin Ernie, and the LOP. I told him we better not talk about that, as the walls themselves may have ears these days. He seemed content with that answer, but I got the sense he'll approach me again sometime. Not sure what will come of that, but I'll let you know if it's anything interesting.

I hope you are in good health? I'll try to send you another letter soon. You can probably get a letter to me by sending it to Devo Construction Company, c/o Audie Zaitsev.

Bye for now, your friend,
Audie

8

It was Sunday, November 14, at ten minutes past nine in the morning. It was looking to be a rather warm and sunny day. Matt Adams was surprised and a bit concerned that Daquan Jefferson had not shown up yet for their once-a-week recurring catch-up chat. They always met by the fallen down statue in what used to be Morgan Park. Daquan had always been punctual, and he usually arrived a few minutes early for everything.

But the extended wait was not arduous for Matt. The trees in the park still had a lot of their leaves, and they were bright orange and yellow in colour, and even flaming red in a few places. The air was unusually still, and the natural mossy smells within the old urban forest were invigorating.

Daquan and Matt had now attended five consecutive Saturday lunchtime Workers Social Club get-togethers. Matt and Daquan were meeting some decent people at the sessions that could easily become their friends, including some attractive and interesting women. The sessions typically ran about two hours, and they were casual, friendly and quite entertaining. They were also multi-racial and multi-ethnic. But most churches and some public schools were still that way.

So, the meetings would probably not have attracted much interest from the VPF had Army Intelligence not suspected for some reason that something *more* might be going on with the social group.

Matt had been told by a few meeting regulars that so far the LOP had not bothered them. But the cadre of the LOP were all volunteers, and apparently most of them were also Friday night binge drinkers and dope smokers who woke up every Saturday morning with a hangover. Harassing non-whites for the good of Cousin Ernie and his fascist state was something that could wait for later in the day, or even another day, when they felt better.

But Matt was now wondering if he had started down the wrong path and would have to look for another 'social club' to check out. If the group meetings were really a front for a nefarious political party, Matt had not seen or heard any evidence to support that notion. The older man who had expressed some interest in talking to Matt about President Wolf and his Loyal Order of Patriots had not attended the last three sessions.

But there was the old man now! He was riding towards him on a bicycle along a leaf-covered, narrow path through the overhanging trees. And the bicycle looked very much like the old borrowed bicycle that Daquan had been using.

The old man rode right up to Matt. The bike wobbled a bit as it slowed down, and skidded to a stop on the wet leaves. Then the old man awkwardly climbed off the ancient, rusty machine.

Matt guessed the man was probably in his early seventies, and a bit arthritic. He was a short, pale-skinned guy with a clean-shaven, wrinkly but otherwise quite ordinary-looking face. He was also mostly bald, with a double chin, and large, tortoise-shell-framed glasses with very thick lenses.

The old man casually looked around as if he was enjoying the natural scenery. Then he said very quietly without looking at Matt, "There's a bench we can sit on, back down the path I just used, and off to the left a bit in a small clearing. This place is probably all right, but the bench is regularly checked-out, and we know it is a safe place to talk. Rest easy, your friend is all right. Okay?"

Matt just nodded, and they set off on foot together to find the 'checked-out' bench. The old man pushed the squeaky bike along as they walked, but he said nothing more until they got to the bench. The old man leaned the bike up against the back of the weather-worn, unpainted, wooden bench, and then he sat down on it, and stared off into the woods. Matt sat down beside him about three feet away, and also stared straight ahead rather than look at the man.

"We intercepted your letter, and we know who you really are," the old man said very quietly.

Matt said nothing in response.

"Don't worry, we know how to open envelopes and re-seal them so no one can tell they've been opened," the old man continued, almost in a whisper. "We put it back in the same mail box you used. It should get to your address okay. But there is no longer an Army Intelligence outfit. Your letter, and every other one you send to that address with the name you used, will reach the Veterans Police Force. They're kind of like the Gestapo was in Hitler's Germany, or the NKVD slash GRU slash KGB were in the Soviet Union, if you know some history."

Matt kept staring off in the distance, and asked quietly, "Who are you, and what do you want?"

"It's best that you never know my name," whispered the old man. "Your secret is safe with us, although I'm sure you're not even close yet to believing anything I tell you. I'm part of a group of let us say 'special patriots'. We are patriotically loyal to no country, rather we are ardent supporters of the *Second Chance* project. Have you heard of it?"

Matt took a quick glance at the old man, and then he said quietly, "Yes, of course."

"Are you in favour of it?"

"Greatly. I mean, it's supposed to save the human species, and other Earth species, right? How can that be a bad thing?"

"I fully agree with you. But our president thinks it's a complete waste of money. Also, it was not his idea, and therefore in his feeble, ignorant and conceited mind it can't be any good. And since he's a vindictive, overly aggressive, pathological lying fool, he's building a rocket to blow it up with a nuclear bomb."

"How do you know that?"

This time the old man turned to look directly at Matt. Matt noted the deliberate change of body position with his peripheral vision, so he turned to look directly back at the old man.

"Our group is pretty small actually," said the old man, almost inaudibly. "We're mostly scientists, and academics. We are funded by what some people in power call the 'benevolent oligarchs'. Have you heard of them?"

"No."

"Well, most of them are not nice guys. Personally, I think benevolent just means some of them are not quite as bad as the others. I think they're all greedy bastards, actually.

"Others in our order are convinced there is an altruistic subset of their network that is driven to help the world. But you don't have to believe that fully to perceive that our goals are remarkably aligned with the whole lot of them.

"They want the *Second Chance* project to be completed because it's making them a lot of money. Most of them have shares in European and Eurasian rocket launching corporations, and in the Moon Base joint venture, and in the worldwide-group of inter-connected, supply-chain contractors.

"And our little, impoverished, but well-intentioned social group wants to make sure the generation spaceship leaves Moon orbit with the right mix of flora and fauna, and the right number of people, and the right people. And we want the spaceship to have the right organizational system, and a superb artificial intelligence system, to be able to survive the long journey, and be useful to the settlers when it gets to its final destination.

"When it gets to its destination after eighty or so generations, we want the inhabitants, or the Tube Dwellers, to be well-seasoned farmers with well-honed survival skills, and well-equipped to deal successfully with true pioneering. And we want them to have easy access to all accumulated human knowledge, so they can quickly rebuild a technologically advanced world, while hopefully not repeating the many mistakes that we have made here on Earth.

"But our social group has not completely given up on the notion that humanity can survive for a while longer here on Earth. So we are also working on another more secretive project, in a very remote location. It is comprised of the most sophisticated seed bank, artificial intelligence control system and data archive ever devised. And the facility will be able to defend itself. The idea is that if all hell breaks loose here on Earth, like we think it will, we would like to give the survivors a little help to rebuild. Further elaboration on this other project is out of the question.

"Now, do you recognize how these projects are essential for saving humanity?"

"Yes. And you haven't told me yet how you know our president will try to blow up the *Second Chance*, or why you think I'm not Audie Zaitsev."

The old man paused to take a long, slow, deep breath. The focused effort made him cough a couple of times. Then he whispered, "The Social Club you have attended is just that, but we do use it as a bit of a pre-screening vehicle, or front, for our real organization. Our rule is we don't talk politics in the Club because we suspect a few regulars are Veterans Police Force spies. We're pretty sure we know who those folks are, and that knowledge can be useful for working various tactical misdirection schemes.

"I recognized you right away. I have a background in let us say, *journalism*. Your eyepatch and forehead scar are obviously distinctive. And there was one very brief mention of your spectacular war exploits in a rather obscure mercenary magazine, complete with a photograph. I'm sure you are completely unaware that a digital snapshot was taken of you during the last Social Club meeting. Facial recognition software confirms that you are indeed Mathieu Adams, and knowing that, we also know you prefer to be called Matt.

"Now, as for knowing what Cousin Ernie is secretly up to, well, let's just say not everyone in government is completely pleased with him, or with what he's paying them. So for a bit of extra cash, they discreetly feed information to our benevolent oligarch partners, and they in turn share what they learn with us.

"The latest news is the Strategic Air Command or SAC is assembling a Vulcan Centaur IVB rocket booster at Cape Canaveral that can easily reach the Moon. It will be disguised as a commercial Earth-orbit satellite launch vehicle. SAC also has a number of secret 'mothballed' thermonuclear warheads they can fairly readily install inside the rocket's rather cavernous nose cone. It does not have to be a high yield device, actually. It just has to be big enough to blow up the *Second Chance*. The real trick is making the warhead steerable from Earth. But the latest word is they have solved that technical problem. Furthermore, the latest report suggests the missile should be ready to launch in less than six months' time.

"Do I have your interest yet?"

"Yes, definitely."

"You have always been loyal to your country, we know that too. And that's a very admirable thing, even when your country has not always treated you very well, especially after you were discharged. Sure, you left the Army with lots of medals. But you can't eat those medals, or get much money by pawning them. And you were disabled while serving your country with distinction, and you had to grab on to a rather distasteful and nebulous, domestic spy job just to stay alive.

"We want you to stay alive, Matt… if you agree to help us.

"I don't want to threaten you unless I have to. But we could take you out *right now* if you answer a straightforward, upcoming question the wrong way.

"You see, I have friends nearby, hidden away, very professionally. You know the art of staying hidden better than anybody, but these guys are pretty good, too. They're kind of like Robin Hood's Merry Men, you know, only with compound hunting bows and flesh-ripping arrows. No one will ever hear their attack. I can tell them to attack using a simple hand signal. And of course they will attack you if you attack me first. By the way, your dead body will just look like three or four others around town tomorrow morning.

"You probably heard that Cousin Ernie banned all civilian hand guns and assault rifles. Furthermore, most cities and towns now won't allow *any* guns of *any* kind inside their boundaries. But lots of hooligans and criminals are running around at night in Akron with clubs, bows and arrows, and knives. Even the LOP thugs are scared of them. You don't hear about this new reality because Ernie and his Secretary of News don't want you to know about it. You're supposed to feel completely at ease and all warm and fuzzy inside, with the comforting knowledge that Cousin Ernie is always looking out for you.

"Now, to help us out, we'll want you and your good friend Daquan to keep attending the Saturday noontime Social Club meetings. Daquan knows who you really are now, and he wants to help us, and to help you. You pick your friends very well. He has not been treated very well either by society, and he has been angered and upset by the alarming resurgence of racism in America. It turns out he is also well-read, and a big fan of the *Second Chance* project. He told us you probably didn't know that, because you two have never talked about it.

"Secondly, we'll want you to keep writing your letters to Mister Cranston P. Snord. Only, we'll want you to let us help you write those letters from now on. You see, we'll want Cranston to believe you're making steady progress with your covert investigation, and that we really *are* a front for an emerging socialist revolutionary party. But we want you to tease old Cranston a bit, by making him believe that we are bigger and more spread-out than we actually are. We also want to divert the VPF's attention, to buy us some more time. Meanwhile, you should be able to keep working at Devo, and keep getting minimum wage, and your room and board.

"As a quick aside, do you know that Devo is short for 'de-evolution'? It has been observed that humanity may be regressing as increasing technology affects who we are as a species. The concept, or rather concern, was put forward by the Luddites many centuries ago, and later on in science-fiction literature, and also by musicians right here in Akron. It's kind of ironic, don't you think, considering what's actually happening with our species, here and elsewhere?

"Now, back on point again. Collectively we may not have much time to work with, because Cousin Ernie has also got SAC building some ICBM's. They're much further along with that covert program than with the Moon missile program. We don't know what Ernie wants to do with his ICBM's exactly, but we have a strong suspicion he wants to completely destroy and permanently irradiate what's left of Mexico City!

"You see, President Ernie Wolf passionately and irrationally hates the Mexicans, and all Central and South Americans for that matter. They're not pure white, you know. And in his twisted mind, they also don't talk the way Americans are *supposed* to talk. And he and his fascist base are vindictive, and they figure 'true' a.k.a. white Americans are fully justified with wanting to end the humiliating stalemate we now have with the Mexicans, and the people further to the south. And Ernie and his fascist cronies are going to kill millions of impoverished innocent people *out of pure spite*!

"So thirdly, Matt, and mostly, we want you to be our *wolf slayer*.

"I think you know very well what I mean by that. We have a notional plan, but we know you're a world-class expert, and can *refine* our rather amateurish scheme, and with a bit of our help, *make it happen*. Then, we'll help you get away, as best we can, which to be absolutely truthful with you, will be limited in extent.

"After you perform the mission, you can go anywhere you want, as long as it's *far away*. But don't ever tell us where you're planning to go, or anybody else for that matter, even Daquan. Because there will be many nasty people out to kill you.

"Okay, that's a whole lot to consider. I am truly sorry about that, but *our need is great*. I can spare a few more minutes if you want to think about it some more. The lads in the woods won't mind that much, either.

"So, here is the basic question. *Are you with us*?"

Matt sat in silence for a few minutes, while staring directly into the forest again. Then he whispered, "What will happen after the *wolf is slain*? I mean, with the government."

This time the old man sat in silence for a few minutes. Then he whispered, "That is admittedly pretty fuzzy. A military coup will probably occur. Our organization includes a few top generals. Ernie has no vice-president, and he likely will never appoint one. The secretary of state would be next in line, but Ernie has *three* of them with split duties, by design. And there is no Congress any more. The members of the Cabinet, or Ernie's inner circle, back stab each other at every opportunity, and Ernie seems to like the continual chaos. There will be a *lot* more chaos, at least initially, if you manage to take him out successfully. That ensuing chaos may present us with an opportunity to help put someone more competent, ethical and humane in place as our president. Truthfully, that may be very naïve on our part.

"To be successful, timing is everything for us. You must tell us a date and a time, and you must stay on schedule *exactly*, and we must be ready to move very fast in response. You'll probably never know more about the actual consequences of your actions than what I just told you *could* happen. But that's a good thing, in case you get caught. Because if you get caught, Matt, you will no doubt be slowly tortured to death."

Matt sat in silence again and thought for another minute or two. Then he smiled, stared hard at the old man, and said, "I wouldn't miss this for the world. What's next, Skipper?"

The old man laughed quietly, and said, "Phew! That's good! Okay, next, we'll send you some interesting stuff to read, by a self-employed, commercial courier. In other words, by a guy on a bicycle. He won't know what he's carrying. The main document will tell you more about how our order believes the world of oligarchs actually works. Burn that stuff right after you read it. The courier will also deliver to you our plan outline, and you'll quickly see that it's just that, a *freaking outline*. But burn that stuff too, as sketchy as it is, right away. And after that, try to plan *everything* in your head without writing *anything* down.

"And then we'll be working for you. You'll tell us what you need, in one-on-one meetings like this one, and we'll try to help you out as best we can. You will likely meet a few people other than me to deflect VPF attention and allay their suspicions. And we'll send you draft letters for Cranston using commercial, trustworthy, bicycle-riding couriers.

"Okay?"

Matt hesitated another few moments, and then he said in his normal voice, "Okay. Let's do it. Can I walk you back to the road?"

"No, I'll leave first, Matt. Maybe sit here another fifteen minutes or so. Robin and his lads will all be well away by then, too.

"I'll see you on most Saturday's. If you nod at me in one of our get-together sessions, I'll know you'll want to talk to someone directly, the following Sunday morning at exactly nine o'clock on this very same bench.

"You better just talk to Daquan at our get-togethers from now on, or somewhere else that won't attract much attention in our fascist, segregated nation.

"That's it. We better break it off now. See you around... Audie."

9

Dear Cranston,

How are you? I hope you got over that cold, or touch of the flu all right?

Things may be looking up for me a bit here. Devo Construction just promoted me, and put me on to their 'cold-patch team'. It means I'm suddenly getting another twenty-five cents an hour, and a little more interesting work. The guys I'm working with are all right. I have a beer or three with them Friday nights after work if I can squeeze it out of my tight budget. I kind of wiped out my savings by buying a well-used bicycle, but it sure makes getting around town a lot easier.

I'm still going to the Workers Social Club noontime 'get-togethers' every Saturday. None of the guys at work know anything about it, and I don't get the sense they're very much interested in it. So, I won't mention it to them again.

I found out from a little old lady member that there's an unwritten Social Club rule that says we can only engage in small talk at the sessions. And if someone wants to tell you their name, they are only supposed to share a nickname with you. I guess we're also not supposed to swear, or talk loudly, or talk about anything controversial, like something political, or a war, or what's in the stores, or what's not in the stores.

But a young, nerdy guy named Squeaker seemed to want to talk to me after the last meeting, so I walked beside him with my bike on my way home. It seems our paths were aligned for a mile or so. He told me our Social Club is part of a network of similar clubs. Apparently the one in Minot, North Dakota is the biggest, or rather it seems to have the most say in setting club rules, and directing volunteer work. And it seems something big might be about to happen there.

Squeaker also told me that for a bit of fun I should put my name in for some of the Club's extra-curricular volunteer activities. Apparently there is an interesting Club newsletter, and a bunch of pamphlets designed to help workers improve their lives. They need to get distributed to very precise locations. And sometimes there is a need to stand up in public somewhere, and yell something out at a certain time to help workers get more money, or better food, or whatever.

Anyway, I told the young man that I was interested. He seemed very pleased to hear that. Then he said someone would get a note to me about where to pick up some documents, and what to do with them, or where to go, and what to yell out exactly. It's all a bit uncertain right now, but if anything more interesting develops, I'll let you know. Maybe one of these Social Clubs is close to you, and you can get involved, too? Darn, I've got to get back to work now. Take care of yourself!

Audie Zaitsev

10

Matt Adams was alone in his smelly and moldy two-room flat in the small, dilapidated camp building at the back of the Devo Construction yard in Akron, Ohio.

It was mid-morning on Sunday, December 5. Matt had just burned the inner Social Club 'plan outline' in his wood stove, after carefully reading it for the seventh time.

Matt had also carefully read and then re-read the twenty-page document that had described the present-day world order. He had burned that document the day before.

The twenty-page document had provided a bit of historical context that Matt found illuminating. But it also seemed to have been written by two authors with diverging opinions.

One section had named the key controlling oligarchs in the world, and categorized them as either benevolent or malevolent.

Matt found that part interesting, but probably a bit too simplistic. The author of that section clearly held the view that the world of oligarchs was either black or white, with no grey. That did not fit into Matt's paradigm that held that human beings simply could not be stuffed into only two discrete categories. In his experience, the distribution of any human trait was a normal curve, or a spectrum of possibilities.

Another section in the document claimed that the benevolent oligarch network had its roots in ancient, secret, wealthy and religious, chivalry organizations. Without providing any proof, it just said that the network had evolved from the Knights Templar, the Military Order of Christ, the Freemasons, various spin-off rich-guy academic cults, and a partnership with a reincarnated Islamic Circassian Caste.

To Matt, that section seemed like a contrarian professor's stretch of imagination.

After some more thought, he concluded the whole subject matter of benevolent oligarchs was something he really did not need to know much about.

Matt was surprised to learn that societal disparity of wealth had been a cold, hard reality for the human species for thousands of years. The one-percent ultra-rich always got richer through political influence or direct control. And the ninety-nine percent poor continually suffered as they tried to survive in an autocratic, capitalistic world run by the ultra-rich. Socialism was a failed experiment left in the dust eons ego. And the so-called middle-class was long gone, too.

Matt did not know what 'better' might look like exactly. But this world sure sucked. He now had a chance to do his bit to help ensure that at least a few thousand decent, healthy, fertile human beings could head off to somewhere far away in space. Their descendants could start somewhere fresh, with new ideas, in a pristine but alien world. Now *that* was something he really wanted to see happen.

Matt used the wood stove in his flat to make another pot of percolated coffee. While sipping some fresh coffee, he started down the rather arduous task of refining the sketchy plan he now retained in his mind.

Matt's assigned job was to assassinate President Wolf, and then successfully escape without *ever* getting caught. In their two-page plan outline, the inner Social Club, or the 'elite', had suggested the best place for the assassination would be at one of Cousin Ernie's upcoming speaking engagements. Even though Ernie had declared himself 'President-for-Life', he still felt the need to periodically rally his fascist base with rousing speeches full of lies and vitriol. The Social Club elite believed Ernie craved attention, and fawning adulation. That character weakness, one of the many he demonstrated continually, created an opportunity, at least in theory. In their plan outline, the elite had admitted it was a very small and rather nebulous opportunity.

Ernie's upcoming speeches were mostly indoors in large sports arenas. Matt immediately ruled those venues out. The security inside those indoor arenas would be intensive. Uniformed and plain-clothed Secret Service agents would be everywhere. There would be multiple advance sweeps through those buildings looking for weapons, explosive devices and other threats. Only people with legitimate passes would be allowed in. Matt would have to present a convincing pass, and get by security somehow, with a rifle. And then he would have to get into hiding somewhere, and make a killing shot from an angle that would somehow skirt Ernie's protective bullet-proof glass shield. All of that might be remotely possible. But Matt figured getting out of the building alive after taking the killing shot, and then safely getting away entirely, would be virtually impossible.

Matt Adams was not suicidal, nor was he fanatical. He now philosophically agreed with the pressing need to rid the world of Ernie Wolf. And he hoped whatever came next for the world would be a bit better than the current mess it was in. On a personal level, he wanted to start up again somewhere fresh, doing something completely different, perhaps farming. And he would like to meet a pretty and loving woman, and make her his wife, and raise a family with her.

It suddenly struck him that he would likely never be able to get his left eye fixed. He was about to become a renegade. He asked himself how he could possibly attract a nice lady while wearing his eyepatch, and continually running away from the VPF.

'All just dreams and fantasy,' he nagged himself. 'Better just deal with the current reality, Matt, as grim as it is.'

Matt noted that there were two outdoor springtime rallies planned for Ernie. One was scheduled for eight o'clock in the evening on Saturday, March 25, 2484 in Duluth, Minnesota, where Ernie was going to open a refurbished dry-dock for lake freighters. The Social Club elite had intelligence that Ernie would give his speech at the renovated dockyard, with his back to Lake Superior. And apparently, Ernie did not like to speak from inside a fully-enclosed, bullet-proof glass box. Rather, he always used a three-sided glass shield with two teleprompters in front of his podium outside of the glass shield. Therefore, his backside would be completely exposed. But that meant Matt would have to take his shot from somewhere out on Lake Superior, from a moving vessel. And the Secret Service and the Coast Guard would undoubtedly be patrolling the lake and the shoreline, and no boat would be allowed anywhere near the dockyard.

The other outdoor rally was planned for two weeks earlier, at eight o'clock in the evening on Saturday, March 11, 2484 in Riverside Park in Detroit, Michigan. Ernie was apparently going to tell his base about his elaborate plan to rebuild the condemned Ambassador III suspension bridge. The bridge was located just to the east of the park, and it was now only being used by brave pedestrians, and desperate or stupid people on bicycles.

Matt decided that the Riverside Park venue was really the only credible opportunity for him.

Ernie would have his back to the Detroit River during his speech. And on the other side of the river, to the southeast, would be the especially rundown and much smaller, ancient city of Windsor, Ontario. Matt thought he might be able to find a suitable, hidden vantage point somewhere on the Windsor side of the river. He would have to personally reconnoitre that shoreline to pick out the right spot, and then put a detailed, practical plan together to make use of it effectively. He wondered if Daquan could help him with the preliminary scouting work. But he put that sketchy idea aside for a moment.

There was an old but fairly large and detailed map of the Great Lakes on a wall in Devo's cafeteria. By referencing that map, Matt figured the shot he would likely have to make would be on the order of eleven-hundred yards or so. But Matt had killed men at over twice that distance. Ideally he would want to use a fifty-calibre rifle like the one he had used very successfully as a long-range sniper. The kinetic energy contained in a speeding fifty-calibre bullet was fearsome. One well-placed shot would be almost explosively lethal.

He could do the sniper calculations in his head for such a weapon, to properly adjust his aim for distance and gravity, and wind velocity. He would be at roughly the same elevation as his target, so he would not have to worry about angle of descent or ascent. He would try to nail down a shooting location from which he could get a good prior range estimate from a more accurate map.

Hopefully he would also have a 'mildot' scope on his rifle, and he could use that to confirm the range estimate knowing that the target was almost exactly two yards tall.

He had memorized a wind table for his fifty-calibre sniper rifle. Fifty-calibre rounds had not changed significantly for centuries. The original design had been superb. So the wind table he had memorized would be valid if the rifle he had to work with had about the same muzzle velocity, and he strongly suspected that it would.

And he was very experienced with accurately estimating wind speed and direction.

But he would have to ask the Social Club elite, and perhaps by extension, the benevolent oligarchs, for help in obtaining such a highly-specialized and restricted rifle. And those folks almost certainly could not obtain for him a modern M209 rifle, the one he was most familiar with. Those weapons were few and far between, and locked-up in ultra-secure armouries on only a couple of military bases. Still, he would tell the Social Club elite that they would have to get him *some* type of fairly equivalent fifty-calibre rifle to enable him to do the job properly. And the current owner of that rifle must be content with the idea that he or she would never see it again.

There was so much more that had to be planned in great detail, like how to travel probably a couple of times between Akron and Detroit without being questioned or searched. And he would have to possess and possibly transport a totally illegal weapon without being detected. And he would like to create some cunning diversions to make people believe, at least initially, that the killing shot came from somewhere else, to buy him some time to get way from the scene.

And he would have to figure out how to get *completely* away, and where to go exactly.

Matt had only a notional idea about how best to escape from the Windsor area. Roadways and railways would be right out. Those would be the first places the Secret Service and the VPF would move towards and secure. But freighters still worked the lakes, carrying iron ore and wheat to world markets via transshipment terminals on the Saint Lawrence River estuary. And lake freighters also moved liquefied natural gas, refined hydrocarbons, bulk commodities and some manufactured goods to and from United States harbours.

Matt had worked three years on a grain-carrying lake freighter, and he still had his expired, able-bodied seaman identification card. But he never kept it on his person with his 'Audie Zaitsev' phony identification cards.

After completing Grade Eleven, the highest grade offered in Baie-Comeau public schools, Matt's father Phillipe had helped him get that lake freighter job. Phillipe Adams had managed the ancient Baie-Comeau grain transhipment terminal, and a 'Laker' skipper with a gambling problem had owed him a few favours. Matt was the beneficiary of that debt settlement.

Phillipe Adams and Maude, his wife, had both died of some kind of infectious disease while Matt was sniping away in Central America. The memory of the loss of his loving parents greatly saddened Matt. He thought his first cousin and once good friend Claude Adams might still be alive, but he had not heard from him in years. Claude had been working as a lumberjack in a forest north of Baie-Comeau when Matt had left to join the Army. If he was still alive, Claude might be able to help him get further away, perhaps to extreme northern Quebec. But that meant Matt would first need to somehow travel safely and undetected all of the way to Baie-Comeau.

There was so much more to work out. And Matt knew he had to break it all down into manageable bits, and take one methodical step at a time.

He decided he would share his initial thoughts and many doubts with his close friend Daquan Jefferson, and hopefully get started on this incredibly risky mission with his help.

11

Matt Adams woke up yelling something. He just had the recurring nightmare again. It was always approximately the same vivid dream, and he could never figure out what triggered it.

He looked at the alarm clock beside his bed. The red LED display indicated 02:01. 'Yes, that's consistent,' he thought to himself. 'I wonder why?'

He threw off the bed covers, and sat up to have a sip of water from the tall glass that he always kept beside his alarm clock. He was sweating profusely, and that always seemed to go with the dream. "I wonder why?" he said out loud.

After a few moments, he lay back down on the bed without covering himself.

He had to admit that he probably knew the answer to his problem. He figured he must have post-traumatic stress disorder to some degree. If that was the case, he was only experiencing two of the dozen or so possible symptoms the Army had warned him about. The recurring nightmare was one. The guilt and shame he felt about the many soldiers he had killed for his country was the other.

He realized that he never talked about what he did in the war because he felt guilty about it. Knowing that the war accomplished nothing but hardship and grief made the feeling of guilt worse.

And the recurring nightmare was centred around other feelings of guilt, too.

When he was fourteen, Matt went to check a trap line in the middle of a Quebec winter with his cousin Claude. Claude was a year older than Matt. Matt's father Phillipe had taught Matt how to shoot, and he had given him a '270' or a twenty-seven calibre, bolt-action rifle, as sort of a 'coming of age' birthday present. Matt immediately started carrying the high-velocity rifle with him whenever he went into the wilderness.

It had been a frosty but clear morning, and the two teenage friends had seen something well off in the distance. It was about one hundred and fifty yards or so away from them, down a snow-covered trail that had been cut in a perfectly straight line through a forest of tall trees. It looked to be an animal that resembled a very large dog. It was standing sideways to the trail, and chewing on something in about the same place that they had set out a trap. Claude had yelled, "*Mon Dieu, c'est un loup*! That's a wolf Matt! And he's wrecking our pelt! Kill it! Quickly!"

Matt had immediately agreed that the creature sure looked like a wolf. The jet-black, scruffy-looking beast had stopped eating, and had just turned its head to stare at Matt and Claude with gore dripping from its jowls.

Matt did not have a scope on his rifle, but he would not need one. It had been sighted-in for two hundred yards, and there was no wind to speak of. He had just quickly knelt down in the snow, worked the bolt to load the chamber, aimed half a foot lower than the heart of the creature and slowly squeezed the trigger. The crack from the powerful rifle had been deafening.

The beast had instantly toppled over.

Matt and Claude had then jogged quickly on their snowshoes to have a look at what Matt had shot. When they had got up to the stricken beast, they could see that it was twitching a bit, but bleeding profusely in the right spot. The shot had been very well placed.

"Hey, it's only got three legs!" Claude had noted with a gasp. "I bet it got its foot stuck in a trap, probably one of ours, and had to chew its own leg off! It's a lone wolf, and maybe a coy-wolf too, you know, a wolf-coyote cross. But I'm no expert. I guess it could no longer keep up with its pack, so the others must have banished it. Poor bastard! The only way it could live was by scavenging. Bloody sad, but at least we put it out of its misery."

Matt knew that Claude had spoken the truth, but the event had always haunted him. He liked wolves, and they almost always kept their distance. They were excellent stalkers, they worked as a team and they were happy with their social status, be it alpha or omega within their pack. If a trap he had set for pine marten and mink had ultimately led to the wolf's suffering and death, well, he felt pretty bad about that.

In Matt's recurring dream, he always killed a soldier with a very long sniper shot. The tactical situations were always slightly different. But the locations were very similar to places where he had actually been. After he had made the killing shot, Matt's spotter would always say to him at the end of the dream, "Hey, Matt, that was a wolf you killed, not a man! And it's only got three legs!" And then Matt would wake up in a state of panic.

Right after experiencing the dream, Matt would always ask himself how killing a three-legged wolf could possibly be worse than killing a human being. He had killed one wolf in his lifetime, and hundreds of human beings. The dream did not make a lot of sense, but it sure bothered him.

Matt lay still for a long while. Eventually he pulled the covers back over himself. Just before he fell asleep again, he wondered if the recurring dream would change, or go away entirely, if he managed to kill an evil bastard of a human being that just happened to be named Wolf.

12

Daquan Jefferson listened attentively and sympathetically as Matt Adams told him about his recurring nightmare. Daquan was giving Matt a long overdue haircut while Matt was talking.

It was raining outside, and it was approaching two o'clock in the afternoon on Sunday, January 16, 2484. Matt had queued up behind two bedraggled, soaking-wet homeless men to get a free haircut in Daquan's drafty, leaky, squatter's shack.

Daquan had been living alone in the crude, derelict cabin for a few months. It was located near the southern boundary of an unused and overgrown City of Akron acreage that decades ago had been a children's hospital. The heavily forested plot of land also formed the southern boundary of a now institutionalized, black ghetto.

Through word of mouth, many desperate, homeless people of all races and ethnicity were taking advantage of Daquan's magnanimous once-a-week offer of charity. The LOP and VPF were paying very little if any attention to what was happening. Daquan figured there probably was not much sport in harassing starving homeless people. On the street outside the downtown barber shop where he worked, he once overheard an LOP thug exclaim to a peer, 'They're all ignorant and stupid, and doomed to early, lice-ridden deaths. They're just like rats, you know. So, I say good riddance!'

The Sunday afternoon charity sessions in his shack took about an hour or two out of Daquan's only day off during a week. But it made him feel good, and he learned a lot about what was really happening in the core of the city. When he worked as a paid barber in the segregated shop downtown, black customers were afraid to say anything to him. But everyone, including Daquan, knew the public place could very well be under active surveillance.

Daquan shared every piece of information that he thought might be important with the Social Club elite. In fact, Daquan was now a junior member of the elite. Matt was made aware of that development, and he was indirectly told by the elite to tell Daquan about his mission, and to actively seek out his help. Daquan was a wise and close friend, and Matt really did not need a prod to involve him.

When Matt was finished talking, Daquan said quietly, "PTSD is a funny thing, Matt. I've heard it's different for everyone. But if completing your mission helps save America, and the *Second Chance*, I'm sure you'll feel better. And you *should* feel better, and move on to something completely different, to put it all behind you. I bet the bad dreams will happen a lot less often in your future."

"I sure hope so, Daquan. Thanks! Listen, have you come up with any ideas about how I can safely make a visit to Detroit and Windsor?"

"Yes, I think I have, but I'll have to go with you."

"Daquan, this is really dangerous business. Giving me advice is one thing, but doing field operations is quite another thing entirely."

"I know that, Matt. But you'll need a good alibi to be able to go there, on the sly. And you can't use public transportation, even if it worked, as the VPF and even the LOP will get suspicious, and check your ID, or even search you. So, you'll have to use the reinstated underground railway, that's all, and I'll need to help you use it. Do you know what I'm talking about?"

"Haven't got a clue."

"Well, before and during the Civil War, escaped slaves were moved up to slave-free Canada by a secret, highly-organized network of people, both black and white, and I imagine some native people, too. Sympathetic people in the network had secret hiding places in their homes that were used as staging areas. They called it the 'underground railway', because it was covert and basically invisible. But it worked.

"And something like it is operating again. It helps people trying to escape fascist persecution, but mostly people of colour, who must pay cash for room and board. What used to be Canada is not as racist or fascist yet as the rest of America, and may never be that way. I understand Cousin Ernie is not as popular up there, not by a long shot.

"Here's what I'm thinking. The elite told me they will give us the bit of cash that we'll need. It's about two hundred miles to Windsor. We'll ride our bikes, say fifty miles a day, so four full days with three overnights. I found out where the safe houses are that might accept us, both along the route, and in Windsor.

"I'll be riding in front. You'll follow behind a hundred yards or so. If I look back, and you're not there, I'll stop and wait until I see you again. When we get to the next safe house, you'll hang back and I'll check it out. I'll come back outside and lean my bike on the front fence or side wall of the house if they'll take us in. Then you'll park your bike in the same place and walk through the same door I used to re-enter the place, say five minutes after me.

"We'll put what we'll need for the trip in backpacks, but everyone does that, so we won't stand out. Lots of regular poor people travel on bikes as you know, so we won't bring extra attention to ourselves by travelling that way. You okay with this so far?"

"Sounds really good, Daquan."

"Okay, great. Now we'll need some good excuses to get say, ah, *two weeks* off work. So, you'll need to think a bit out of your sniper-man box for a minute.

"To have any chance of getting away with this you'll need to look different, Matt, after you pull that rifle trigger. That eyepatch is a dead giveaway. We know there is no way we can get you a functional working replacement eye. But I checked around, and there's a guy in Detroit, a barber actually, that does surgery on the side. You know, he'll take out a bullet for you if you get shot by the VPF, or the mafia or whomever.

"As an aside, I understand that in the middle ages some barbers also performed surgery, as crude as it was. What goes around, comes around, I guess.

"Anyway, one of my customers told me that his uncle had this Detroit barber dude install a *glass* eye for him. That's what they used to do before bionic options became available. It will be purely cosmetic. Under close inspection, it won't look natural. It might point off slightly in the wrong direction, for instance. And you'll still have your scars.

"But with a bit of make-up, and wrap-around dark sunglasses, no one will be able to tell you have a glass eye, or your scars, I'm sure of that.

"So, after the surgery, you'll go back to wearing your eyepatch. You might need to let everything the Detroit barber does to you heal-up anyway. When you go back to Detroit the *second* time, on your own but with my arrangements, you could do it without the eyepatch, and with the make-up and the sunglasses. You okay with this part of the plan, too?"

Matt hesitated for a long moment, but then he said, "Yes, okay, Daquan."

"Okay, great. Now, I've already told my boss that I need two weeks off. I basically told him the truth, that a close friend needs some eye surgery done in Detroit, on the sly, and that my friend needs my help. He's cool with it.

"I think you should tell Devo that your eye socket is really bugging you, and Veterans Affairs has you on a never-ending waiting list. But a freelancing surgeon told you he can help you out, for cash. Don't say that the surgeon is in Detroit. And you'll say that after the operation, the surgeon thinks you'll need a couple of weeks to heal up so you won't get infected.

"Devo will probably check with the VPF before they say 'yes'. But you'll tell Cranston in a letter the very same thing. They might say 'no', but I bet they'll say 'yes'. The elite thinks the VPF still considers you a worthwhile and rather inexpensive asset. And you're proposing to do something on your own tab that you probably really do in fact need.

"So, what do you say to all of that, Matt?"

"It all does sound pretty good, Daquan. Thanks!"

"Okay, no sweat. Hey, I'm all done with your haircut now. You look like a respectable pirate again!

"You better get out of here now, and come back next week, say for a shave, so grow a beard. I'll assume we'll be able to leave together the next day. If not, we'll target the following Monday.

"Oh, and, Matt, you'll need a different excuse to go to Detroit the *second* time. If you quit your job, the VPF might get suspicious. So, I think it will be better for you to get fired or laid-off by Devo for not giving Cranston enough juicy stuff. I'll work on that idea with the elite."

13

Dame Heather Farquhar was both the Chairman of the Board and Chief Executive Officer of Moon Base Corporation. The Moon's twenty-thousand or so people, including Moon Base employees and their families, used GMT, or Greenwich Mean Time. It was now eight o'clock in the morning GMT on Monday, January 17. Heather was waiting impatiently in her office for a very private meeting that she had just requested.

In fact, Heather was so anxious with worry that she simply could not manage to stay seated behind her large, ornate desk. Instead she was unconsciously pacing around the richly furnished suite, completely unaware that she was also mumbling to herself.

Heather was startled by a soft rap on the frame of the door to her office. But she quickly gathered herself together, and said quietly, "Jürgen, thanks for dropping by on such short notice. I know how busy you are. But I just could not wait any longer for an update from you, and I certainly could not wait until our regularly-scheduled Wednesday morning meeting. So, please come in, close the door, and sit down, ah, over here, in the lounge area."

Jürgen Mayer was the Chief Operating Officer of Moon Base Corporation. He had been born on the Moon, in the South Pole Base hospital. He and his CEO now occupied the only two private offices in the base. The base had been built into the lip of the large South Pole crater. A mine extracted water ice towards the bottom of the crater. There were also a number of industrial facilities scattered around the interior, concave surface of the crater.

Jürgen had never left the Moon, and he loved to be referred to as a 'real loonie'. He was a very experienced electro-mechanical engineer, and an exceptional manager of people and facilities. He was forty-five years old, and looked to be about that age. He was six feet tall, and very fit. He also had excellent posture. He could move about very quickly and expertly in the Moon's one-sixth gravity field, with hardly a noticeable bounce to his step. He still had a thick head of wavy hair, but it was now mostly gray with just a few flecks of black. He also had a handsome, Saxon face, which was made far more interesting by a fascinating network of creases and wrinkles. His most striking feature however was a pair of brilliant blue eyes. Fortunately he had never had to wear eyeglasses, or even think about laser surgery.

Heather Farquhar had a PhD in astrophysics and an MBA, both from the University of London. She was a proud 'LBC' or 'Loonie by Choice'. She had been working as a senior executive on the Moon for twelve years. She had been the CEO of the Corporation for five years, and had just recently been appointed Chairman of the Board of Directors as well. She was fifty-two years old, and petite. She was not exceptionally pretty, but she always dressed well, and she carried herself with regal grace, even in low gravity. In fact, she was a second cousin of the reigning King of England, not that anyone cared about things like that any more. She still had a few freckles, and long red hair that she braided and then pinned-up in a spiral bun. And she had green eyes that were very hard to see through her oversized, purple eyeglass frames with their thick lenses.

The two top executives sat down facing each other with a narrow walnut coffee table situated between them. Heather leaned forward, and asked quietly, "So, how does the new stuff look, Jürgen? Is there anything missing, or was anything damaged in transit?"

"It has all checked out perfectly," Jürgen replied with his clear, booming, baritone voice. Then he smiled and added, "Just like the previous six shipments. So, we're now ready to start assembly. In fact, we've already begun."

Jürgen could tell that his boss was excited, and he liked her the better for it. In fact, he had the greatest respect for Heather Farquhar, and all that she had done to advance the *Second Chance* project in the face of an endless series of political, financial and logistical obstacles.

"So, will the Earth-side lava tube be adequate to house the device?" Heather asked with concern.

"At one and a half kilometres, we think it will be *just* long enough for the fully assembled weapon," Jürgen replied happily. "The device will be powered by its own dedicated fusion reactor, the one we installed on the same side of the South Pole crater last year. The weapon came with an elaborate charge generating and storage system, and enough mercury to fire it fifty or so times."

"Hopefully we may never have to fire it at all," Heather said quietly with a shake of her head. "However, our benevolent oligarch friends and financiers on Earth believe that President Ernie Wolf is only a couple months away from launching his Moon missile. How certain are we that this weapon could destroy that missile, or rather the steerable thermonuclear warhead that it will deliver into Moon orbit?"

"The Russian inventors tested the weapon secretly, and shared the test results with us through the oligarch network," replied Jürgen succinctly. "It should work exactly as they promised it will."

Jürgen had a rather refined 'loonie' accent, which had a Germanic twang to it. The official language of Moon Base was English. Most 'loonies' had European or Eurasian ancestry. Jürgen had studied the German language to find out more about his ancestry, and everyone knew that he liked to use German expressions to add a touch of elegance to his speech.

After taking a moment to order his thoughts, Jürgen elaborated by saying, "The shooting device is basically a particle accelerator. Our particles will be mercury nuclei moving at near light speed. So, when the particles hit their warhead target, the massive kinetic energy transfer will superheat the surface of the device, and deeper ionization effects will fry the internal electronics.

"The key step-change that occurred during the highly-secretive, technical development of this weapon was the refinement of an amazing four-dimensional, high-precision, targeting system. For the system to work properly, we will have to install ancillary tracking facilities in four remote locations. They will be equidistant from each other, and twenty kilometres away from the South Pole. Thankfully, they will not have to be manned facilities."

Heather nodded, and then she sat quietly for a long moment, lost in her own thoughts. Then she asked with obvious concern, "Can we *really* keep all of this secret, Jürgen?"

"Yes, I believe so," he replied confidently. "Other than you and me, there are only the twenty-six people on the weapon assembly team who are fully in-the-know. They are all 'lifer loonies', and frankly, they're all *fanatical* about protecting Moon Base, and the *Second Chance*. They will also quickly job transition to become our firing team. They all know we have to keep this special project completely secret, at least until we actually fire the weapon for the first time.

"Thankfully, it will be fairly easy to isolate the firing team members as a group. They have their own camp now, and have just moved into it with their immediate families. All outside communication from the camp has been banned, and that restriction will remain in place at least until the weapon is fired for the first time.

"As for the weapon and targeting system facilities, they all look very much like our other facilities. The 'sharp end' of the weapon, if you will, is retractable. It's actually a coaxial, flexible tube that is shaped and aimed by robotic arms that are sort of like 'Canadarms' on a space station. None of this 'sharp-end' assembly will be seen until we decide to fire the weapon in anger."

Heather seemed to like Jürgen's answer, and politely nodded again. Then she anxiously addressed what was really on her mind. She reached across the narrow table and grabbed hold of Jürgen's left forearm. Then she looked straight into his eyes and asked, "Can we have it all ready *in time*, Jürgen?"

Jürgen patted her arm, smiled and said, "Yes, I believe so, Skipper. Everything is modular, and well-designed for the many peculiarities of lunar construction. I think we'll have it all ready in six or seven weeks.

"There is one residual risk, however, that we will just *have* to accept, unfortunately. And that is, we can't *test fire* the weapon because that would reveal it to Cousin Ernie and our other Earthbound enemies. We do not believe any of our enemies and detractors have spies on the Moon. But collectively they *do* have spy satellites around both the Earth and the Moon. So, we'll just have to depend on thorough diagnostic checking, and a bit of good luck."

Heather took a long, slow, deep breath, and did her best to say correctly in German, "*Dann alles gute, Herr Mayer.*"

14

Matt was sitting by himself on the old, solitary wooden bench in the secluded glade near the heart of Morgan Park. It was five minutes before nine o'clock on the morning of February 13. It was cool and clear. Matt was wearing a woolen jacket and a pair of woolen gloves.

The winter had been like all winters now. There had been very little snowfall in Akron, Ohio, and a thin covering of wet snow never stayed on the ground for more than an hour or so. There was now even a smell of spring in the air, and the bare-branched deciduous bushes and trees all had large, well-developed buds.

Matt heard the creaky old bicycle approaching before he saw it. The old man wobbled to a stop behind the bench. He was probably a bit overdressed for the above-freezing air temperature they were currently experiencing. He was wearing woolen mittens, a weather-worn lambskin coat, and a rather comical old-style lambskin aviator cap. The old man grabbed on to the back of the bench to steady himself as he dismounted from the bike. Then he leaned the bike against the back of the bench, stretched his back muscles with a groan, and then sat down on the bench about three feet away from Matt.

As usual, the old man was strictly business. He said in a whisper, "We have secured a suitable weapon for you."

"What kind of rifle is it?" Matt asked, also in a whisper.

"It's an antique, I am told, from the collection of a benevolent oligarch living in the US. It's a bolt-action McAllister MAC-50 K1-Z2. It was made in Flagstaff, Arizona in 2419, but apparently it is in mint condition. It weighs 26 pounds. It has a hydraulic recoil mitigation system in the buttstock. It has a fiberglass stock, and a bipod. It has a rotary pistol-grip and a clip for five, fifty-calibre rounds. It comes to us with five rounds of expertly re-recrafted .5 DMG 12.7 millimetre by 99 millimetre ammunition. It has a Zeitzer and Bausch 5-25 by 56 telescopic sight. Oh, and we have not been able to secure a night-vision scope, or a pair of night-vision binoculars for you as you requested. But we believe your target will be very well illuminated with floodlights.

"Do you know this weapon? And will this all be satisfactory?"

"It will probably do the trick all right. I obviously have no direct experience with this particular weapon."

"Has it been fired recently? And has it been *precisely* sighted-in, also recently? I will not have the opportunity to do that myself."

"Yes, the oligarch owner told us that just before transit he personally and expertly sighted the weapon in for exactly two-hundred yards. And he had a sharp-shooting expert friend of his confirm his scope adjustments. The owner has a large estate in a rural area. He hunts deer on the acreage, so gunshots are heard all of the time there. I must not elaborate further."

"Okay, I can work with that. I've fired similar weapons, but again, not this particular weapon. The model is famous, with an effective range of over two-thousand yards. Have you got an improved estimate of the range for me? And do you know the muzzle velocity of the rifle?"

"Using accurate maps, we estimate that it is 1168 yards from the river-side of the old windmill you picked out to the back of the stage where Cousin Ernie will be standing. So you'll probably want to add a couple of yards to that number, using your own judgement, with direct visual references I imagine you will see through the scope? That is your business of course, as you are the expert.

"Now, I was told the muzzle velocity of the rifle is 2800 feet per second. Is that acceptable?"

"That's perfect. It means I can use familiar algorithms. Now, I'll need the manuals for the rifle and for the scope, to adjust the minutes of angle of drop on the scope for the range of the shot, and also, and separately, the spin driftage. And it always helps to know the particular 'do's and the don'ts' for any weapon. They all have their peculiarities."

"The owner said that what you might need for instruction has been taped to the stock. I believe he made specific reference to what you were just talking about."

"How will I acquire the weapon?"

"It has been placed exactly where you wanted it, together with the tube of glue you wanted. I was assured that the weapon was handled very gently in transit. It is now behind the wooden panel slats that you marked out for us, near the uppermost window that faces the river. The weapon was placed expertly, and the expert did it at night. He is sure that he was not observed."

Matt looked a bit sceptical, so the old man reluctantly added, "He works as a commercial security guard. His employer has a contract with the present-day village of Windsor, and they check the property on the third night of every month, for vagrants and vandals. His work for us did not require a bribe. He is an elite Social Club member. I have probably said too much. But I know you need to believe your weapon will be there for you, and that it will do the job properly.

"The transit expert said you picked a great spot. The windmill is an historic replica that has been replaced three times over the last five centuries. As you know, it is located in a now overgrown and heavily-wooded area that used to be a city park. The neighbouring apartment buildings are all deserted. Windsor is not much of a city any more, as you saw for yourself with Daquan.

"What will you do with the weapon after you use it?"

"I'll put it back in the same spot. I'll glue the cover panels back in place. The owner, or this security guard, must *never* try to retrieve it. Forensic analysis of rifling grooves will positively link the weapon to the killing round, which they will no doubt recover almost immediately.

"What about the flash-bang grenades?"

"You told us you only want to return to the windmill once, to make the shot, and then get away from the scene as quickly as possible. So, you'll have to carry the three grenades with you to Detroit and Windsor, and place them yourself beforehand in the spots you select. The radio-controlled triggering device is now stashed in the wall beside the gun and the tube of glue. The bombs will go off simultaneously when you depress the trigger lever.

"Do you have an escape planned-out and put in place?"

"Yes, Daquan helped me with that. But I must not elaborate further, like you've correctly said to me a few times about other matters."

"Good. Keep it a secret. Anything else right now?"

"I need to cut my ties with Devo Construction without raising suspicion. And I'll need a bit of cash to cover operating expenses, and to get away afterwards. It might take me a month or more to reach where I want to go."

"We'll send the cash to you tomorrow by courier. It should be more than enough. You are about to earn it, but we don't want you to feel like a wealth-craving mercenary. And we'll also send a suitable draft letter to you by the same courier. You can copy it in your own hand writing and then mail it to Cranston. The dominos should fall quickly after that.

"You're still wearing your patch. How's your eye coming along?"

"It's healed up now, and it no longer hurts. The patch will come off the night of the shooting, and then stay off."

"And you have a plan to get to Detroit and Windsor?"

"Yes, Daquan set that up during the scouting trip we made together. I'll be staying in the same places as last time, and riding my bicycle again. I'll be dressed as I am now, in worker's clothing."

"We may be at war again soon. We know SAC now has an ICBM ready for Cousin Ernie. It is uncertain how this development will complicate things for us. The Moon missile is also advancing quickly, perhaps more quickly than we estimated. So, time is of the essence. You *must* succeed, Matt, and stay exactly on schedule."

"I won't fail the cause, sir."

"We know you won't. And we wish you the very best of luck. Now, I better go. You should wait twenty minutes or so before leaving."

Matt shook hands with the old man, and watched him leave. He sat on the bench for another thirty minutes before starting his solitary walk home.

15

Dear Cranston,

I hope you remain in good spirits?

I must admit I'm a bit down in the dumps. You, see, I've had a bit of a falling out with the Social Club here in Akron.

I didn't see it coming. It seems a Club member overheard me telling a non-member that 'something big' was about to happen in or near Minot, North Dakota.

It was all pretty innocent. I was just having a sip of coffee at an outdoor kiosk, and small talking with someone I didn't know about the weather and such. The young lady mentioned she was from North Dakota where it has been a lot colder lately. That's when I said I heard there was going to be a big demonstration near the SAC base in Minot to protest the return of missiles and nukes to the area.

Well anyway, someone from the Social Club must have been nearby and overheard what I said. Two elders in the club told me not to come to any more Saturday noontime get-togethers. That's a real downer, because I really enjoyed those sessions.

I'm not sure what I'm going to do now for a social life.

My job with Devo Construction is okay, but it's becoming a bit too routine. I'm bored silly half the time. I know more already than the cold-patch team supervisor. I think I am more than qualified to do the job, and my supervisor's job for that matter. But promotions are based on seniority apparently, not ability or potential.

It would not upset me too much if Devo let me go. If they do, I suppose I'll head back to Texas. I kind of got to like that place. And I heard there may be some decent work opportunities in the Houston area.

So, not sure where my next letter will be coming from, or when you'll get it. But I promise to actively keep in touch with you.

Your friend,
Audie Zaitsev

16

Jose Jimenez was not his real name. He knew it had been used in the distant past by an American stand-up comedian who made a living making fun of the way recently immigrated Hispanic people talked. But very few present-day people had seen those ancient, televised comedic routines. So the false name was as good as any other one that he could have selected.

Jose was a spy and a terrorist. He worked for an oligarch that lived in Acapulco, Mexico, and who did most of his illicit business in Mexico City. Jose's current assignment placed him in Houston, Texas. Jose found that he fit in very well in that city. For a long while it had been about one-third black, one-third white and one-third Hispanic. Now a mixed population predominated.

As always, Jose travelled on an old bicycle to the bonded customs warehouse on the industrial canal south of Texas City. The bicycle had an electric motor assist. Because the rickety bike could cruise at an astounding and rather terrifying thirty miles per hour, Jose always wore a helmet when he rode it.

Jose was forty-one years old, and he was short and wiry. He looked very much like he had Mayan ancestry.

He had short black hair, a prominent hooked nose, dark skin and dark eyes.

Jose was wearing a pair of faded and patched-up blue jeans, and a frayed but clean, white tee-shirt with a breast pocket. He was holding on to his helmet while an overworked US Customs agent flipped through his manifest. The balding young man was sweating profusely in the hundred-degree heat. He glanced at Jose for a second and asked gruffly, "What's that you're holding, bubba, your crash helmet?"

"Oh, I hope not," replied Jose with a straight face using an intentionally thick Hispanic accent.

The old joke was completely lost on the busy young man. He finished scanning the document, and then he snapped, "Okay, two pallets of canned tomatoes from Italy. And you are…?" He was now glaring intensely at Jose.

"My name Jose Jimenez."

"Let me see your passport, Jose."

Jose pulled a US passport out of the breast pocket on his tee-shirt and handed it to the customs officer. The agent looked at the document carefully, and studied Jose's face intently again for a few moments. Then he handed the document back to Jose.

The passport was a very good forgery. The customs agent could have confirmed that it was a forgery by accessing the immigration department's computer database. But he was outside of the bonded warehouse, and well away from his sweltering, un-air-conditioned office. He could also have thoroughly inspected the two pallets of cans. But he was behind schedule. US Customs was now underfunded and understaffed like every other government agency.

Instead, the customs agent just asked, "So, what are you going to do with all of those wop tomatoes, Jose?"

"Oh, I make a lot of salsa, Senor, in my lunch wagon," replied Jose. "These tomatoes, they are the very best. And my salsa, it is also the very best. I wish you could try some right now, Senor Officer, and I know you would agree. But my wagon, she is far away, up in Katy."

Just then a small electric-powered delivery truck backed into a large bin of oranges nearby, and toppled it over. Oranges were suddenly rolling around everywhere on the roadway by the loading dock.

The customs agent yelled at the driver, "You stupid freaking nigger! Watch where you're going, asshole! Now, get out of that filthy truck, and put every *goddam orange* back into that bin! Move it!"

The now frantic agent returned his attention to Jose and mumbled, "Those oranges still have not cleared customs. So, I'm going to have to watch that guy carefully. You got a vehicle to help you, Jose?"

"Si, Senor Officer, a truck, she is waiting by the gate, all I have to do is wave at the driver."

"The duty is one hundred bucks, all in cash."

The US had bi-lateral trade agreements with about two-dozen Far Eastern and European nations, including

Italy. Jose knew there was no duty owing. But corruption was a way of life now everywhere. He simply reached into his back pocket, pulled out an unsealed envelope and handed it to the customs agent.

The customs agent looked in the envelope, flipped through the contents and noted Jose had given him one hundred fifty dollars in well-used, small denomination bills. He simply nodded, put the envelope in his back pocket, and said quietly, "Okay, load up your two pallets, and get the hell out of here, Jose." Then he said more loudly, "And you better tell your truck driver not to run over any of those oranges! Or back into any bins himself! Geez, what a *freaking* day this is turning out to be..." He trailed off as he ran over to supervise the comic, chaotic, runaway orange retrieval operation.

It all had been carefully staged.

Jose worked quickly with his Hispanic truck driver to offload a small forklift that was attached to the back of the panelled, two-and-a-half ton, LNG-powered truck. Then they efficiently moved the two pallets of canned tomatoes inside of the truck. They re-attached the small forklift to the back of the truck. Then the driver drove the truck away with its load of canned tomatoes, and Jose put his helmet back on and rode away on his electric bicycle.

Jose knew there was a cavity inside the stack of cans on one of the pallets they had just acquired. Inside that cavity was the fissile core for the cylindrical 'secondary', or fusion part of a thermonuclear bomb.

Jose had two accomplices, and they were the two truck drivers that had just helped him clear customs without detection. The three men now had everything they needed. The next step was to complete the assembly of the radiation-implosion, two-stage, fission-fusion, 380 kiloton device. When it was ready for deployment, it would weigh a little over a thousand pounds. They could use the bigger truck to deliver the weapon to any ground location they could drive to, as long as they could avoid detection.

Mexico did not have missiles. But it would soon have a fully operational nuclear bomb on US soil. And they had a crude but effective means of delivery, too.

Jose knew that his oligarch boss was not eager to blow up downtown Houston. But if Cousin Ernie did something stupid, like launch an ICBM at Mexico City, well, Jose and his two fellow patriotic hombres would not hesitate to comply with an order to retaliate in kind.

17

President Ernie Wolf would only leave the White House to speak at Veterans Party rallies, which were all extensively, and of course favourably, covered by state-controlled television and radio networks. Ernie was afraid to appear in public more than that. He had recurring nightmares about being assassinated by the unfriendly international network of oligarchs.

Ernie was still very selective about the people he listened to. The VPF, and the remnants of the once powerful CIA, continuously supplied him with domestic and international intelligence. But usually that intelligence did not agree with Ernie's fascist paradigms, which stemmed from a street thug's gut instinct. So he usually blew off intelligence reports without even reading them.

It therefore fell upon the four members of Ernie's very tight inner circle to attempt to positively influence Ernie's thinking. They wanted him to maintain a semblance of economic stability and security in the nation to in turn maintain his power base, and to protect their own interests of course.

Ernie no longer attended full cabinet meetings. However, those protracted and complex meetings still occurred on a weekly basis. Ernie now left it up to his inner cabinet members to manage those extended team sessions, while ensuring that Ernie's interests were always front and centre in everyone's mind.

But every Monday morning, Ernie would meet with the members of his inner cabinet for an hour or so. He no longer invited state media to cover the start of these meetings. The only people in attendance were the head of the Secret Service, and his three secretaries of state. There was never any prior agenda, or any written minutes kept of their discussions.

The head of the Secret Service, and the leader of the Veterans Party, was Thomas Fitzgerald, who the president affectionately referred to as Tommy. No one else would dare call the man Tommy. He was an ex-mob hitman, with a fierce temper. He was also an overweight, flabby, ugly brute, with a heavily-scarred face from knife fights in his youth that could have gone better from his perspective. Thomas also controlled the LOP. And he controlled many nefarious businesses, which fed a lot of money to himself and the president. He was a fanatical supporter of Ernie. He was openly homosexual, and people who knew him well thought that he might actually be in love with Ernie. But Ernie quite openly preferred women, and the more licentious the better.

Thomas was also, and secretly, a paedophile. Or, at least he thought it was a secret.

Frank Palermo was a secretary of state, in theory on par with his two peer secretaries of state. He ran the VPF and that federal police organization's efficient torture and concentration camps. He also ran the CIA, and the judicial system. He was a competent lawyer, and a superb organizer. He had once been a New York mafia boss consiglieri. Ernie liked him because he kept all of Ernie's many perversions and affairs, including the brutal rapes, out of the public eye. Frank was also completely ruthless, and believed in torture as a great way to terrorize and pacify the general population, and extract useful information before ending the life of an 'undesirable'. But Frank was not sadistic. Everything with him was strictly business. Torture and terrorism were not mindless perversions. They were purposeful. The ends justified the means. And the end would be Frank as an oligarch, or even the next president. Anyone that stood in his way was placed on his secret, 'undesirable' list.

Poppy Beauregard was another secretary of state. He ran the Treasury and the Internal Revenue Service, the Department of the Interior, International Trade, Agriculture, Commerce, Energy, Labour, Transportation, the Diplomatic Corps, and Customs and Immigration. He would also have run Education, Health, Urban Development and Human Services, but Ernie had no interest in what he considered, 'wasteful, 'touchy-feely, socialist kinds of stuff.' Poppy was a certified general accountant who also had mob connections. He was also an oligarch, the malevolent kind, with personal wealth in the billions of dollars. Ernie trusted him because he was probably not motivated to skim much money from government coffers, and therefore from Ernie.

Sidney Lefebvre was the third secretary of state. He ran the Defence Department, including SAC, the Coast Guard, NASA and Veterans Affairs. He was a retired Army three-star or lieutenant general, and a rabid hawk like Ernie. He had grown up hating the Navy, and now made sure it did not get much funding. There was now only an East Coast Fleet and a West Coast Fleet, and two divisions of Marines. He saw some value in the Air Force, but only for tactical support of the Army. He only gave SAC enough money to meet Ernie's demands for a few ICBM's, and a Moon missile. And he considered NASA a waste of money, other than for making and launching a few replacement communication, GPS and spy satellites. He hated *everything* about the international joint venture Moon Base Corporation, and the *Second Chance* project.

Ernie continually reminded Tommy, Frank, Poppy and Sidney that they were all in line to be the next president. He told them he would only name his successor on his deathbed. The four men were obsequiously polite with Ernie and with each other during inner cabinet meetings. But Ernie knew they were continuously at each other's throats outside of those weekly, private sessions.

And Ernie liked that. He believed in survival of the fittest. And the members of his inner cabinet knew full well that he held firmly to that simple, brutal philosophy.

It was ten o'clock in the morning on Monday, February 21. Ernie started his inner cabinet meeting by asking Sidney Lefebvre for a SAC status update.

"Well, we have one Minuteman VI ready to go, Mister President," Sidney said proudly. "We should have two or even three more operational by the end of March."

"I can't start a war with only one goddam missile, Sid!" Ernie yelled. "What the *hell* is the hold-up?"

Sidney recoiled at the rebuke, then replied quietly, "The old underground silos in North Dakota are the problem, Mister President. The reinforcing bars in the concrete walls of the silos have all corroded through centuries of contact with ground water. And the ancillary underground facilities are all very complex, and we have to make sure everything we re-install will work properly."

"What do we need underground silos for, anyway?" Ernie growled.

"Well, Mister President, we want hardened launching sites that probably could withstand a pre-emptive or retaliatory nuclear strike. Frank says no one else has nukes or delivery mechanisms, but I say we can't know that for sure. And we haven't had a mobile intermediate-range option, or a submarine-launched option, or a bomber option, in our nuclear arsenal for over two centuries now. And as far as I'm concerned, the *goddam Navy* must stay *completely* the hell out of this SAC business. It's a money disposal pit!"

"Well, what about the Moon missile, Sid?" Ernie asked a little more respectfully.

"I am very pleased to say that it is actually now ready to go, Mister President," Sidney replied happily. "We completed the project well ahead of schedule with a lot of hard work and dedicated resources."

"How soon can you launch it?"

"Ah, well, hmmm, on say two days' notice from you, Mister President?" Sidney questioned himself out loud. He had not been expecting that question today.

"Well that's *much better*, Sid old buddy!" Ernie barked happily. "I'm completely *fed up* with this gang of oligarch wankers and their annoying death threats. We need to teach them a lesson they'll never forget! And completely wipe out that *Second Chance* monstrosity! It's wasting the world's resources, and interfering with our trade balance."

Then Ernie added impulsively in a cavalier manner, "So, I want you to launch that Moon missile first thing Wednesday morning, Sid."

There was a long moment of stunned silence in the room.

Frank Palermo was the first to react. He stayed remarkably calm while observing, "That action will almost certainly start a world war, Mister President.

And it will be us against the whole freaking world. The oligarchs will undoubtedly all join up against us. That's because they'll be *extremely pissed* that we wrecked their massive, lucrative, business joint venture."

"You sound just like a chicken-shit *wimp*, Frank!" Tommy Fitzgerald yelled as a direct taunt.

Before Frank could react out loud in anger, Poppy Beauregard interjected smoothly with, "That's a bit extreme, Thomas, now isn't it? And I think that outburst was completely uncalled for, frankly.

"But I personally don't see a big problem with this plan of yours, Mister President.

"A *limited* war would be highly stimulating for our tired, old economy. We're probably overdue for one, actually. I think we could limit the reaction to this surprise attack by being proactive with some advance communication. I think Frank could write a very nice letter for you, Mister President, and then deliver a signed version of it to all of the oligarchs in the world over the next few days.

"I think all it has to say, really, is that we have nukes again, deliverable by ICBM's. We don't have to say how many nukes and missiles we have exactly, nor should we. 'Keep them guessing' is always a good strategy! They'll *imagine* we have quite a few nukes and missiles, if we act boldly like this.

"I suggest that with one simple letter we could completely reinstate the deterrence of mutual self-destruction. And I bet the rest of the world will mostly just blink at us when the *Second Chance* is blown to bits.

"To close, Mister President, once again, I don't believe Frank is a *wimp*, far from it. But I bet a whole bunch of these oligarch guys turn out to be just that."

"What do you say, Frank?" Ernie asked with a big grin. He was really enjoying this exchange. "Are you warming up to this idea of mine yet?"

Frank was a really smart guy, and he knew he was now completely isolated in the room.

"Yes, I'm now okay with it, Mister President," Frank said calmly. "I think it's a fine plan. I can have all of the letters on your desk for your signature right after lunch. That is, as long as we don't go overtime today."

"Well that's just great, Frank," Ernie said happily. "And you know, that's all I really wanted to talk with you guys about today. So, you can have a little more time to work with, Frank.

"And *everyone* can start thinking about how to get the most out of a *nice little war*!

"Great *team work* as usual, guys! This meeting is hereby adjourned."

18

It was late in the evening Moon time on Monday, February 28. The COO of Moon Base Corporation, Jürgen Mayer, was sitting beside Traktor Volkov, the lead engineer of the particle-beam weapon project. They were the only people in the firing-system control room. Both men knew they were about to find out if the weapon would actually work.

Jürgen felt he should have greater belief in a positive outcome. Traktor continuously exuded confidence in the device. He had been a senior member of the research and development team back on Earth, and he had supervised every aspect of the assembly process on the Moon. He had also supervised the comprehensive and methodical diagnostic inspection of the very complex weapon system.

That knowledge should have made Jürgen relax just a bit. But he found that he simply could not do that.

In addition to experiencing a classic case of the jitters, Jürgen was feeling a bit of shame. He knew that he had virtually wasted an entire week selfishly wondering how he would deal with a colossal failure. And as a result, he had been getting very little sleep.

But Jürgen was wide awake now, and trying very hard to suppress his growing anxiety.

"How much time until we... until we reach the trigger point, Traktor?" Jürgen asked as calmly as he could manage.

"Is about over North Pole now, Director Jürgen," Traktor answered without a waver in his voice. He spoke with a fairly thick Muscovite Russian accent. "Estimate twenty-seven minutes, right over us."

"And the weapon is ready?"

"Fully charged and loaded. Tube end deployed two hours now. All aiming control arms working properly. Anyone looking from space can see it now, that is, if they know where to look. And lava tube fully evacuated one hour now."

"And the target has not deviated again from its north-south orbital path? No more course corrections?"

"Nyet, still same altitude as *Second Chance*, one hundred, twenty-two point seven six four miles. Two more orbits, direct hit. Might not even *need* bomb. Target orbital insertion and course corrections expertly done. Impressive, even for *Amerikanskaya teknologia. Izveniti*, Yankee technology."

The *Second Chance* was holding its orbit precisely over the Moon's equator. In thirty years' time, when it would leave on its eighty-plus generation mission, it would first aim for a near miss of Mars. A gravitational assist maneuver, and the resulting 'slingshot effect', would change and correct the course of the huge vessel, and increase its velocity considerably, all 'free of charge'. Mars would essentially carry the *Second Chance* briefly along with it on its orbital path, and by doing so, transfer some of its enormous momentum to the much less massive spacecraft.

The Americans had placed their thermonuclear warhead in a polar orbit around the Moon. That meant that it would eventually sweep over the entire surface of the Moon, and with a few cunning course corrections, set up a very close encounter with the *Second Chance*. That close encounter was now imminent.

"We got a few minutes. Coffee, Director?

"Ah, sure Traktor," Jürgen answered after a moment of hesitation. He doubted that coffee could make him feel any *more* anxious. He was about to burst at the seams.

Jürgen held out his metal cup as Traktor readied his thermos bottle. Jürgen's hand was visibly shaking. Traktor gently grabbed hold of his wrist to steady it, and deftly poured half-a-cup of steaming black coffee into the cup.

Jürgen looked with embarrassment at Traktor. Traktor just smiled, and said quietly, "Is okay, Director, you look like I feel, believe me."

After taking his first tentative sips, Jürgen was amazed to find that he thoroughly enjoyed the coffee. It was a good brew, and it invigorated him. For some reason it also calmed him down a bit.

"Above horizon one minute, Director. Tracking camera should be aimed at right spot."

After a minute, Traktor said calmly, "Da, there it is. We have good lock on it. Still fire nearest approach to weapon?"

"Yes, fire the weapon when the warhead is right over us, or rather at its closest approach to us. That is a *direct* order, Traktor. I take full responsibility for whatever happens now." Jürgen was surprised at how he had issued that critical order without a waver in his voice.

"Roger, I just gave your order in turn to computer. We just watch now. Image should gradually improve on screen with auto-focus."

"*Dann alles gute*, Traktor Ivanovich."

"*Spaseeba*, and good luck to you too, Director. Computer is counting down."

After a few more moments, Traktor chanted calmly, "Five, four, three, two, one...

"Confirm weapon has fired! Look, target is *glowing* now! And *wow*! Target has *blown up*!

"No longer have camera lock. Pieces all about same size, I guess, and dispersing radially."

"Yes, I can see that, Traktor."

After taking a moment to dispel some lagging disbelief about what had obviously just occurred, Jürgen said quietly, "Okay, Traktor, please notify the *Second Chance* about what happened. Everyone needs to remain in a safe refuge area, just like we are doing here in Moon Base. I'm not entirely sure how long they'll have to stay there, however. Maybe a couple of hours?"

"I think I should tell those people four hours minimum, Director, just to be on safe side."

"Yes, *do* that Traktor."

It still had not fully sunk in yet. Jürgen felt completely numb.

After Traktor had sent a brief text message to the *Second Chance*, he stood up, and offered his hand to Jürgen. Instead of shaking it, Jürgen grabbed Traktor and pulled him into a bear hug. Then he yelled, "That was freaking *great*! Well done!"

Traktor was suddenly laughing with joy as well, and he said happily, "*Spaseeba*, Director! Now, I better go say same thing to rest of team. And I tell them to retract the aiming tube, and put it back safely in its cubby hole."

"Yes, please do all of that, Traktor. And I better go tell Heather, that is, my boss, the CEO. Then I'll have to make a few phone calls with her to Earth, no doubt.

"I'll let you know when we have a full debriefing meeting scheduled with you and your team, Traktor."

19

Ernie Wolf was waiting for the 'confirmation' phone call in the Oval Office. He had instructed Jody Philpott, his Secretary of News, to invite the state television news agency in to cover the 'glorious event', live and in prime time. The television crew and the lead reporter were doing final sound checks when Sidney Lefebvre and two SAC generals suddenly appeared in the massive doorway to the office.

The three men just stood in the doorway. When Sidney could see that he had the president's full eye contact, he shook his head very slightly a few times, and then made a very subtle beckoning motion with his right hand that was hanging down by his side.

Ernie was startled by the unscheduled intrusion and the hand signal, but he immediately stood up in what he thought was a casual manner, and said with a chuckle, "Nature calls, folks. Don't worry, I'll be back in a minute."

When he got to the doorway, Ernie spat in a harsh whisper, "What the *hell*, Sid… ?"

Sidney shook his head again very slightly, turned around and started to walk down the wide hallway. The two SAC generals followed behind him very closely.

Ernie took the cue, and sauntered down the hallway, like he really was on his way to the men's room, and in no great panic about it.

About two-thirds of the way down the hallway, Sidney and the two generals abruptly turned right into an empty break-away room that the press sometimes used for non-presidential interviews. Ernie took a nonchalant look around to see that no one was paying close attention to him. Then he also went into the breakaway room, and quietly closed the door behind him.

"So, what the *hell's* going on, Sid?" Ernie barked angrily. "You were *supposed* to call me, *remember*, and I was supposed to put you on the speakerphone, *remember*?"

"It blew up, Mister President," Sidney replied very quietly. He looked very anxious, and even a bit nervous.

"Well, that's what it was *supposed* to do, wasn't it? It was a freaking *bomb*, right? Or did I miss something?"

"It blew up over the Moon's South Pole, Mister President, thousands of miles away from the *Second Chance*."

"How the *hell* did that happen? Some moron push the wrong button or something? You got a bunch of *amateurs* working for you, Sid?"

"No, Mister President. We had it right on track for direct interception in about two more orbits. We believe there was no malfunction. We think that either a kinetic energy weapon, or a beamed energy weapon of some kind, was used to destroy it. We've obviously just started our investigation, so it's too early to make any definite conclusions."

"What the hell is a 'kinetic energy weapon', Sid?" Ernie asked in almost his normal voice. He was starting to grasp the implications, and he was also starting to feel a bit anxious himself.

"Kinetic energy is half the mass times the velocity *squared* of a moving object. A hand-thrown rock has a bit of kinetic energy. That's why it hurts if it hits you. But a rock launched at say, *twenty-thousand miles per hour*, will completely wipe you out.

"A conventional missile can do the same thing as a big speeding rock. The trick is finding a way to hit a target moving at say, the same high speed as your missile, which is also on a different trajectory. The US has worked on the problem at various times. But we've never been able to get something to work reliably enough to get overly excited about the weapon concept."

"So, you're now looking for a missile or rock launching device, or something like that?"

"Yes, Mister President. But as you know, we've had to cut back a lot on our surveillance systems, with the economy in the dumps and all. But we believe the launcher, if it exists, was probably not in space. We believe we have accounted for most objects in orbit around the Earth and the Moon. But there is a *lot* of space junk out there, so maybe we missed something?

"The launcher could also have been positioned on the surface of the Moon. We have only one operating lunar spy satellite. But if it was not looking in exactly the right place at exactly the right time, it probably didn't see anything."

Ernie stumbled over to a cushioned metal chair in the little room, and sat down hard. He looked to be in a bit of a daze. After a long moment, he mumbled, "So, what about the other thing, Sid? What was that you were talking about, a ray gun or something?"

"Yes, it could have been something like that, Mister President. The US has played around with energy and particle-beam weaponry ideas a bit too. It was once called 'star wars technology' because it all seemed very far-fetched, you know, just comic book stuff.

"As far as I'm aware, we have never commissioned weapons resembling star wars stuff for active service. And we're not aware that anyone else has either. If there is now a working energy or particle-beam weapon on the Moon, it must be well-disguised. We're checking through all existing, recent spy satellite images, of course. And we've got our only working spy satellite up there on the look-out for it in real time. It's in a polar orbit, so it sweeps the entire lunar surface, eventually. The Moon keeps the same side pointed at the Earth while it circles our planet about every twenty-seven days. That means it revolves around its axis once every twenty-seven days or so."

Sid had a close look at the president's face and body language. It was easy to tell Ernie was suddenly very confused, and maybe even a bit disoriented. So he asked quietly, "Can I suggest an immediate course of action for you to consider, Mister President?"

"Yea, sure, Sid, whatever."

"Have Frank look into the causes of this catastrophe too, as a high-priority intelligence gathering effort. Someone out there knows what *really* happened. And they might also know if this could be made to happen again, either on or around the Moon, or elsewhere."

"Elsewhere, as in 'on the Earth', or 'over the Earth'?" Ernie asked with a quiver in his voice.

"Yes, Mister President. This technology might allow someone to blow up an incoming MIRV, or multiple, independently-targetable, re-entry vehicle, like the one we have on our Minuteman VI missile. If so, I think your strategic defence plan is a sound idea. You know, where you said let's wait until we have *four* ICBM's completely ready to go before we start our limited war.

"That strategy will give us some options to work with, should this weapon be used against us again. And if it *is* used again, we won't be completely vulnerable, or caught with our pants down if there is a counter-attack. And if we can see the weapon in action, we also should learn more about who we are up against, and possibly even how to defeat them."

"Yea, thanks, Sid. Good idea. Let's get Frank on the line right now. You better do the talking, though. I'm not very technical, you know.

"Oh shit, I better call Jody first, and have her clear out the Oval Office. She'll come up with the right excuse to use."

Ernie seemed to suddenly perk up a bit, and added flippantly before he started pressing numbers into his cell phone, "And you and your SAC boys better get working on another Moon missile, Sid. If you find a big rock launcher or a ray gun or whatever on the Moon, we'll want to take it out right away.

"Oh wait, this thing might wipe out our warhead again, right? So, you'll just have to figure out how to prevent that from happening, that's all. Anyway, you better get started on all of that, as a top priority. Now where was I... ?" He trailed off while trying to find Jody Philpott's telephone number in his cell phone's contact list.

The two SAC generals stared with horror at Sidney. Sidney just shrugged, and waved his right hand a few times towards the door to indicate that they should leave him alone with the president.

20

It was approaching eight o'clock in the morning on Wednesday, March 1. The weather was a bit chilly, but clear. Matt Adams was almost ready to head out on his bicycle. He hoped it would be the last time he would ever see the Devo Construction yard in Akron, Ohio.

Matt's bike had two leather saddlebags on either side of its wide rear wheel. The bags were filled with his meagre possessions. He was also wearing a backpack filled with layers of clothing, dried food and fresh water.

As Matt was about to climb aboard his bicycle, he saw a courier quickly approaching him on a similar bicycle. So, Matt held on to his bike, and waited to see if the courier might be looking to deliver something to him. He quickly recognized the courier as Luke, the skinny teenage guy that had often delivered documents to him.

"Morning, Mister Audie!" Luke said happily in greeting. "Glad I caught you. I have a letter for you." He then opened the flap on his handlebar pouch, pulled out a sealed white envelope, and handed it to Matt. Matt noted that the envelope was simply addressed to 'Audie Zaitsev'.

"Oh, okay, thanks Luke. Ah, sorry, I can't tip you today. I've got to save up now. You see, I lost my job yesterday."

"Ah, you've always tipped me pretty good before, so no sweat. Gee, that's too bad about your job, Mister Audie. Where are you heading?"

"South, I guess. Probably make my way back to Texas, eventually. I liked it down there. Houston might be all right, from what I hear."

"Well, it might be a little *warmer* down there, in the wintertime anyway. It also might take you a good long while to get there from what I hear."

"No doubt about that, Luke. Well, I better get started, don't want to waste sunlight.

"But say, now that you're here, Luke, would you do me a favour? Would you take a letter back for me, to the person that sent me the letter you just brought?"

"Sure, no problem."

Matt fished a sealed, oversized envelope out of a saddle-bag, and handed it to Luke. It was addressed to the 'Social Club Convenor'. Luke then slid the envelope into a compartment inside one of his own saddlebags. The envelope was too big for his handlebar pouch.

Then Matt said pleasantly, "Thanks, Luke. Now, you take really good care of yourself!"

"You too, Mister Audie. Bye now, and good luck!"

"You too, Luke!"

Matt watched until Luke was well out of sight. He folded the letter-sized envelope he had just received in half, and tucked it into his coat pocket.

About two hours later, Matt steered his bike into a little clump of bushes and small trees beside the road. He was well outside Akron now, heading for Cleveland. He got off the bike, and leaned it against a tree. He pulled his water bottle out of his backpack, and had a few sips.

Then Matt pulled the envelope out of his pocket, and opened it up. There was only a folded-up, single piece of paper inside the envelope. Matt opened the letter up. The handwriting was a bit sloppy, but Matt was able to read,

'Tomahawk attack worked. Peaceful full Moon tonight, Kemosabe. Patawomec on warpath though. Expect heap big trouble next full Moon. Aztecs very worried. So good hunting.'

Matt took a quick look around. No one was anywhere close to him. So, he carefully ripped up the letter into tiny pieces and put them all in his coat pocket. Then he got back on his bike, and then back on the road heading north.

Every now and then as he was riding along, he pulled some of the little pieces of paper out of his pocket, and tossed them into the wind.

21

Matt Adams did not check into an 'underground railway' safe house when he got to Detroit on the morning of Sunday, March 5. Instead, he crossed over the dangerously decaying and corroding Ambassador III Bridge, and rode into Windsor.

Matt was really pleased that no LOP thugs or VPF officers had stopped him or questioned him on his long journey from Akron. He had always tried to travel close to other bike riders. He figured a solitary rider might draw more attention from the authorities, and from vagabonds, especially if the rider was obviously carrying a lot of gear like he was. Thankfully, he was also not the kind of person that the LOP or thieves would ordinarily choose to harass.

As a result, he figured no one knew where he was now, other than the Social Club elite, and Daquan.

It had been really hard to say good-bye to Daquan. He had naively thought that a handshake would be enough. But Daquan had pulled him into a hug. And they had both been choked-up a bit. After all, they had been through a lot together. They promised to keep in touch, somehow. But both men knew that could never happen.

Matt simply had to completely disappear for everyone involved in this deadly work to have a chance at survival.

Matt rode south through what long ago had been the conservative, clean and safe city of Windsor, Ontario, and its suburbs. He rode for almost an hour-and-a-half. He kept the Detroit River in sight the whole time. There were very few people about. The ancient urban areas, and the previously farmed countryside, were basically wilderness areas again.

Just north of the hamlet of Amherstburg, Matt turned right on to a muddy trail that led down to the river. There had once been a marina on the site. There was still one partially-collapsed wooden dock at the water's edge.

An old black man lived in a cabin nearby. He was probably a squatter. Daquan had negotiated a boat rental deal with the man for Matt.

The old man said he remembered Matt vaguely, but he didn't remember being paid. Daquan had thought the old man probably had dementia, but was basically honest. Daquan had said both of those attributes might be advantageous for Matt. If the old man *could* remember the boat rental for a while, but then forget about Matt completely, that would all be good.

So, Matt paid the old man again.

The old man promised, again, to put the square-ended fibreglass boat in the water for him sometime during the afternoon of Saturday, March 11. Matt used a thick, greasy, blue pencil, and wrote in large letters 'BOAT RENTAL SATURDAY' at eye level on the inside of the crude wooden door of the man's shack. Then he asked the old man again not to forget about him.

The old man said he would try, really hard, not to forget. Then he gave Matt the simple little key device that would let him use the electric outboard motor. The motor would be secured to the back of the boat. The old man also promised that the battery for the motor would be fully charged, and he told Matt not to worry about that either.

Matt said good-bye to the old man, and then rode back up the trail to the road. There was thick forest on the other side of the road. Matt rode north for about three hundred yards until he found a rough, narrow trail heading off to his right. His bike was a 'fat bike' design, and it could handle cross-country excursions fairly well. So, Matt turned and carefully rode up the trail a hundred yards or so until he found a little clearing. He decided he would put up a simple lean-to shelter there, and make it his camp.

Matt took the saddlebags off his bike, and then settled in for the night.

The next day, late in the afternoon, Matt put on his mostly emptied backpack, and rode his bike north along the road to Windsor. When he got there, he then rode his bike back across the Detroit River. Right after crossing the Ambassador III Bridge, he turned left and rode beside some railway tracks. After a few minutes he could see that Riverside Park ahead of him was already cordoned-off.

There was a paved road that went down to the river on the nearest or eastern edge of the park. Matt decided to avoid that road for now, as there were some people walking about on it.

Matt rode further along the side of the tracks, just past the park on his left, until he found a narrow dirt road that went down to the river. At the riverbank, he pulled his bike into some bushes, and then waited there until dark.

Matt was pleased to find there was still enough urban light pollution in Detroit for him to feel his way around. And he was very practiced at working in the dark.

About an hour after sunset, Matt climbed a tall spruce tree, and set up one of his flash-bombs near the very top of it.

Then he made his way back to the road on the other side of the park. The road was completely deserted now. So, he rode down the road to the riverside. And then he climbed another tall spruce tree, and installed his second flash-bomb near its peak.

Matt then made his way back to the Ambassador III Bridge, and crossed over it to return to Windsor. He only passed one pedestrian on the bridge. The young man did not even look at him, and he was walking very fast. Matt figured the roads at night in Detroit and

Windsor were probably as dangerous as they were in Akron.

At the Windsor side of the bridge, Matt took a look around to see if anyone was in the area. The coast was clear, so he carefully made his way on his bicycle along a convoluted dirt path to get directly under the bridge. He found that there were two rows of well-braced but rusty I-beam columns holding up the long ramp that led to the suspension bridge. Matt secured his third flash-bomb to one of the vertical columns near the riverbank. He made sure that the grenade-like device could only be seen from the riverside. Even then, he decided it would be very hard to spot.

Then Matt rode south on the Windsor side of the river. It was just after midnight when he found his lean-to again in the pitch dark.

He lit a fire, and made himself a luxurious dinner of canned ham, canned brown beans and canned peaches.

He had enough food to last a week. But he was down to just dried food again, unfortunately.

It was now just a waiting game. But he had learned how to be patient as well as stealthy. It was just part of the deadly-serious business of being a sniper.

22

Just before six o'clock in the evening on Saturday, March 11, Matt Adams took off his eyepatch. He would never wear it again. Then he dabbed some flesh-coloured make-up on his forehead and around his left eye to hide the scars as best he could.

The light would be fading in a couple of hours, but he decided to wear his brand-new pair of wrap-around sunglasses until he just *had* to take them off. But it would be almost dark by then, and no one would be able to see his face very well. He had a thick, brown beard. But with the help of a little mirror and a pair of scissors, he cut it off. And then he gave himself a close shave with a razor and some soap. He figured people who saw him would be less likely to make special note of a clean-shaven face.

Then he put everything he had, including his backpack and his saddlebags, under the cover of his lean-to shelter.

He was wearing the clothes he used to wear when he worked for Devo Construction. So, in that respect, he looked just like most of the other men in the area.

Then Matt got on his bike, and rode north.

There were only a few trucks using the road. There were a few people riding purposefully somewhere on bikes, and a few people walking quickly and nervously somewhere on foot. But for the most part the road was unusually quiet.

Matt figured many people had now made their way over to Riverside Park to secure a good spot to hear President Wolf speak, and to see him in action. If a person was fortunate enough to be able to afford a television, and they were lucky enough to have electrical power, they might have invited friends and family over to watch the state-controlled broadcast. And some people would no doubt be listening to Cousin Ernie on a radio set. That was what Matt was going to do, with the help of a cordless earpiece.

The condemned windmill was in a wooded area that a century or more ago had been Windsor's Mill Park. Matt reached the edge of the overgrown area of the old park in a little over an hour.

There was a dirt pathway leading into the interior of the heavily-wooded acreage. There were no signs to warn people away, or fences to keep them out. The place had simply returned to wilderness, complete with feral dogs and cats, and foxes and rabbits.

Matt pushed his way through thick, prickly undergrowth for a hundred feet or so. Then he got off his bike, and leaned it against some thorn bushes. He got down on his belly, and worked his way quietly towards the windmill.

Matt watched the windmill carefully for about half an hour until it was almost pitch dark. He was certain there was no one about, and if there were homeless people or vandals inside the condemned building, they were not making themselves visible through the broken windows or making any noise. So, he crawled over to the building, and started to climb up its side to a completely smashed-out window on the uppermost level. The window was on the side of the building that faced away from the river towards the old city of Windsor. There were a lot of useful holes and cracks in the rotten wooden cladding, so climbing the outside wall was fairly easy.

Actually, all of the windows in the building had been smashed-out. As a result, wasps, birds and bats had made the place their home. But they went about their business without reacting to Matt's presence.

There was no one in the building. There was some fresh-looking graffiti on the walls, however. So, other trespassers had visited the place since Matt and Daquan had been there.

Matt got down on his hands and knees and crawled over to the window that faced towards the Detroit River. He peeped over the window sill, and was extremely pleased to see that he would still have a clear view of Riverside Park.

The park was well lit-up with floodlights. And the back of the stage was clearly visible to his one functioning eye.

Matt crawled away, and then stood up when he was sure he could not be seen through the river-side window. The city-side window looked straight into a wall of tall, dark, trees, so he was not concerned about it. Then he walked over to the northeast interior wall. He looked around for the marks he had made with Daquan. They had used a can of grey spray paint that had been left in the building by vandals. They had only made three small circular dots with the spray can on three horizontal panel boards, just above eye level. Sure enough, the dots were still there.

Matt pulled a wobbly, wooden bench over to the wall, stood on it carefully, and pried the three panels loose with a pen knife. He carefully set them aside, and then reached down between two studs he had exposed in the middle of the opening.

The rifle was there, resting vertically on its butt.

Matt grabbed the barrel firmly with his right hand, and carefully eased the heavy, massive rifle up and out of the cavity.

It was a magnificent weapon, and very similar to the one he had been issued in the Army. He figured you really could not improve on an excellent design.

Before looking it over, he saw that the flash-bomb trigger device, and the tube of glue, had both been taped to the fore-stock of the weapon. He took the ancillary items off of the weapon, and set them aside.

He then went through his well-practised drill of thoroughly checking over an unfamiliar weapon.

It looked and even smelled brand new. It had obviously been well cared for, by someone who really knew guns, and treated them tenderly, with something approaching love. It was as clean as a whistle, and properly lubricated and oiled.

Some typewritten notes had been taped to the stock. They provided an algorithm and tabulated values for adjusting the range setting on the scope. They also indicated the proper spin-drift setting for the scope that matched rifle to bullet. Matt checked the spin-drift first, and not surprisingly, the scope had been set correctly.

Matt then got down on his hands and knees again, and dragged the wooden bench over to the window that faced towards the river. He found some wood splinters, and shoved them into cracks in the leg joints to take out most of the wobble in the bench. He had noted before that the bench was just a little higher than the height of the window sill. He was glad that vandals had not stolen or wrecked the bench. It would greatly help him to steady his aim.

He sat down with his legs crossed and placed the bipod of the rifle on the bench. He made sure that the end of the barrel would still be inside of the building. There would be a brilliant flash when the weapon was fired, but hopefully that flash would only be seen from the river side. There would also be an ungodly loud bang, but there was simply no avoiding that. Long-range snipers did not use silencers. Predictable, precision, high muzzle velocity was everything.

He used the scope to locate the stage that had been set up in Riverside Park. It was still well lit up with tall banks of floodlights.

It was a dark, partially-cloudy night, with about a quarter moon. The weak, intermittent moonlight was reflecting off the ripples on the surface of the water flowing in the wide river. There were other weak and wobbly reflections on the river water from the lights of the city. The power seemed to be mostly 'on' in Detroit. Matt figured Cousin Ernie had probably insisted upon that for his big production.

President Wolf had not yet appeared, but it looked like his arrival was imminent. There were helmeted Secret Service guys in black battle uniforms standing on each side of the podium. There were also two teleprompters set up in front and on either side of the podium. Matt could see that a protective glass shield had been set up directly in front of the podium. Thick glass shields had also been installed on both sides of the podium. But the back of the podium was wide open. This confirmed that Matt would have a clear shot, as long as Ernie stayed behind the podium and did not move around too much.

Matt looked carefully at a Secret Service guy. If the man was about six feet tall, the 'Mil dots' on the scope confirmed that the range he had been given was about right. So, he changed the range setting on the scope to correspond to 1170 yards. And he hoped again that the rifle had been properly sighted-in, and that the scope and rifle had been handled gently in transit.

The wind had dropped off, but Matt figured it was still about sixteen knots. He had practised guessing wind velocity for many years, and he was pretty good at it. The wind was steady, and moving away from him, at about a forty-five degree angle, from left to right. So, he would use three-quarters of the wind table value he had memorized for his very similar, Army-issued, fifty-calibre rifle. He did the math in his head, as he always did. For this range, the full value was 28 inches. So, he would put the crosshairs right on his target, and aim 21 inches up wind. From photos, Matt knew Ernie's shoulders were about 20 inches wide. So, he thought, 'Centre of his back at heart level, width of his shoulders to the left, and just a hair more. Bingo.'

Matt pulled a little battery-powered radio out of the front left pocket of his coveralls. Then he put the radio's cordless earpiece into his right ear. He turned the radio on, and tuned in the station that would broadcast the speech.

The announcer was saying that President Wolf had arrived in the park, and would soon be up on stage.

Sure enough, about ten minutes later, there was Ernie, up on stage, and waving madly to the crowd. Matt could hear the roar of the frenzied crowd from his distant location across the river. He figured it must be a very large crowd.

The Secret Service agents quickly steered Ernie behind the protective glass. It appeared that Ernie did not like to be steered by anyone. Then Matt could see the two teleprompters spring into life in front to the podium.

And then Ernie started to speak.

Matt was amazed at the disgusting garbage Ernie was saying. It was sickening, and very alarming. It was clear he was not reading what was on the teleprompters.

But Matt was mostly focused on what Ernie's routine was when he was speaking. He was jumping around a lot, and pointing at people, and swaying and turning one way and then the other.

But Matt noted that whenever Ernie got into an especially passionate rant, he would thrust both fists high up into the air, and stare at the heavens. And while he was doing that, the rest of his body was perfectly still.

Matt retrieved the flash-bomb trigger device, and got back into his well-braced, cross-legged position. He put the trigger device on the floor, and carefully positioned his right toe on the lever-like switch without depressing it. He took the radio earpiece out of his right ear, and put a plastic earplug in each of his ears.

Then he noted there was a lake freighter moving downstream in the Detroit River, from his right to his left. It was passing just now under the Ambassador III Bridge. He immediately realized that if he could time this *just* right, he could create yet another distraction, and more confusion about where the killing shot had come from.

He repositioned the rifle, and got set. He skillfully worked the bolt to place a massive, fifty-calibre round into the firing chamber. He quickly glanced out of the window again to note where the ship was. It was now getting close to blocking his shot! And he could tell visually that Ernie was getting worked up again into a lather. Matt took a deep breath, fully exhaled and held his breath.

There! Ernie's two fists shot up into the air!

Matt deftly positioned the crosshairs on his target spot. Then he gently and smoothly squeezed the trigger while depressing the flash-bomb trigger lever with his right toe.

23

President Ernie Wolf was really impressed by the large turnout for his speech. He asked the senior Secret Service agent sitting beside him in the presidential limousine how many people were in the park. The agent told him the Secret Service figured there were about five thousand people in the crowd, and they were all confirmed loyal supporters.

Ernie loved big crowds, and that number seemed way too small to him. With Ernie, during his presidency, everything just *had* to be the biggest and the best *ever* in the long history of America.

Ernie moved around in a massive, black, LNG-powered, amour-plated, sports-utility-like limousine. His Secret Service driver slowly eased through the crowd. Then he smoothly executed a three-point turn, and stopped the SUV directly by the left-side stairs to the stage, with the front of the vehicle facing the crowd.

A dozen or so uniformed Secret Service agents lined both sides of the stairway. About the same number of uniformed and plain-clothed agents were stationed on the stage itself.

Two plain-clothed agents got out of the SUV and looked around for a minute. Then one of the agents opened the back right door of the SUV, and Ernie got out. The crowd instantly erupted with loud applause and screaming.

Ernie walked up the stairs to the stage, while waving to the crowd. He was grinning like a mad fool, and obviously enjoying himself. He loved to give speeches, but only to enthusiastic supporters. And this crowd sure seemed to be enthusiastic and supportive. It helped that only ticket-paying Veterans Party members had been allowed into the park. But Ernie always overlooked embarrassing facts like that.

Ernie seemed to want to dawdle a bit and wave at some sign-waving people in the crowd. So, two plain-clothed agents gently grabbed hold of his elbows, and urged him to stand behind the podium. Ernie shook them off with obvious disgust, and then thrust both of his fists high up into the air. The crowd went wild.

Then Ernie adjusted the microphone on the podium and got ready to start his speech. He paid no attention to what was being displayed on the two teleprompters positioned for his use on either side of the forward-facing protective glass shield. He usually liked to wing it, and speak informally.

When the crowd noise subsided a bit, Ernie said in a booming, clear voice:

"So, here we all are in the grand old city of Detroit, Michigan!

"They still make cars here, did you know that? Electric ones, but that's okay. I've never believed in all

of that climate change crap, no, never did. But, electric cars? Well, whatever, I guess.

"By the way, we'll just have to see if the climate actually does change. And what's wrong with warmer anyway? But we'll see. We'll see what happens.

"But here we are, and it's great! And you're great, and I'm great. And America's now great, because of me.

"So, that's what forty-thousand patriotic people look like! The Secret Service told me that was the head count for tonight. Seems much bigger than that. But wow, still, what a great turn out! So, thanks for coming, folks!

"We're here to mostly announce funding to build the Ambassador IV Bridge. I just signed the executive order. So it's going to happen. Believe me. And we're going to let the old bridge stay up a while longer for the use of pedestrians and bicycles. But the holes in the roadway, and the missing railings? They'll all be fixed. Believe me.

"You know, Ontario used to be part of Canada. We never had as much trouble with Canadians as we still do with Mexicans. But still, a lot of illegal stuff and very nasty people used to come into the United States from Canada. And the Canucks didn't do anything to stop it! Right at this very border crossing. Massive problem. Huge. And the Canucks always started trade wars with us. Tried to dump inferior products at jacked-up prices. But we put the Canadians in their place, and let them

become Americans. Reluctantly. But history is history. They lost, and we won. That's it. End of story.

"Now, as for the Mexicans, they still need to be put in their place. Forever. We kept building bigger walls, but we just could not keep them out. So we wiped their brown asses in a war, and pushed the border five hundred miles further south. And then we mined the crap out of the border, on their side. But they're still sneaking into our country! At night, because they're all cowards. And they're all drug dealers and pimps. And they molest children and animals. Even cute little cats and dogs. Bad people. Very bad. Believe me.

"So, what the Mexicans don't know is that we have nukes again. On missiles. Lots of them. Big ones. The biggest. Can go anywhere. Mexico City? Piece of cake for us.

"And we have missiles and nukes that can go to the Moon too!

"So, the Mexicans and the Moon men and the idiots building that monstrosity of a spaceship better watch out! Who do they think they're messing with? I'm Ernie Wolf! The greatest world leader, ever! And my enemies are just money-grubbing oligarchs! And I'm the president of the United States! For life! And I'm not going to take it any... "

The fifty-calibre bullet struck Ernie in the centre of his back. It shattered his spine and then blew open his heart. The squashed bullet then deflected slightly and exited Ernie's chest three inches to the right of his sternum. It then ricocheted off the protective glass screen in front of the podium and flew off behind the stage.

Blood and gore spattered on to the front protective glass screen. Ernie fell directly forward onto the podium, and then immediately slumped to the floor of the stage.

The crowd moaned in unison and then went completely silent. Then people started screaming.

The Secret Service agents were all running around in confusion, on the stage and in front of the stage. They were pointing at people, and striking some people to the ground with the butts of their rifles.

Two plain-clothed agents grabbed hold of Ernie under his armpits and dragged him face-down over to the top of the stairs. Then two other agents grabbed hold of his ankles, and the four large men hustled him down the stairs and quickly into the waiting SUV. Then the SUV started away. It quickly picked up speed, and struck a few people to the ground in its haste to get away.

The crowd was now in full panic mode. Everyone raced towards the main gate. The guards at the gate could not contain them. Uniformed Secret Service agents started firing at the crowd. But that only made the panic worse.

The television and radio broadcasts abruptly stopped. After a few minutes, the television network started to show an old sitcom. And the radio station started to play classical music.

24

Matt Adams was well prepared for the massive recoil from the powerful rifle, but it was still an awesome jolt. The butt recoil mechanism helped, but his shoulder still took a major thump. And the barrel leapt upwards wildly. His ears were immediately ringing from the concussive crack of the rifle, even though he was wearing ear plugs.

Matt quickly put the rifle back on target. He saw that Cousin Ernie had fallen directly forward onto the podium. That meant the bullet had struck his body somewhere along the centreline of his torso. Then he saw Ernie slump to the floor of the stage. And then he saw the blood-spattered protective glass.

Then the bow of the passing ship blocked his view. But that was really all he could safely allow himself to see anyway. Someone might catch the reflection off the lens of the scope on the rifle, if they had somehow traced the crack of the rifle to his well-hidden and darkened location. Matt knew that was unlikely. The 'beauty' of an ultra, long-range shot was that it was very difficult to know where it came from. One could really only *suspect* a sniper's location, based upon likely hiding places.

And Matt was in an *excellent* hiding place, and it was high time to get the hell away from it.

He moved quickly but efficiently. He worked the bolt to discharge the spent cartridge. A fresh round went into the chamber, but he put the safety catch on. He wanted to minimize how many things he handled and had to wipe down. And he had never touched any of the rounds in the magazine.

He crawled away from the window, dragging the rifle and the wooden bench with him. He stood up, pushed the bench up against the northeast-side wall, and carefully stood up on the bench. He pulled a rag out of his back left pocket. Then he methodically wiped the rifle down to completely remove all his fingerprints. He firmly held on to the butt of the rifle with the rag still in his right hand, and lowered it back down into the wall cavity, pointy-end down.

He found the flash-bomb trigger device, completely wiped it down with the rag and threw the little box into the wall cavity.

He found the tube of glue, and squeezed glue on to the face of the exposed studs, and on to the innermost edges of the bordering wall-panelling. Then he screwed the lid back on the tube of glue, wiped his finger prints off of it and threw it into the wall cavity.

He found the spent cartridge, wiped it down with the rag, and threw the cartridge into the wall cavity.

He removed his two earplugs, wiped them down with the rag, and threw them into the wall cavity.

Then he threw the rag into the wall cavity.

And finally, he very carefully pressed the three panel boards back into place.

He dragged the wooden bench over to the southwest-side wall and left it there. He took one last methodical look around to confirm the place looked exactly like it had before. Then he walked over to the window facing the old city.

Everything looked clear outside, and there were no unusual sounds. So, he quickly climbed out of the window, and made his way carefully back down the side of the building.

When he got to ground level he immediately flattened himself right out on the damp ground. He listened carefully for another couple of minutes. The only sounds he could hear were screams and yells from across the river, and muted rustling sounds from small animals moving about in the bracken nearby. So he crawled along the ground until he was a hundred feet or so away from the old windmill and into thick trees. He got up into a crouching position for a few seconds and looked all around again. It was still all clear, so he rose to his feet and walked calmly and quietly toward his bike.

He found his bike exactly where he had left it. He pulled it away from the prickly bushes, and pushed it back on to the dirt roadway. It was still all clear, so he got on his bike and rode away.

He forced himself to ride at his normal speed. If anyone had seen him before on one of his journeys, they would not suspect he was up to anything different this time. Of course, since he was unknown to people, no one around here would ever have known what he was up to.

He headed south, staying as always within sight of the river. He could hear helicopters in the air now on the Detroit side of the river. There was still a lot of yelling and screaming over there, and now the unmistakable, sporadic crack of gunshots. He figured he must have caused a lot of panic, and maybe even a riot. And now there was a lot of shouting noise from behind him too, maybe on the Ambassador III Bridge itself.

But he kept his eyes forward, directly on the road. It was still very quiet, and very dark. There were a lot of loose gravel sections, and deep potholes and wide cracks in the road.

After he had travelled a few miles, he heard a siren, but it was coming from well behind him, and it was moving away from him.

After travelling another few miles, he took a glance at the river to his right. The lake freighter he had seen before had almost slowed to a stop in a buoy-marked channel. Matt figured it must actually be in hard reverse to resist the current. There was a Coast Guard cutter nearby, all lit-up with flood lights, and it was launching a semi-inflatable boat.

Matt suddenly felt sorry for the crew of the freighter. They were about to be put through the wringer. The ship would probably be ordered to a dock, and then searched thoroughly. And in this evil, fascist world, the crew would probably be tortured, possibly to death, even if no evidence was found to support a notion that the killing shot had come from somewhere on the vessel.

After travelling another mile, Matt saw someone running along the other side of the road, coming towards him. It was a man wearing a track outfit and a fluorescent vest. The man casually waved at Matt, so Matt waved back at him. Matt figured the guy was out for a late evening jog! That meant the world was as nutty and normal as ever, at least in a few places.

Matt also passed two pedestrians walking side-by-side ahead of him on his side of the road. When he got closer, he could see they were a teenage couple, holding hands. Matt casually said, "Hello!" to the frightened boy and girl as he rode past them, and they both gasped "Hello!" back to him.

About two miles north of Amherstburg, Matt saw a man standing on his side of the road, looking his way. The man suddenly held up his right hand in a stop sign. The man was obviously a civilian, and he was not wearing a 'LOP' armband. At the last second, the man stepped right into Matt's path. Matt swerved to the left and struck the man full in his face with a right forearm smash. The guy instantly howled with pain. Matt looked back and saw that the guy was now staggering down the road in the opposite direction with his hands to his face. Matt figured he was a common thief, who was now a common thief with a busted nose.

Matt was back at his lean-to shelter in the woods in a little over an hour. He had no intentions of staying very long at his old campsite. He put the saddlebags back on his bike. Then he put all his camp garbage into the saddlebags, and added a few rocks. He kicked apart his lean-to, and spread his camp fire ashes around. Then he put on his backpack and rode his bike back to the north-south running road. He pedaled the few hundred yards south to reach the dirt lane that led past the old man's shack and then down to the river.

There were no lights on in the shack, but it was pretty late in the evening now. And Matt didn't know if the old man was connected to what was left of the electrical power grid. He knew that he had an old diesel generator, but fuel was no longer available.

Matt mentally crossed his fingers and rode down to the riverbank.

He almost cried out loud with joy and relief. There was the boat, tied up beside the nearly-collapsed dock. And the electric motor was on the back of the boat, with the propeller pulled up out of the water.

Matt laid his bike down on the ground, and gingerly walked out along the dock. There was a bit of moonlight still, so he had a weak, silvery-light to see by. He looked down into the boat. He decided it definitely was more of a canoe-shape than a boat-shape. And it would probably be a bit tipsy like a canoe. 'Something to remember at all times', he lectured himself.

The old man had correctly hooked up a large wet-cell battery to the motor. He had also left him an old wooden paddle to use.

The canoe was about seventeen feet long, and rather beamy in the centre. It was probably based on a traditional freight canoe design. Matt went back and picked up his bike. It was a heavy load, but he figured the canoe could manage it all right. He stepped carefully along the dock, and lowered the bike down into the centre of the boat. He positioned the bike on its side, resting it on the portside gunwale. He grunted once out loud from the strain of the awkward work. But he looked around again, and there was still no one in sight. And there was no activity at all on the river.

Matt laid his backpack in the aft of the canoe in front of where he would be sitting. Then he undid the bow line from a rusty little cleat on the dock, and tossed the crappy nylon line into the bow. Then he gingerly stepped into the centre of the canoe behind the bike, and sat down, straddling a narrow mesh seat and facing the port-side. He fished the little key out of a pocket on his backpack, and then put it in the starter slot on the motor. A little red LED light immediately lit-up on the motor. Matt twisted the end of the tiller a bit, and watched the propeller smoothly turn for a few seconds. He knew he was in business.

He put the propeller down in the water, and then wiggled around to untie the stern line from another cleat on the dock. He laid the frayed nylon line at his feet. Then he gently pushed away from the dock, and put the motor in high speed.

The boat was facing into the current, so Matt angled his course a bit to vector himself straight out from shore.

Just before he got to a marked shipping channel, he steered the boat right into the current. Then he reached forward and started working the bike over the port-side gunwale. It was a really awkward struggle. He decided he would have to temporarily lock the tiller in place to complete the job safely. When that was done, he used both of his hands to flip the bike over the side of the canoe into the water.

He pulled away a few feet, and then followed the bike as it floated down river. It did not stay afloat very long. The saddlebags quickly filled with water, and the bike sank completely out of sight. Matt figured the bike would go right to bottom, and stay there in the filthy muck, hopefully forever.

Matt was now travelling along with the current. He could see his destination now, Bois Blanc Island. It was the last island in the Detroit River. This part of the river might have been called an estuary had Lake Erie been salt water and tidal. The only remaining marked shipping channel ran right along the eastern side, or Ontario side, of the island.

Matt steered the canoe for the nearest part of the long island. He could see that the island was heavily forested, and completely dark. Daquan had found out that no one lived there any more. It had once been a getaway place for Canadian summer vacationers. Centuries ago there had even been an amusement park there.

Matt saw a little sandy cove on the 'bow' of the island, and he headed for that spot. He gave the boat a burst of speed and lifted the propeller out of the water. The boat glided up on to a narrow sand beach and gradually came to a stop.

Matt finally breathed a sigh of relief. He grabbed his backpack and carefully walked down the centreline of the canoe to the bow. Then he stepped off the canoe on to wet sand. He laid his backpack down on a dry rock. Then he pulled the canoe right up off the beach and further along into some bushes. He tied off the bow line on a small tree trunk. He would not have to worry about tide here, but he figured the river level would go up and down a bit when big ships passed nearby.

He grabbed his backpack and made his way up into the forest. After a hundred feet or so, he found a small clearing, and immediately started to make a lean-to shelter. He was also going to risk a small fire, and cook up something warm to eat before he lay down to sleep. He also would set up his camp so that he would get a bit of reflected heat from the fire to warm up the interior of his lean-to.

He figured it was going to be a cool, clear night. But he also figured he would have to put the fire completely out by daylight. Smoke above the tree line would reveal his presence on an island where supposedly no one lived.

As he was stumbling around gathering branches and bracken in the darkness, he decided once-and-for-all that he would stay on the island for at least one full day. He wanted things to cool down a bit before he took the next risky step towards real freedom, and hopefully, blissful obscurity.

25

Sidney Lefebvre was the first secretary of state to arrive at the White House. It was just after ten-thirty in the evening on Saturday, March 11.

Sidney was uncharacteristically wearing his retired, immaculate, three-star general uniform, complete with its many medals. The uniform was in the old US Calvary style, and it looked very smart.

Sidney told the attending Secret Service agents that he was now the commander-in-chief. They knew the president had just been confirmed dead, so they did not challenge Sidney's claim. Then Sidney told the agents that he would make use of the Oval Office, and he instructed them to usher the other two secretaries of state into the Oval Office as soon as they arrived. And he specifically ordered the Secret Service agents not to admit Thomas Fitzgerald, their boss, into the Oval Office until his presence was directly requested by the three secretaries of state.

Frank Palermo and Poppy Beauregard arrived together at the White House at around eleven-thirty pm. They had been attending the same formal dinner party with their wives, and they were wearing very stylish, black tuxedos.

When Frank and Poppy were admitted into the Oval Office, they noted with disgust that Sidney was sitting behind the president's desk, and he was using the huge, multi-button desk phone.

Sidney saw the angry expressions on their faces, and he said into the telephone handset, "Okay, call me back on this number when you can confirm the result."

Sidney stood up and motioned the two new arrivals to join him in the adjoining lounge area in the cavernous office. Sidney said to them in a rather cavalier manner, "Sorry, fellows, I didn't mean to imply anything, just wanted to use the phone."

Frank replied in a sarcastic manner, "Cell phone doesn't work again, right, Sid?"

"As a matter of fact, it doesn't, Frank," Sidney said a bit defensively.

When they were seated, Sidney asked, "So, you guys both got a call from Tommy too, confirming that Ernie is dead?"

"Yes, and also that there is still a riot of sorts going on in Detroit," Poppy said quietly with a shake of his head. "This is goddam *horrible!*"

"So now what?" asked Frank bluntly with an expressionless face and no discernible sign of emotion in his voice.

"Well, we all know that our President Ernie Wolf did not name a successor," Poppy observed using his typical, upper-class manner of speaking. "Maybe he left a will, or some other legal document that we don't know about. But for now, the leadership of the United States falls upon the three of us, that is, *together*, as a sort of triumvirate."

"Or a triad," Frank replied bluntly. "Except for Sid, we two should respect our mob heritage, after all, Poppy. Triads don't hold together very long, if you remember. 'Families' only get along with each other if they all perceive a benefit. But eventually someone figures they should get more than the others, and they will try to get the upper hand. You know, Tony will hit Luigi, and Luigi will hit Freddo, and Freddo will hit Tony. And everyone will lose, big time."

"Right, so this can only be an interim but necessary arrangement until we have an election for president," Sidney said with a growl. "And we better include Thomas Fitzgerald on the ballot. He's head of the Party anyway. And I bet he's pacing around outside right now like a madman, demanding his *own guys* let him in here. We've got to manage him very carefully, or he'll create a *lot* of trouble for us, and for the country."

"I think that makes a lot of sense, Sid," replied Poppy stiffly. "Frank, any leads on who may have done this terrible deed, and how they did it?"

"Nothing concrete yet, of course," Frank snapped. "It just freaking happened, right? We've found the bullet that was used. It was a fifty-calibre. That's massive, so Ernie didn't have a chance. He was shot square in the back. So, a cowardly act, but damn professional. The shot may have come from a passing ship. We're checking that out, and some of Sid's people are helping us out with that effort.

"Some people in attendance said they saw shooters in two tall spruce trees on the Detroit-side river bank. But the angles are all wrong, and we've found nothing yet to support that claim. Some other bystanders said the shot came from under the Ambassador III Bridge, on the Windsor side. That makes a lot of sense, but we're still checking that out."

"You used the word 'professional', Frank," Poppy said with a waver in his voice. "Does that mean this was a mob hit?"

Frank hesitated for a moment. Then he said, "Ernie may have made a few enemies that we don't know about. The sniper *may* have been a mafia guy, or a mob guy hired by someone else. Right now though, I strongly suspect our oligarch buddies are ultimately behind this."

"You don't really mean 'buddies', do you, Frank?" asked Poppy with a look of horror on his face.

"Of course not!" yelled Frank. "I was being sarcastic!"

Just then the phone on the president's desk rang. Everyone just sat there. After the phone rang three times, Frank said, "That will be the phone, Sid. You were waiting for a call, right?"

Sid was in a bit of a daze, but he jumped up and said, "Yes, I was!"

He went quickly over to the desk and picked up the handset. Then he said loudly, "Yes, this is Lefebvre. What is it?"

Sid listened for over a minute. He started to look increasingly angered by something that was being said. Then he yelled, "How could it blow up on its own while on descent into target? How is that even possible?"

Another minute or so went by. Then Sidney suddenly looked like he had experienced instant shellshock. He mumbled into the mouthpiece, "Okay, keep me posted. Better use my cell phone next time. I think it's working again."

Sidney stumbled over and re-joined the others. He looked completely shattered.

"What the hell was all that about, Sid?" asked Frank angrily.

Sidney looked at the other two men in turn. He was obviously in a state of disbelief. Then he shook his head a few times, and mumbled, "The missile never reached its target. Disintegrated about forty miles above Mexico City. No one knows how. Yet, anyway."

"What *fucking* missile?" yelled Frank angrily.

Sidney initially recoiled in reaction to Frank's emotional, obscene outburst, then he said defensively, "I *am* the new commander-in-chief you know. If I want to launch a freaking missile, I'll launch a freaking missile!"

"If you've started a war, Sid, when we're so messed up like this, you may have doomed us all to oblivion,"

Poppy said with obvious anxiety. After a long moment, he seemed to experience a blinding flash of the obvious. Then he suddenly looked very angry himself, and he yelled, "This was a *political ploy*, wasn't it, Sid? If the country is at *war*, then they'll want a *wartime president*, right? You bloody fool!"

Sid made a lunging motion at Poppy, but Frank rose up quickly and pushed him hard back into his seat. Then he yelled, "Cool it! Both of you. There's too much at stake, damn it."

Everyone stewed in their own juices for a minute. Frank seemed to recover first, and he said calmly, "Okay, no more unilateral actions, Sid. Right? Or anybody else for that matter, until the presidency is decided. Okay?"

Sid quietly replied, "Okay, Frank. Sorry, Poppy."

Poppy mumbled, "Yes, okay, too. Forget about it, Sid."

Frank smiled, and he took a deep breath. Then he said calmly, "We better invite Tommy in here now, guys. Remember, 'Keep your friends close, and your enemies closer.' Right?"

26

Matt Adams stayed under cover during the day, and peeped through the trees at the activity on the Detroit River. He mostly focused on the upstream or northerly direction. He was looking for an opportunity to board a vessel heading south.

It was noontime before the first Great Lakes freighter went by, but it was going north and away from him in the Amherstburg Channel to the right of Bois Blanc Island. It was a bulk carrier named *Ironman II*. Matt figured it was probably headed for a port in Wisconsin to pick up a load of taconite pellets.

In the distant past, there had been two well-maintained, well-marked channels at this location in the Detroit River. Ships travelling upstream had used the Amherstburg Channel, and ships travelling downstream had used the Livingstone Channel. But with decreased shipping volume, and lack of government funding, only the Amherstburg Channel was still operating. This meant that ships would have to alert other ships over the radio when they were approaching the channel. Otherwise, a collision or a grounding would be likely.

Matt could not even tell where the Livingstone Channel once had been, but he remembered it had been to his left, on the western side of Bois Blanc Island.

A lake freighter went by just before dusk, but it was also heading north using the Amherstburg Channel. It was a typical bulk carrier. The name on the back of the ship had mostly worn off and Matt could not make it out. Ships were now as poorly maintained as the river channel.

So, Matt concluded that there was very little shipping traffic on the Detroit River. Matt did not know if that was the norm now, or somehow linked to the assassination of President Ernie Wolf. So far he had not seen any ships moving south. He thought that could mean the Coast Guard was holding up ships in Lake St. Clair just north of the Detroit River, and conducting thorough searches there.

At about ten o'clock in the evening, Matt saw a lake freighter approaching from the upstream direction. It was within the Amherstburg Channel. It was a well-lit-up bulk carrier of the standard length and width to be able to make safe use of the locks in the Welland Canal. The locks were 800 feet long, so these kinds of lake vessels were no more than 740 feet in length. But that meant that this vessel was probably heading for a port on Lake Ontario or the St. Lawrence River. And that's what he was looking for.

Matt had already placed his backpack in his canoe. He also had the canoe on the beach, ready to launch, with the bow in the water. He quickly stepped into the stern of the canoe, and shoved it away from the beach with his right foot. Then he started the electric motor, and headed upstream.

He could now read the name on the bow of the approaching lake freighter. The vessel was the *Baie Comeau III*. That sounded really encouraging. Matt figured it was almost certainly a grain carrier, heading for the transshipment terminal in Baie-Comeau, Quebec. His luck was still holding out.

The steel sides of a lake freighter are smooth and vertical. But there were three lines hanging down on the starboard side of this vessel. They were all dangling like skipping ropes. Matt figured the ship had recently been boarded, and probably was ordered to provide tie-off points for an attending Coast Guard launch or cutter. The base of the catenary curve of one of the ropes was only four or five feet above the water line. Matt decided he would try to grab a hold of it.

He put his backpack on. Then he put the electric engine in full speed, and steered on a vector that he thought might take him to the correct intercept point. The ship was making about six knots, and he figured the canoe might be making ten knots, so it would be nip and tuck.

The canoe started to rock and sway in the wake of the bow wave as he approached the massive vessel. It was towering over him in the weak moonlight. But after a few in-and-out swerves, and a few near capsize disasters, he finally got right under the rope he was looking for.

This was the critical moment. But he knew it was probably his only chance for survival.

He stood up and grabbed the rope with both hands. The canoe suddenly swerved hard to the right, and he kicked it away.

He was now waist deep in rushing water. The strain was enormous.

But he worked his way aft along the rope. Finally he was clear of the water. He pulled himself up the side of the vessel. It required all of his immense strength. He found he could get some traction with his boots on the rough and blistered sides of the ship, so that made it slightly easier.

When he finally got to the gunwale, his arms were just about ready to give out. And his hands were bleeding and rubbed raw from the death-grip squeeze he needed to hang on to the greasy, bristly rope.

He made one last, mighty lunge, and just managed to swing his right leg over the two-foot thick, starboard-side gunwale. He tumbled to the steel, painted deck, gasping for air.

After a minute or so, he struggled to his feet. He turned around, and found with a shock that he was staring right into the face of a massive, bearded seaman. The beastly fellow was wearing a pair of well-worn but clean orange coveralls, and a greasy red floater vest.

"That was neat trick, buddy," the sailor growled. "Brave, but foolish. If your puny dingy had stayed close by, I'd throw you back over the side. But I ain't no murderer.

"We better go show you to the captain, though. Skipper Bob might order me to throw you back, but then your death would be on his hands, not mine. We'll head forward, matey, you first. And you better go up those stairs ahead of us on the left."

The steel stairs led to the closed door of the ship's bridge. When they both reached the small steel platform at the top of the stairs, the seaman growled, "You wait here, bucko. Remember, there's no place to hide on this ship. So don't try anything stupid."

The seaman then went through the door to the bridge, and closed the door. Matt waited outside for five long minutes. He thought he could hear some yelling inside. He wondered what his fate would be.

The seaman came back out through the door with another man right behind him. The other man was in a mercantile officer's uniform. He looked angry, and he was about to say something to Matt, but he stopped short. Then he looked carefully at Matt's face, smiled, and said, "Hello, Matt! Long time, no see!"

Matt thought he recognized the officer. But he could not place a name to the familiar face. Then he guessed, "Yes, hello, we served together for a while, didn't we, on the… *Herbert T. Lemaire*?"

"That's right! I'm Gerard Gaspard, now First Officer on this vessel.

"This might change a few things. But we'll just have to see. I'm not the captain. You must remember how the pecking order works on a freighter.

"Matt, this is Able Seaman Jean Parizeau. Jean, please go have a cup of coffee with my old shipmate Mathieu Adams. Matt is an able seaman too, or he was, anyway. Stay with him please, in the galley. When we're completely clear of the channel and out on Lake Erie, the captain will want to talk to him."

27

Matt leapt to his feet and stood at rigid attention when Captain Robert Lemieux stormed into the galley. Seaman Jean Parizeau immediately stood up as well, but quickly went to get a second cup of coffee.

Captain Lemieux marched over and positioned himself just inches away from Matt. Lemieux was a big, bald, burly, middle-aged man with a ruddy complexion. Their eyes were at about the same level. Lemieux also had bad breath.

But Matt did not flinch.

Captain Lemieux wheezed into Matt's face, "What are you doing aboard my ship, stowaway?"

"Looking for work, sir."

"Can't line up at a Grain Shippers Incorporated office like everyone else?"

"No money, sir. Can't get to Thunder Bay, or Baie-Comeau."

"What were you doing in Detroit?"

"Looking for work, sir. And starving, I guess."

Captain Lemieux stepped back a couple of paces, and looked carefully at Matt, from top to bottom.

"Got any ID?" he growled.

Matt was holding on to his expired able seaman certification card, his passport and his US Army veteran identification card. He handed the three documents to the captain.

The captain looked everything over carefully, then handed the documents back to Matt. Then he ordered, "Go fetch me a coffee, Adams, and then sit down and talk with me."

The cook had the cup of fresh black coffee ready just as soon as Matt got to the serving counter in the galley. "He likes it black," the cook whispered to Matt as he handed over the steaming cup. He also gave Matt a reassuring wink.

Matt sat down opposite Captain Lemieux, and then carefully slid the cup of coffee across the table to him. The captain picked up the cup by the handle. Then he blew on the hot coffee three times while staring over the rim of the cup at Matt. Then he put the cup back down on the table with a thump, and asked quietly, "Were you honourably discharged?"

"Yes, sir."

"Why? Get tired of it?"

"Wounded, sir. Shrapnel, the last time."

"Saw some front line action then?"

"Yes, sir. In Central America. First Ranger Battalion."

"That where you got those scars?"

"Yes, sir. Lost my left eye, too. They gave me a glass eye. But I can still work. I *know* I can."

"You know a Phillipe Adams?"

"Yes, sir. He was my father."

"Was? What, is he dead now? I thought he retired... "

"No, he never got to retire. He and my Mom both died, sir, at about the same time. Of something infectious, apparently. I was in a battle, and could not get back for the funeral. I haven't been back since, actually."

"Phillipe was a fine man. Always a straight shooter, never any issues at the transhipment terminal when *he* was in charge."

Matt did not reply. The thought of his father choked him up a bit, and it showed on his face.

Captain Lemieux seemed to soften a bit. He said quietly, "First Officer Gaspard thinks you're okay. And he's a hard man to please, just like I am.

"We got a real shake down by the Coast Guard at the head of the Detroit River. Something about a 'special alert'. Something big must have happened, because there's just cheesy music on all of the radio stations. And just special interest junk on the news broadcasts. Ship-to ship and ship-to shore radio work is all strictly business now, too. No more chatter allowed on any frequency. Anyway, I have no intention of going anywhere near a port until I get to Baie-Comeau.

"So here's what I'll do for you. I'll get you to shadow Jean Parizeau around for two days. If he says you're still 'able', then you can stay on with us until

Baie-Comeau. We are two hands short, as it happens. They skipped out on us while we were loading in Thunder Bay, the bastards.

"I can't offer you pay, because you're not officially hired. The office has to do that, and they would rather we went shorthanded. Times are tough everywhere. But you'll get room and board, and the grub's good aboard my ship. How does that sound?"

Matt smiled and said, "I understand the situation. I could not have hoped for anything more than that. Thank you, sir."

"Okay, I'll tell the purser what the deal is, and get him to assign you a bunk, and some protective gear."

Then Captain Lemieux looked around the galley to locate Seamen Jean Parizeau. He was chatting amiably with the cook. Captain Lemieux bellowed, "Hey, Jean, come over here, will you? We have a new recruit for you to check out and keep out of trouble."

28

Pablo Cortez was pleased that the very expensive missile defence system that he had bought to protect Mexico City had worked. In fact, it had worked *exactly* as the oligarch network had promised him it would.

He remembered that they had told him not to worry because the same system had just worked on the Moon. But that was a secret he was expected to keep to himself if he wanted to stay in the 'club', and to stay alive.

But he *had* been worried. The President of the United States was a lunatic, and he hated Mexicans. So, Pablo reciprocated by hating the president, and Americans.

Pablo was both a malevolent oligarch and a Mexican patriot. He was also a drug lord. He loved tequila and rich food, but he never got drunk, and he rarely overate. He stayed lean and fit by running three miles every day. And he did not use his illicit drugs. He made his fortune by manufacturing and transporting those illegal drugs, but those poisons were made to sell to the dregs of American society. He took their money, and the drugs killed a lot of them. And he felt pretty good about that.

He lived in a large estate in Acapulco. It was really a feudal fortress, surrounded by a fifteen-foot high concrete wall, topped with razor-wire. There were eight fifty-caliber machine gun posts stationed on top of the wall, cunningly positioned to enable overlapping fields of fire. He also had an anti-aircraft battery with six surface-to-air missiles and a couple of twenty-millimetre cannons installed within the compound.

But he knew he was now a marked man. So he decided to spend most of his time in Mexico City, where he felt it would be safer. The Acapulco fortress would be kept just as it was, but it would now be a ruse. He would go completely undercover. Only his two captains would know where he was at any given time. Point forward, they would meet with him separately and in person, and always in different, very busy and public places.

He considered his two captains completely trustworthy. They had all been toughened-up together as teenagers in a Mexico City street gang, and Pablo had saved their lives a couple of times each.

Pablo had been born a peasant, and he missed some aspects of that simple lifestyle. Okay, as he had grown to be a man, he had learned to like French cuisine, powerful electric Ferrari's, the best red wine, expensive cigars and loose, beautiful women. But in Mexico City he would carry around lots of cash, a switchblade and a pistol. So, fulfilling his fits of lust would never be a problem. He figured he would not really miss his confining and arguably cowardly Acapulco estate.

When he was fully incognito and settled into his new routine, he told one of his captains to send a message to Jose Jimenez.

Through his captain, Pablo Cortez told Jose Jimenez that it was time to settle an old score on behalf of Mexico.

29

It was just before ten o'clock in the morning on Thursday, March 30. Commandant Lamar Petrie of the Veterans Police Force in Cleveland, Ohio had efficiently dealt with his most urgent matters, and decided to read the paper mail in his inbox while sipping a cup of coffee.

His adjutant had just placed a fancy silver tray on the side of his desk. Petrie used some silver tongs to put two lumps of demerara sugar in the Chinese porcelain cup on the tray. Then he poured hot Columbian coffee into the cup from a silver-plated thermos jug. Then he looked again with disgust at the huge stack of letters and memos he would have to read.

This was a daily routine, and it went with the job. The silver serving set that he had confiscated from a rich felon took away some of the drudgery.

To help him out, all of his mail was pre-opened and pre-screened. His administrators would even suggest a classification for each document, and a recommended course of action, to expedite the overall process.

He reached for the letter at the top of the pile. It was hand-written and undated. A carefully-opened, postage-stamped envelope had been properly stapled to the back of the letter. The envelope was addressed to 'Cranston P. Snord', at a Cleveland address that US Army Intelligence had once used before their role had been usurped by the VPF. Petrie had not expected to see another letter from this particular agent.

He noted that the post mark over the postage stamp indicated the letter had been mailed on March 12, 2484, from St. Louis, Missouri. So, it had taken over two weeks to get to his desk. Still, that was better than average for delivery time. He knew his very efficient staff would never be on the critical path timeline. So he wondered for a moment if the train service might be improving marginally.

Then he studied the letter carefully. It read:

Dear Cranston,

I thought you might be curious about where I was headed. I looked for a job in St. Louis, but it's pretty desperate here. Not that El Paso or Akron were much better of course. The local VA Office suggested I could try Houston. Apparently food processing is picking up there, and a plant or two might be hiring.

The VA Office also said I had to have a fixed address to start collecting my disability pension again. That might be one of the new rules? But I don't know what kind of place I could rent to be able to have a fixed address, as my money is running out fast.

So, if you get wind of any other work like I had up in Akron, please send a letter to me care of the

Department of Veterans Affairs, Downtown Centre, Houston, Texas.
I hope things are working out better for you,
Your friend,
Audie Zaitsev

Commandant Petrie noted that someone on his staff had stamped 'HAND WRITING MATCHES' on the letter below the signature. And probably someone else on his staff had stamped 'PROJECT TERMINATED' further down on the letter. There was also a hand-written note paper-clipped to the letter that suggested it should be placed in the project file, then the file officially closed and sent away to the remote offsite storage archives.

'Well, that was a complete waste of effort and money,' he thought to himself. 'Just another amateur Army Intelligence wild goose chase.'

He could not have cared less about the ultimate fate of one Mathieu Adams, a.k.a. Audie Zaitsev. Like thousands of other homeless, unemployed people, he was probably heading for a quick demise. Petrie knew there was nobody looking for workers in Houston. The place was depopulating by the day.

So he scribbled his signature in the right spot on the routing note to indicate that he approved of the recommendations made by his supporting staff. Then he placed the letter in his 'out basket', and reached for the next document in his 'in basket'.

30

It was almost one o'clock in the morning on April Fools' Day, Saturday, April 1.

Jose Jimenez was standing in the back of the two-and-a-half ton panel truck with his black helper, who went by the name of Carlos Santana. Jose's Hispanic helper was driving the truck. They called him Julio Iglesias.

Jose had a thing for ancient history. He also had an obscure sense of humour that was lost on most people, including his two uneducated but otherwise capable helpers.

Jose and Carlos were both holding on to straps that were fastened to the ceiling of the cargo hold. Both men had their eyes fixed on the device.

The finished form of the device resembled a pressurized tank lying on its side. It was a metallic cylinder about ten feet long and three feet in diameter. The ends were outwardly-curved hemispheres.

The device was strapped with metal bands to two wooden pallets. And the two pallets had in turn been securely pinned to the floor of the cargo hold.

The ride from Katy, Texas had been protracted. There were many bumps in the road, and the men *definitely* did not want to disturb their cargo in any way.

There was a little sliding window between the cab of the truck and the cargo hold. Suddenly Julio yelled through the open window, "We're almost there, boss! It's going to get bumpy! I got to go slow now!"

"You take your time, Julio!" yelled back Jose.

"I will boss!"

The ride was indeed pretty rough for about five minutes or so as the truck crawled along at walking speed. They obviously were no longer on a proper roadway. Then Julio abruptly stopped the truck, and turned off the LNG-powered, internal-combustion engine. Then he said quietly through the open cab window, "We're right where you wanted it to be, boss. The coast is all clear, too. Not even a drunken student to be seen anywhere. I think it is exam time, or something."

"Right, then let's get going, amigos," replied Jose.

The electrical power was off in this part of Houston again. But there was just enough moonlight to see by. The truck had been positioned in what used to be a park on the grounds of the University of Houston in central Houston, Texas. The area was now a field of tall weeds and prickly bushes. Some of the brown and bone-dry vegetation was as tall as the truck.

Julio walked around to the back of the truck and opened up one of the big vertical doors. Then Carlos and

Jose handed down three bicycles to Julio. Each bike had a dis-connectable electric motor drive, and a fully charged, extra-large battery.

Carlos climbed down from the cargo hold. Then Jose said to his two helpers standing below him outside of the truck, "Okay, it is ten after one now. I'm flipping the toggle switch. Okay, it is flipped. So, we now got eight hours to get as far away from here as we can."

Jose climbed down from the cargo hold, and said, "Okay, Julio, lock the truck doors with the fob. Okay, good. The windows are up, right? Good. Now throw the keys in with the bomb. Okay. Carlos, close the big door. Okay, put the padlock on it. Good. Now give me the key."

Jose took hold of the little key and then threw it away as far as he could.

"Okay. Now, let's get the hell out of here, upwind. If we three are lucky, we will see each other again, in the Cantina Americana in San Antonio.

"Now remember, we must go by different roads. Adios, compadres."

31

It was about seven o'clock in the morning on Sunday, April 2. The three secretaries of state had spent the night together in the bomb-proof bunker far below the White House.

They were just finishing a breakfast of fried eggs, bacon and toast.

Frank Palermo pushed his plate away first, and he had a close look at his two peers while they were finishing up. He was completely disgusted with both of them, but as usual, his face did not reveal any emotion.

Sidney Lefebvre looked up to see that Frank was staring at him. He pushed his plate away too, stretched out his back and arms while yawning, and then asked quietly, "What's on your mind, Frank?"

"So, we lost Ernie, and now we've lost Houston," Frank snapped. "That's what's on my mind."

Sidney just glared back at him.

Poppy Beauregard quickly finished his last mouthful, and wiped his mouth methodically with his napkin. Then he pushed his plate away too, and said in a professorial way, "Yes, losing Ernie was certainly a huge loss for the nation. And losing Houston! Yes, well, that of course is extremely sad, too. But the place was in steep decline. Down to about five hundred thousand people, we think. Most people there were starving, and less than one-quarter were white. So, we can recover from this blow, I'm sure of it. But losing the Port of Houston, yes, well, that will hurt commerce, a bit."

"Did you get an update on the radioactive fallout?" asked Frank. He had never stopped staring at Sidney.

"Yes, it's definitely in Beaumont now," replied Sidney in a nonchalant manner. "It's expected to show up in Mobile any time now. It will probably go past New Orleans, eventually. But probably not much further east than that. It was a crude device. You know, inefficient, and dirty in the fallout sense."

"And you've confirmed it was not delivered by an ICBM, a bomber, or a cruise missile?"

"Definitely not. Nothing from the air, that's for sure. We can tell these things, you know."

"So, ground-based detonation. *Driven* to ground-zero, presumably. And you've confirmed it was not one of our own? We're not missing any nukes?

"No, we're pretty sure about that. And we make them better than anybody else. We know what the yield and fallout signatures look like, too. This one doesn't fit at all with what we have modelled for our own gadgets."

"You're 'pretty sure'. Well, that makes me feel a whole lot better, Sid."

"Frank, come off your high horse, will you?" asked Poppy aggressively. "The real question is who did this, isn't it? And how about *you*? Have *you* got any leads for us yet? I mean about who might have killed Ernie, too? It seems to me you're the one who's been dragging his butt. So, I think you should *lay off* Sid until you correct your own failings!"

Frank slowly turned his head to stare hard at Poppy. He waited until Poppy started to look uncomfortable. Then he said calmly, "Ernie's killer was a sniper. Professional. Not a mob guy. All the Dons came to us right away with personal assurances of innocence, and offers to help us in any way they can.

"The sniper set up three incendiary devices to confuse the Secret Service, and it worked. When the flash-bombs detonated, they looked and sounded like a high-calibre rifle going off. We found conclusive forensic evidence that two incendiary grenades had been set up high in riverside spruce trees on the Detroit side of the river, on opposite sides of the stage. Another one was set off under the Ambassador III Bridge on the Windsor side. By correlating the eye-witness reports, the three devices all went off at the same time, and exactly when the bullet struck Ernie.

"So, everyone at the time suspected there was more than one sniper. And they all thought a sniper was *definitely* on a ship passing close by on the Detroit River. But a comprehensive search of that vessel has turned up nothing. And no crew member on the ship coughed up anything useful for us, even under torture.

"But we looked hard at the trajectory of the fifty-calibre bullet that went right through Ernie. It hit him square in the back. So, we demarcated a stretch along the Windsor side of the Detroit River where the sniper may have been located, and we searched *every* possible location from where he could have made the killing shot.

"And yesterday we found the rifle. It was stashed behind some panelling in a condemned replica windmill. The site was an old tourist attraction, replaced about three times over the years. The weapon is an antique, but still totally lethal, and obviously very effective. The bullet-to-rifle ballistics match up perfectly.

"So, we know the rifle we found definitely fired the killing bullet. And only one shot was fired from it. The spent cartridge was found with the gun.

"We have no leads at all on where the weapon came from. It is definitely not a weapon that can be registered any more. Long-range hunters would love to have it, but a fifty-calibre bullet makes a mess out of anything it hits, so they would like it more for trophy 'bragging rights' than to acquire some edible wild meat.

"No US museums or collectors have reported a theft of such a weapon. It could have been smuggled into the country. But we also come across illegal domestic gun collections from time to time. They're out there. America has always liked its guns.

"The sniper wiped everything clean. He threw the radio-frequency triggering device for the three incendiary grenades into the wall cavity with the rifle.

The device itself might be a lead. It looks like something the KGB has used, and that was based on an MI-6 creation.

"So, the sniper may have been a foreign agent, or a mercenary paid by a foreign country, or by an unfriendly oligarch, which means *any* oligarch the way things stand now between us and the rest of the *whole freaking world*.

"The sniper got clean away, somehow, right through our dragnet. That confirms he was a professional.

"Now, there was a veteran sniper working for us as a low-pay undercover agent in Akron. That's not exactly close to Windsor. After six months we fired him. He turned up nothing really useful for us.

"But he mailed a letter to us from St. Louis the day after the killing. There are no commercial airplanes any more, of course. And only a military transport plane from St. John's, Newfoundland landed in St. Louis on the day of the killing, and nothing landed there the day before, or the day after. So, that's a bust right there. He could not have got to St. Louis so fast by ground transportation.

"In the letter, the guy said he was looking for work, and heading for Houston. If he made it there, he's burnt toast now. But we don't think he could be our man for the reasons I just outlined."

Frank stopped to think for a long moment. Then he said, "No, the more I consider this matter, the more I think we'll keep tabs on this guy anyway. Yes, I'll set that up.

"As for the bomb, it must have been either smuggled into the country intact, or it was assembled here by experts. They could have been terrorists, or traitors, or foreign agents, who worked with stolen or smuggled-in components. No one has claimed responsibility yet, so they probably never will. And, probably like the assassination, I think it was meant as a message to America, and now to 'we three'. The perpetrators are telling us, 'You mess with us, we will mess with you.'

"To take it a bit further, I believe the oligarch's have sent us a harsh, indirect message that I believe we must heed. They're telling us, 'Don't launch any more missiles at any of us, or at the Moon or at the *Second Chance*.'

"The other piece of intelligence I will share with you is that the South Pole Moon Base now has a fully operational, particle-beam weapon. It fires particles of mercury at near light speed. It has an unbelievably accurate targeting system. It wiped out Ernie's Moon-missile warhead, and that was a *damned* impressive feat of high-tech wizardry.

"And something similar has been set up in Mexico City. It wiped out Sid's ICBM re-entry vehicle. Again, we can only *dream* of being able to do something like that.

"And we think a similar weapon is being set up in Moscow, and another one *may* be installed in London.

And not coincidentally, the world price of mercury has just sky-rocketed. In fact, it's now considered an exceedingly rare element.

"And that's what I think, guys. That's all the latest news.

"So, Poppy, a sniper rifle, a nuclear bomb, foreign agents and maybe even a sniper probably crossed through borders you're supposed to be defending for us. What are you doing about that?"

"God damn it, Frank, so now you're starting on *me*?" yelled Poppy angrily. "Save your unfounded accusations for the campaign trail! And if you make any of this public, well, you've just given us *lots* of fresh material to use against *you*. So, you better watch it!"

Sid just laughed, and then quietly chuckled, "Good one, Poppy."

Frank abruptly stood up and said calmly, "Right. I'm going upstairs to make a campaign TV commercial. And then I'm going to get a little work done at my little side desk inside the Oval Office. Let me know if we're having our evening get-together down here again."

Then Frank turned around and walked towards the elevator, leaving Sid and Poppy aghast. They were both staring at his backside with their mouths open. Then Poppy said nervously, "Well, I'm not leaving this place for today, anyway. How about you, Sid?"

"No, I'm staying put too today, that's for sure," Sidney said with a shake of his head. "If Frank wants to pretend he's the hero type, let him, I say."

32

It was almost midnight on Thursday, April 6. Frank Palermo was sitting in the passenger seat of a black SUV with very dark, tinted windows. He and the three crack VPF officers sitting inside the large, roomy vehicle were all wearing the same outfits. They each wore a flat-black helmet, a bullet-proof vest and the black, military-style uniform of a Secret Service agent on special guard duty. Their vehicle was parked on a brick-paved alleyway about one hundred yards from the gated entrance to a large mansion. The mansion was a famous, grand old structure in an affluent suburb of Washington, D.C.

There was a bus full of similarly-garbed VPF officers parked immediately behind the SUV. The bus was a converted prisoner transport vehicle. It had recently been painted entirely flat black. It also had newly-installed, very dark, tinted windows.

Suddenly Frank's cell phone rang. The other three men in the SUV could not avoid hearing his side of the conversation.

"This is Palermo, go ahead.

"Great. Coroner confirmed it?

"Okay. How is the guy, fully on side with us, or what?

"Okay, great. Ask him if he drinks, and where he likes to go.

"Okay, take him there, and buy him as many cocktails as he wants. Have a few yourself. Good work. It's our turn now. See you afterwards."

Frank turned off his cell phone, and put it in his vest pocket. Then he said calmly, "Okay, we're on, you guys, let's go."

The four men all quietly got out of the SUV. The driver opened up the back hatch, and issued everyone, including Frank, an assault rifle with a large, curved magazine.

In response to the visual cue from Frank and the three officers in the SUV, the twenty 'special tactics' officers quickly poured out of the bus and assembled into two ranks. Each of those men was also handed an assault rifle. Frank and his three elite VPF officers then joined up at the front of the squad.

Then Frank gave a 'forward ho' arm signal, and the group marched off in an orderly manner.

They turned left on to the road to the mansion, and quick-marched straight for the front gate.

A Secret Service guard at the gate was startled by the loud noise that their heavy boots were making on the brick road surface. He had almost been dozing, and he was trying to quickly recover his wits. He stumbled out of a brick-clad guard shack on the right side of the open, massive, wrought-iron gate. Then he stopped and looked with confusion at the rapidly approaching squad of Secret Service agents. Frank saluted the guard and stopped to talk to him while waving the two ranks to pass him by.

"Orders!" Frank yelled to the guard. "Boss wants reinforcements!"

"I heard nothing about this," the guard growled angrily. Then he turned, started to pull his automatic pistol out of its open holster and yelled at the departing squad, "Hey, you guys… "

His verbal challenge was cut short by Frank. The guard had forgotten to put on his helmet, and Frank had clubbed him very hard on the back of his head with the butt of his rifle. The guard fell to the ground, unconscious.

Frank then ran to catch up with the squad. They had all formed up in a huddle near the huge front door of the mansion.

In a hushed voice, while trying to catch his breath, Frank told the group of excited men, "One Secret Service guy… on each floor… we think. Might be more. No need for silence now. Take them all out… if they resist. I'm heading for the master bedroom… with my three guys. We'll follow you. Okay, let's move."

Two especially burly VPF officers quickly battered open the front door of the mansion with one mighty swing of a hand-held, heavy metallic ramming device. Then the squad poured into the mansion.

Frank and his three men were the last to pass through the now wide-open, double front door. They charged up the right side of a double, very elegant, spiral staircase with Frank leading the way.

At the top of the stairway, Frank turned right down a wide hallway with very high, ornately moulded ceilings. Frank stopped at a closed, right-side, double-door near the end of the hallway. Frank pointed at the door. The largest officer with him stepped forward, and Frank said quietly, "Kick it open, Fred. We'll cover you."

Everyone readied their assault rifle, and Fred, the big tae kwon do expert, savagely kicked the door between the two knobs. The door flew open with a loud bang, and Frank charged into the room followed by the other three men.

They all immediately stopped short, and pointed their automatic rifles at Thomas Fitzgerald. Thomas was wearing a tacky, fluffy, vertically-striped robe. The covers on the super-sized bed in the huge suite were all in disarray. Thomas yelled angrily. "What the *hell* is this? You can't come in… "

Just then they all heard the sound of two long bursts of automatic gunfire. The loud burping noise had come from the level below.

Now Thomas suddenly looked more frightened than angry. Frank noticed the *en suite* bathroom door was shut. Frank yelled, "Who's in the bathroom, Tommy?"

"No one," Thomas growled as calmly as he could manage. "And don't call me Tommy, *Franky*."

Frank said quietly, "Same drill with that door, guys. I'll cover Tommy."

'Fred the Giant' then went over to the bathroom door. When the other two officers had their rifles ready, another tae kwon do kick from Fred burst the bathroom door open. There was a strangled scream from inside the bathroom, and then silence.

Frank yelled, "Check it out, Fred!"

After a minute, Frank yelled from inside the bathroom, "Hey, it's just a naked kid! Male, maybe fifteen. He's beat up pretty bad. Looks semi-conscious."

Frank glared with disgust at Tommy. He felt like pulling the trigger right then. But first things first. He wanted to play this out, fully.

Frank quietly murmured to the officer right beside him, "Phil, wrap the kid up in a towel, and carry him out of here. Get him some medical attention. Then when he's ready, talk to him. And remember, I said *talk to him*! Don't use force, he's just a kid, right? Get his name, find out if he's got parents, and if so, get somebody to contact them. Then ask the kid to tell you what was going on in here. Be really nice about it. And get the interview all on video. We'll probably use some of it later. Okay, get moving."

When VPF Officer Phil had left with the dazed, bleeding teenage boy in his arms, Frank said quietly to

Thomas, "Okay, Tommy. It's all over. I'm running the country now. And you're out."

Thomas yelled, "I told you to stop calling me *Tommy*, asshole! And how can you be fully in charge…"

"Sid's gone!" Frank yelled to cut him off. "Yep, he was taking Air Force Three to a rally in Los Angeles. Had the wife along with him. Engine trouble or something. *Terrible* tragedy. Crashed in northern New Mexico somewhere. No survivors."

Before Thomas could reply, Frank added in his normal voice, "Yep, and Poppy. Poor Poppy. Hit and run maniac got him outside his favourite restaurant. Didn't kill him outright though. But the paramedic in the ambulance may have made a mistake, somehow. Over-dose injection of pain killer did him in. *Terrible* tragedy."

"I'm still head of the freaking Party!" Thomas yelled. He was shaking with anger now. "And the Secret Service! And the LOP, *goddam it*!"

Frank noted the two remaining VPF officers both had their guns levelled right at Thomas's heart. And they looked completely disgusted with the old pervert.

Frank smiled at them, and seemed to relax a bit. Then he said, still in his normal voice, "Tommy, you *serve* the president, and the Secret Service *protects* the president. And the Party and the VPF *support* the president.

"And I'm now the *president*. And by now, every Secret Service agent has been personally approached by a VPF officer. Even the guy at your front gate, if he's conscious again. It should be no surprise really that so far *every agent* has agreed to whole-heartedly support the transition of power. They now report to *me*, you see, and they know they are going to be joining the ranks of the VPF. They have been granted job security in a world of unemployment. The choice was pretty easy for them.

"So, there will no longer be a Secret Service. And there will no longer be an LOP. Those guys are all being arrested, as I speak. They are not armed, of course, so that part of this operation is relatively routine VPF work. And they are all going to be sent to re-education camps. Some will come through it okay. Others, maybe not so well.

"And as for the *Party*? Well, it will get rolled into Veterans Affairs. They don't know it yet, but the Party will become a social club. All of their functions will be state-sponsored. They'll get beer and food, and the use of poker tables, playing cards and pool tables. If they are members, honourably-discharged and homeless, they'll still get their veterans pensions. I don't foresee any major problems with that part of this operation, either.

"So, now we finally get to you, Tommy. What should we do with *you*?

"No one has a problem with homosexuality. I know I don't. Gay people are just a segment of our population, and an innate part of our species. That's all. No big deal, *for consenting adults*.

"But *paedophilia*, Tommy, everybody's got a *big* problem with that. And you're a god damn, murdering *paedophile*, Tommy."

"Bullshit, I ain't no… "

Frank cut Thomas off with a yell, "I was the head of the VPF, Tommy! Remember, you idiot? We've tracked you for months. We've got the photos, the videos, the sworn testimonies and the coroner's reports."

Thomas suddenly looked like a very sick, sad, beaten-down old man.

Frank shook his head, and said quietly, "You were loyal to Ernie though, Tommy. And he didn't want the VPF to do anything to you. So, in honour of Ernie, I'll give you a way out, if you want.

"You can put a Secret Service pistol to your temple, right now, and blow your brains out. We'll all swear it was suicide, and we won't have to lie about that. And then we won't show your *real* life-story on national television.

"Or, if you really are stupid, you can keep resisting us, and we'll shoot you to death, *right now*, for trying to escape. And then we'll be sure to put Jody Philpott's very fine biographical production on prime time.

"So, what's your pleasure, Tommy?"

"You can *fuck right off*! You're just a *punk,* compared to Ernie! And you ain't no president either, and… "

"Let him have it!" Frank yelled.

Frank and the two VPF officers standing beside him then emptied their magazines into the large, bloated and corpulent body of Thomas Fitzgerald.

33

It was almost ten o'clock in the morning on Saturday, April 18. Daquan Jefferson had just started to give a tall, handsome, middle-aged black man a haircut in the Broadway Barbershop in downtown Akron, Ohio.

Daquan knew his customer was the leader of a notorious criminal organization. But he also knew the man was well-liked in the community, especially by elderly people who he befriended with magnanimous gifts of charity. He was tied into the black market, and he was providing healthy food and other necessities of life to the people living in the downtown black ghetto. He was making a tidy profit, of course. But profiting from free-enterprise was still okay in fascist America. If the free-enterprise was relatively harmless, but nefarious, and one was careful about engaging in it, well, that just reflected a person's wily intelligence. And of course, creative and tasteful bribery was now well received.

The radio stations had been playing nothing but classical music, or silly popular songs, since Cousin Ernie's assassination on March 11. Everyone knew something really serious was happening in their greater

American society, but everyone also concluded it was best not to talk about it.

Suddenly, instead of another pop song on the radio, there was the sound of a trumpet blaring. So, the owner of the barbershop turned up the volume on his old radio receiver. Then they all heard:

"We interrupt this program to bring you a special announcement from the President of the United States. We ask every citizen to stop doing whatever they are doing, and to listen very carefully to what our new president has to say to us."

Daquan stopped using his clippers, and sat down on the empty adjacent customer seat in the shop. His customer did not voice any objection. Then everyone in the shop listened very carefully to the announcement:

"This is your president speaking, Frank Palermo. The last few weeks have been very troubling for our nation. I apologize that it has taken so long to tell the American people what has been going on. But I am very pleased to say things have now stabilized, and I hope things will start getting a lot better in very short order.

"We have still not solved the cowardly murder and assassination of President Ernie Wolf. We have found the murder weapon, however. It is an antique and very rare, bolt-action, fifty-calibre rifle. An expert sniper used it to shoot our former president in the back from a hidden position on the Windsor side of the Detroit River. There were no fingerprints on the weapon or on the spent cartridge. There was one unused round in the

chamber, and three unused rounds in the magazine. There was one useful fingerprint on one of the unused rounds, but it does not match anything we have on record. We ask that any citizen with any insight into this killing come forward immediately, and share whatever you think you know, or even suspect, with a VPF officer.

"There have been two other tragic deaths that I am very sorry to have to report today.

"Secretary of State Sidney Lefebvre, and his lovely wife Amelia, were both killed when Air Force Three crashed into a New Mexico desert. They were on their way to a presidential campaign rally that was set to occur in the Rose Bowl III in Pasadena, California. The cause of the airplane crash is still under investigation, but the incident looks very suspicious. Unfortunately, the United States has many enemies. I will return to discuss this alarming reality in a few moments.

"And Secretary of State Poppy Beauregard was struck to the ground by a hit and run driver. The driver has not been located, but eye witnesses reported that he or she had been driving their SUV very erratically. So, the individual may have been drunk. Poppy was said to have been alive when he was en-route to hospital in an ambulance. But he died after receiving a massive injection of morphine. The paramedic claims that a simple mistake in the heat of the moment led him to use the wrong dosage. He is currently under arrest, awaiting trial. The judge will decide if he is telling the truth.

"There is one other matter of note. I personally led a squad of VPF officers in the arrest of a notorious murderer and paedophile. Thomas Fitzgerald was in the process of abusing a young boy when we charged into his home. The poor, deeply traumatized boy has subsequently told us what Thomas did to him that evening. Thomas was killed when he resisted arrest. At eight o'clock this evening, a documentary will air on television that will describe in great detail the kind of disgusting, perverted murderer Thomas Fitzgerald really was. The film is very graphic, so parents are strongly advised not to allow their children to see it.

"So, folks, by default, I am now your president.

"The United States is in a state of emergency. We are almost at war with a number of nations. In the interest of our national security, and to get us completely out of this mess, I will do this job for two, four-year terms. Rest assured, I will want to retire after serving my country in this manner. This is a very stressful job.

"I am a businessman. So, I will run the United States like a business. I cannot promise anyone true prosperity. But if you keep your nose clean, and work hard, you should be able to get by okay.

"It is an open secret that the world is actually run by oligarchs. I probably will qualify as an oligarch when I retire from the presidency. And my successor will be an oligarch, so the United States can compete effectively on the global stage. I will leave it up to the club of American oligarchs to decide who my

replacement will be, by whatever process they decide to use. May the best man or woman win that critically important contest.

"In the next few days, I will be contacting the greater, worldwide network of oligarchs. I will ask to attend their next meeting, wherever and whenever that may be. If they extend an invitation to me, I will try to make the peace with them.

"I believe wars are wasteful, harmful and stupid. They are bad for business, and again, I am a businessman. I hope that we can all reach a mutually beneficial, lasting, business arrangement.

"For reasons known only to himself, President Ernie Wolf tried to destroy the Second Chance generation spaceship, but he failed. I cannot elaborate, because it involves state secrets.

"And right after President Wolf died, for reasons known only to himself, Secretary of State Sidney Lefebvre tried to destroy Mexico City, but he failed. Again, I cannot elaborate because it involves state secrets.

"I want to assure the American people, and the other nations of the world, and the international network of oligarchs, that the United States under my leadership will not be the one to break the peace. Furthermore, we hope to re-join the lucrative Second Chance international joint venture, and help see the exciting project through to completion.

"Also, to improve efficiency and to save millions of hard-earned taxpayer dollars, most of the agents of the

Secret Service have now become Veterans Police Force officers. The professional officers of the expanded VPF can keep me safe as well as they can keep everyone else safe in our great nation.

"I have never been much of a fascist. So, the Loyal Order of Patriots has been disbanded, and its members are undergoing rehabilitation. And the Veterans Party will become an honoured society of veterans. We will honour their fine service to this nation by building halls for them all across the country, where they can meet, have a few laughs with their comrades, enjoy a few beers, and play cards or whatever. All of that will be on our tab. It is the least we can do for these fine, patriotic Americans.

"And finally, my fellow Americans, I want you all to feel like you are now part of a large, supportive family. If you are my friend, I will be your friend. And if we encounter an enemy together, please help President and Don, Frank Palermo, to kick his ass.

"I wish you all a pleasant day. Good-bye for now."

There was a prolonged and rather awkward silence in the barbershop. The radio started to play another pop song. Everyone was trying to recall and assimilate all of the startling new information they had just heard.

Daquan's customer was the first person to speak again. He growled loudly, "Come on, Daquan, my man! Finish the damn job!"

Daquan jumped up and started to work efficiently with his comb and pair of scissors. His customer then yelled, "*President and Don* has a nice ring to it, don't you think? Now, I wonder how long it will take for me to become an oligarch... ?" He trailed off with a laugh. But everyone in the shop knew he was asking himself a very serious question.

Daquan clipped away in silence while he started to wonder if the Social Club elite would consider the outcome of this amazing series of events as a success.

Later that evening, just before he fell asleep in his squatter's shack, he concluded that the members of the elite would be a lot happier now. The *Second Chance* probably had a secure future, at least until it left on its perilous, multigenerational mission in about thirty years' time.

Then he wondered what his good friend Matt Adams was up to. He hoped he was all right.

34

Matt Adams helped the crew of the *Baie-Comeau III* unload the bulk cargo of grain at the Baie-Comeau transshipment terminal. And then he helped tidy up the ship from top to bottom.

It had taken six-and-a-half weeks to travel from the western end of Lake Erie to Baie-Comeau. There had been frustrating delays at every lock. The locks were under-manned, and almost every one of them had some kind of mechanical or hydraulic issue that either slowed their operation, or required some kind of significant repair before it could be used.

Finally, at four o'clock in the afternoon on Friday, April 28, Captain Robert Lemieux declared the voyage complete. He sent the regular crew members away on two weeks of furlough and told them all to pick up their pay packets at the local Grain Shippers Incorporated office.

Matt was the last crew member to leave the ship. He had his backpack with him when he approached the temporary ramp that led down to the dock. First Officer Gerard Gaspard and Captain Robert Lemieux were both waiting for him beside the ship-end of the ramp.

Captain Lemieux shook Matt's hand, and said pleasantly with a broad smile, "Well, you worked very hard, Mathieu. You proved to be a very able seaman. I cannot promise you a job with Grain Shippers, but please use me as a reference if you want to make an application. But I hear you might be headed for Montreal, by some means or another?"

"Yes, Captain," Matt replied quietly. "There's nothing waiting for me here in Baie-Comeau. But thank you for letting me use your name as a reference. I really appreciate it! And for a while on your fine ship, I had a decent place to sleep and good food to eat. And I made a few friends among the members of the crew. I see Jean is waiting for me down on the dock. He wants to buy me a beer, or something."

"Okay, Mathieu," Captain Lemieux replied with a smile and nod of his head. Then after a moment he added in a sombre tone of voice, "Listen, we had to make note of you in the ship's log. That's the law. If you're running from something, that may make things worse for you. But that's none of our business. If you're not running from anything, there's a small company office in Montreal. Keep us in mind, sailor."

Matt smiled in return, and said, "Thanks, I will, sir."

Then Matt shook hands with Gerard Gaspard. Gerard looked a bit tongue-tied. But he pulled a thick, folded-up envelope from his back right pocket, and handed it to Matt. "Something for you from the officers and crew of the *Baie-Comeau III*. It's a bit less than what your regular pay would have been. But we hope it will help you get to wherever you decide to go next."

Matt was overwhelmed by the generosity. It was completely unexpected. After a moment he managed to stammer, "Thank you both, so much. And please thank everyone else for me. I will miss them."

Then Matt came to rigid attention and smartly saluted the two officers.

Seaman Jean Parizeau was waiting for him on the dock near the end of the ramp. He waved at Matt to follow him.

When the two seamen were outside of the secure area of the port, and well away from security cameras and guards, Jean let Matt catch up to him. Jean shook his hand vigorously, and slapped him on the back jovially. Then he said with a laugh, "Well, we're both free for a while now! So, you didn't get arrested, and they gave you some money in the end, right?"

"I think so, Jean," Matt said quietly. He was still reeling a bit from receiving the thick envelope. "I haven't looked yet in the envelope they just gave me to see how much, though."

"Well, don't do it out here in the open, that's for sure," Jean said quietly while looking around suspiciously. Then he boomed, "Come on, Matt, I know a safe but fun bar nearby. You're going to buy the first round. And you're going to thank me again for not throwing you back in the Detroit River."

Matt laughed, and then he asked, "Okay, but can we visit a store on the way? I need to buy a few things, mostly food items."

"Sure, Matt, I know a good place along the way," replied Jean with a puzzled look. But he did not say anything else. Matt was about to leave somewhere on his own, and what he needed to get there was his business.

About an hour after Matt had left the ship, First Officer Gerard Gaspard finally managed to get a connection with a relay station in Rimouski to the southwest. He found he had to use the transhipment terminal's more powerful radio-telephone to complete the call. Then he faxed a copy of the ship's log for the segment that covered the recent voyage from Thunder Bay. The log extract would make its way to the Grain Shippers Incorporated head office in Montreal, Quebec. Then, as required by law, it would be shared with the VPF via their Montreal outpost, and the Coast Guard.

35

Very early in the morning of Monday, May 2, Claude Adams woke from a weird dream. He heard a loud noise coming from outside of his unpainted, very basic, wood-clad bungalow. He listened intently for a long moment. Then he concluded there was an unusually loud racket coming from the hen house. But there were no other sounds.

He rolled out of bed, trying very hard not to disturb his wife, Madelaine. But she stirred, and murmured, "What is it, Claude? And what *time* is it?"

He looked down tenderly at his wife of twelve years, and the mother of their two kids. Then he looked at the little clock beside their bed, and said softly, "It's about two in the morning, my dear. I think that fox has come back. I better go out back, and check it out."

"Okay, try not to wake the kids."

Claude bent over to kiss Madelaine on the forehead, and watched her as she quickly fell back to sleep.

He sat down on a cushioned chair in the bedroom and pulled on his coveralls. Then he went to the closet. He pulled a couple of twelve-gauge shotgun shells out of a little wooden box he kept on the top shelf.

He made his way quietly to the mud room by the back door of the house. He always kept a side-by-side, double-barrelled, 12-gauge shotgun on a rack over the door, well out of reach of the children. They were both good kids, a boy and a girl. He knew they would never touch his gun, but keeping it way up high made him rest a bit easier.

He broke open the breach of the shotgun, slid the two shells into the chambers, and snapped the breach shut.

Then he grabbed a flashlight out of a drawer in the mud room, checked that it worked okay, and went out the back door.

He was not trying to be stealthy. The hens and the rooster were making a hell of a racket now. He wondered if the fox was actually inside the hen house.

But he first shone his light all around the building, and was totally shocked to see that a large man was standing back in the shadows on the right side of the building, staring back at him.

Claude levelled his shotgun at the trespasser, and barked, "Who are you? And what do you think you're doing? Stealing my chickens?"

"It's me Claude, Matt," replied the intruder, almost in a whisper.

"Matt?" Claude asked more quietly. Then he put the flashlight beam right on the man's bearded face. As recognition set in, he gasped, "*Mon Dieu*, it's Matt Adams!"

"*Bon soir*, Claude, I wasn't trying to steal your chickens, I swear. But I'm in a bit of a bind, and I could use some help. I stirred the birds up a bit because I thought the noise might bring you out here, to talk to me."

Claude looked around, and noted that everything except the hen house was still and quiet. Then he lowered his gun, and said, "Why don't we go into the house Matt, so these poor birds can settle down?"

"Can we just move away, and stay out of sight, Claude? I don't want anyone else to know that I've been here."

Claude thought for a moment, then he pointed at a trail that led back into the woods, and said, "We can use my work shed. Let's have a talk in there."

Claude kept the beam of his flashlight low, and led Matt back to his shed. When they got inside, Claude closed the door, and handed Matt his flashlight. Then he struck a match to light a kerosene lantern. When the light from the lantern was steady, the two men looked carefully at each other.

Claude was the first to speak. "That beard suits you. But I don't like those scars. From the war?"

"Yes, lost an eye too. But a lot of other guys came away from it in far worse shape. And a lot of my buddies were killed."

"I should have written you, Matt. I'm sorry. I guess I got caught up in my own problems."

"Serious problems, Claude?"

"No, common problems that everybody faces these days. The demand for lumber has been weak for decades. I still cut down hardwood trees, and work my own little sawmill. I air-dry the stuff, and sell it to people who make furniture. And I trap furs, and sell the pelts. And Madelaine and I have a huge and amazing vegetable garden, and we raise chickens, like you saw and heard, and a few pigs and goats. But we've gone a bit hungry a few times."

"You're making me rather jealous, Claude. That all sounds pretty good, except for the 'sometimes hungry' part. I'm sorry to about hear that."

Claude smiled, and said, "It doesn't happen very often, thankfully. Now, what kind of trouble are you in, Matt?"

"I'm pretty sure the VPF are after me, Claude. You see, I did something for our country that some people probably won't like. I don't want to tell you any more than that. It might get you in trouble.

"I hopped on a freighter in Detroit, and worked as a seaman until it got here, or rather a few miles south of here, to Baie-Comeau. We arrived on Friday. I got drunk with a shipmate Friday night, and slept in the back of a bar. I left before my friend woke up, and started asking around for you. It took a while to get a solid lead. But a shopkeeper in Baie-Comeau said she knew your wife, and gave me directions to your place. I walked to the start of your lane on Route 138 in the dark yesterday, and set up a lean-to shelter near the road junction. I left my backpack there. Then I walked here fairly carefully, making sure no one saw me. And I watched your place for a while to see if the coast was clear before trying to talk to you.

"You know that I've always been an honest man. I still am, but I've been through a lot. And I want to start up again, and put it all behind me. I've been thinking Montreal might be a good place to live. But we're a long way away from that place. I'm on foot, as you can see, and I was wondering if I could buy a bicycle from you. I see you have a couple, here in this shed."

"You are my cousin Matt. I won't take any money from you, not when you're in a bind."

"Thanks very much, Claude, but I *need* to give you something, so you can tell the VPF under oath that you sold me a bicycle just to get me out of your life. And I want you to promise me you'll tell them *exactly* what we talked about here tonight. You can't lie to these people, Claude. They are all-powerful, and some of them are, quite frankly, sadistic bastards."

Claude nodded in agreement. He had never had an actual run-in with the VPF, but he knew people that had. And it had not been pleasant for them.

Then Clause pointed at a newish-looking bicycle leaning against a side wall in the dusty shack. Then he said, "I've never been as big and strong as you, Matt. I find that fat bike is a bit on the heavy side for me. And the helmet hanging from the handle bars is way too big for me. Would you like that bike, Matt, and the helmet?"

Matt had a close look at the bike. It was a beauty, with eighteen gears, really large rims, outrageously fat and knobby tires, and a rugged-looking spring suspension system. It also had two leather saddlebags and an aluminum handlebar rack. Matt mumbled, "The bike's perfect, Claude."

"Then it's all yours for ten bucks."

"It's worth fifty times that, at least."

"Well, that's too bad, that's my price, take it or leave it." Then he looked a bit sheepish, and asked very quietly, "That is, if that's not too much for you?"

Matt laughed and pulled his wallet out of his front pocket. He handed Claude a ten-dollar bill, and said, "Sold! Thanks so much, Claude. This will really help me out."

Then Claude asked, "Do you need anything else, Matt? For camping?"

Matt saw an old hatchet laying on a work bench beside a newer one. Then he said, "I'm pretty well equipped, with a buck knife, sharpening stone, some things to cook with, matches, sleeping bag, et cetera. But could you afford to part with that old hatchet?"

"Sure Matt, I just ground a new edge on it. It's made of good steel, actually. It didn't really need the touch-up job."

Matt put the hatchet in a saddle-bag on the bike. Then he offered Claude his hand. But Claude would have none of that. He gave Matt a big hug. Then he said, "Come in and say hello to Madelaine, Matt, and meet

my two kids. They've never met one of my relatives..."
He trailed off with a wavering smile. He looked on the verge of tears.

"I can't, Claude. I'm truly sorry. You have to keep my visit a secret, you see, until the VPF shows up to talk to you."

"When do you think that will happen?"

"Hopefully not for a few weeks. By then, I should be a long way away, if not in Montreal."

"Will there be a way to keep in touch with you?"

"I think the best I can do is to mail you a letter from time to time. And if it's safe to give you a mailing address, then perhaps you can write me back?"

"You bet I will."

Then Claude snapped his fingers when he remembered something, and he said. "Wait, I have something of yours, that I bet you could use." He went over to the back wall of the shack, and pulled a long, leather-covered bundle off a high shelf. It was covered in a thick layer of dust. He grabbed a rag and wiped the dust away.

Then he handed the bundle to Matt, and said, "It's your old 270 rifle. You left it with your parents, remember? After they died, well, I took it for safekeeping, until I saw you again."

Matt undid the long zipper on the cover pouch, and had a close look at the weapon. It was in perfect condition.

"Here, let's strap it to the handlebar rack, Matt. I've got some extra shock cords."

They worked together to strap the rifle securely to the bike.

Then Matt said with a smile, "Okay, Claude, I better be going now. You've really been a good friend, as always. And a sight for sore eyes."

"*Bonne nuit et bon voyage, mon ami.*"

36

Claude Adam's rustic bungalow was about seven miles north of the ancient Quebec 'Kings Highway', or Route 138.

It was almost sunrise when Matt Adams returned to his lean-to shelter. He had set it up in the neighbouring woods where the muddy lane to Claude's house terminated at Route 138. Matt retrieved his backpack and moved some stuff in the backpack to the two, leather rear-wheel saddlebags on the bike.

Matt had layers of clothing to match the weather. He had some tinned ham, dried fish, moose jerky, an assortment of dried beans and dried vegetables, yellow peas, rice, and dried fruit. He figured his food would last about a week. He also wanted to buy a couple boxes of ammunition for his rifle as soon as he could.

The little old lady shopkeeper in Baie-Comeau that had told him where the Adams lived had also given him some critically important advice. Matt had deliberately prefaced their brief conversation by telling her that he had not yet decided if he was going east, west or north. She had told him that if was going north, he could probably buy things he might need in the hamlet of Relais-Gabriel on the eastern edge of Lac Manicouagan.

She said that Lac Manicouagan was remarkably circular in shape, but one could only see that by looking at a map. She said it was the site of a huge prehistoric meteor or asteroid strike. She thought the hamlet of Relais-Gabriel might be his last opportunity to shop until he got to what might be left of the ancient mining town of Fermont near the Labrador border, if that's where he ultimately decided to go.

If Matt had turned his bicycle right on Route 138 to make the very long journey to Montreal, at least five long days and two hundred and fifty miles later he would have passed through Quebec City. Montreal was another one hundred and sixty miles beyond Quebec City.

Matt did in fact turn right. But he only stayed on Route 138 for a little more than four miles. Then he turned to the right again and headed north on the ancient and far less travelled Quebec Route 389.

He figured it would take him about nine grueling days to travel the three hundred and fifty miles or so to his first destination, Fermont, Quebec. He suspected the road ahead would be a lot rougher than Route 138.

He planned to cross the state border just north of Fermont into Newfoundland and Labrador. The road then became Route 500 or the old Trans-Labrador Highway. It went on to pass through the ancient town of Labrador City, and beyond.

He suspected Route 389 might be washed out through centuries of neglect, or even overgrown in a few places. But he had never travelled on the road very far as a youth. And the shopkeeper in Baie-Comeau could not help him at all with a recent road report. She had said that she had never been on Route 389 herself. And she had added cryptically that very few people she knew could claim to have ever used it.

Matt would be carrying a heavy load. And a man trying to travel quickly with such a load would attract attention to himself. So, his plan was to go at a steady, safe pace, and avoid falling off his bike, to avoid damaging it.

But he also figured he would be glad to be wearing a helmet on this long, essentially off-road, journey in the wilderness.

37

VPF Commandant Lamar Petrie was just about ready to leave his office and call it a day. He was greatly looking forward to the weekend. He was recently divorced, and had just made a date with a charming woman that surprisingly seemed interested in a senior, workaholic, VPF officer.

It was almost six o'clock in the evening on Friday, May 5. And it was summer-like in Cleveland now.

Petrie was very pleased with himself, perhaps absurdly so. He believed the VPF detachment under his direction had executed another perfectly flawless and highly-efficient week of police work. Okay, the work had all been routine in an impoverished city in decline. But the record would stand for itself.

As he was packing up his valise with some weekend reading material, the phone on his desk rang. He could see that it was an incoming call from his adjutant. He almost blew it off to head for the door. But he reminded himself that in his position he must be professional at all times. So, he picked up the handset, and said curtly, "Yes, what is it, Emanuel?"

"Sir, I have… or rather you have… the *president* on line two, waiting to talk to you, sir!"

"The president of what?" replied Petrie flippantly.

"The President of the United States, sir!" Emanuel replied with a weird combination of horror and disbelief in his voice. "He's waiting on line two for you, sir."

Lamar Petrie dropped his valise on the floor. Then he stared with his own sudden horror and disbelief at the glowing yellow 'line two' button on his desk telephone. He forced himself to take a slow, deep breath, then he pushed the yellow button. He tried to speak calmly, but his voice cracked when he said, "Hello, this is Commandant Lamar Petrie."

"This is President Frank Palermo, Commandant," he heard in reply. "I'm calling you from the Oval Office in the White House. Your adjutant formally and correctly confirmed this connection is legitimate. So, I am who I say I am. Okay?"

"Okay, Mister President."

"Okay then. You remember a contract Army Intelligence agent named Mathieu Adams?"

"Ah, yes sir. We handled his reports in this office when the VPF took over the project."

"Right. Well, I put a special flag on him, and he just showed up in the system again, in a remote place called Baie-Comeau. That's in Quebec."

"Okay. That's a bit strange, sir."

"It's goddam strange! And you haven't made anything easier for us, Petrie. You sent his project file to the dead letter office."

"Ah, if I remember correctly, I sent his file to the offsite archival records facility in Cincinnati, sir."

"Right, where it went into a stack with a billion other paper documents to collect dust and turn yellow with age. And you never digitized his file."

"Ah, we don't normally do that, sir. Not for covert operations. And certainly not in this office, sir. I assure you that we know our business here."

"All right, all right."

There was a long pause, then the president said, "Okay, back on point, Commandant. Can you guess how Adams got to Baie-Comeau?"

"No sir, no idea. That would be a long journey from Akron. I don't know how one would do that, actually, especially if one was poor, like this guy was."

"He climbed on to a lake freighter in the middle of the night at the southern end of the Detroit River, right in an active shipping channel. The ship was underway!"

"Really?"

"Really! And do you know *when* he did it?"

"No sir, of course not. You have me at a disadvantage, sir, with respect to intelligence."

"Yea, well, I'm having my doubts about your *freaking* intelligence, all right, Petrie. He got on the ship a little over a day after President Ernie Wolf was assassinated."

"Oh God, no… "

"Oh God, *yes*! Now, your ass is in a major bind, Commandant. But I'm going to give you a way to recover, and save your career, and maybe your life, too. You're one of the few people on the planet in the know about this. And we're going to keep it that way. Now, here is what you're going to do… "

38

It was midnight on Friday, May 5. It was also closing time in the little cantina. The burly bartender was wiping down tables. Pablo Cortez was the only remaining patron. He was sipping on some straight tequila at a little round table in the middle of the restaurant area. As expected, right on time, one of Pablo's captains, Pedro Alvarez, strolled into the Mexico City back-street establishment, and took the seat opposite Pablo.

Pablo had decided to speak only in English to his two captains. And they always met in carefully-selected, seedy meeting places. Yes, speaking in English in public did reveal an unusual proficiency with a foreign tongue. And yes, by extension, some bystanders might perceive their conversations as sinister. But the choice of communication vehicle would usually create some security for them. Most people foolish enough to eavesdrop on their conversation would probably not understand a word that was said.

Pablo looked carefully at Pedro. As usual, Pedro stared back at him with a blank, unreadable look on his face. His emotions had always been impossible to discern from tone of voice or body language. Then Pablo asked pleasantly, "So, how's business?"

"Flat, maybe a little down."

"You promised me you would do better. Is there competition?"

"The same as always. People have less money, that's all. Even for bad habits."

Pablo became aware that the bartender was now cleaning the table directly behind where he was sitting. But he dismissed the peripheral intrusion.

"Your performance is unacceptable. Perhaps I should... "

Suddenly the bartender had a wire around Pablo's neck and tightened it just enough to hurt really bad, but not quite enough to cut into the skin, or constrict blood vessels or the windpipe. Pablo started to resist violently, but Pedro scolded him with a wag of his right index finger. Then he said quietly, "No, no, no, that will just quicken your death, Senor."

Pablo froze into a rigid sitting position. His eyes were bulging with horror and intense anger.

Then Pedro said, "You helped us make some money, but you always held back too much. You are greedy and selfish. So, I have split your turf with Captain Felix Estevan. He is now a very happy man.

"And your secret man, Jose Jimenez? He held out very well under torture, I am told. But his compadres? Not so much, it seems. They spilled their refried beans in the end. And now they are all dead. The ghost of Sam

Houston, he is a happier Texan now. But he is still very angry about what you did. You will not enjoy meeting him in the afterlife.

"And Don Palermo? He is very happy now, too. He has given me and Felix some new rules, and some new business opportunities. And now we are all friends.

"And now we will slice off your head. Adios, el Diablo de Acapulco."

Pedro made a quick slashing motion across his throat, and the bartender savagely ended the life of Pablo Cortez.

39

It took Matt Adams five days to travel the 200 miles or so from Baie-Comeau to Relais-Gabriel. Matt had decided to set up a temporary nighttime camp just south of the hamlet so he could enter the place on the morning of Sunday, May 7.

Route 389 had been gravel-covered and fairly smooth in some places, and just a muddy trail in others. The ancient bridges across faster rivers had been maintained just well enough to allow people to carefully walk over them, or in his case, walk over them while pushing a heavy bicycle. But floods had cut away bridges across some smaller streams and brooks. Matt had to ford those streams, but it had been fairly dry recently, and the water had not been too deep.

The only person Matt saw on this leg of his journey was a guy riding a horse just south of Relais-Gabriel early on Sunday morning. The man was heading north towards the hamlet, so Matt hung back a few hundred yards to avoid having to talk to him.

But it was encouraging to see someone with a horse. A horse was a very expensive luxury item everywhere in the United States. It would not be easy to feed a horse properly, or to take proper care of it. And you could not make a trip like Matt was trying to make on a horse. There was not much sustenance to be found in a boreal forest for a large herbivore. How moose achieved the feat had always struck Matt as rather miraculous.

Matt was pleased to find that there was indeed a combination general store and trading post in Relais-Gabriel. He was able to find what he needed for foodstuffs, and he bought as much as he could carry along with him. He included some dried and salted lake fish to provide some protein, and some wild berry preserves for vitamins.

The pleasant, middle-aged, male shopkeeper had only spoken French, which was not unusual in the interior of Quebec. English was the only official language in the United States, but that law was very hard if not impossible to enforce in what had become a third-world country where people lived everywhere, even in virtual wilderness.

Matt had asked the shopkeeper how he managed to stay stocked-up. The man told him local hired men helped him with that, using dog-sleds in the wintertime when the trail to the south became a safe-to-use ice road. Dog sleds hauled fur pelts and frozen wild meat south to Baie-Comeau, and then returned with the stuff for his store. He said he had a large warehouse that he drew upon. And there were two local market gardeners who sold him fresh produce and canned preserves in season.

Matt had then asked the shopkeeper for the ammunition he wanted. By law, Matt had to show him either a valid non-restricted firearm permit, or a veteran's card. Matt had shown him his veteran's card. The shopkeeper had dutifully noted the transaction, along with Matt's name and social security number in a ledger. Matt had asked him what happened with that information. The shopkeeper had smiled and said that by law, ledger entries had to be faxed once a week to a VPF office. But then he added the shop's radio-telephone was broken, so it was uncertain when he could comply with the edict.

The shopkeeper had not asked Matt where he was going. But after Matt had paid him with cash, he watched as Matt rode off to the north. Then he added that piece of information to his ledger entry.

As soon as Matt left the hamlet, the road drastically degraded into little more than a narrow, sometimes boggy and rocky trail. About a mile north of Relais-Gabriel, Matt heard a noise off to his right. He rode a little further and came upon a clearing. It was filled with freshly-sawn stumps, so it had obviously been cleared fairly recently. There was a log cabin in the clearing, as well as a shed and an outhouse. There were stacks of firewood everywhere, and a steel pipe coming out of the roof of the cabin. There was smoke coming out of the steel chimney, presumably from a wood stove inside of the cabin.

Matt was sure he heard a woman scream something from within the cabin. Then a man flew out of the neighbouring shed, carrying an axe. The bearded, burly young man was staggering like he was drunk, and bellowing obscenities in French. He charged at the door, and threw his entire weight at it. He rebounded off the door, and fell to the ground. Then he staggered to his feet, and started wailing on the thick wooden door with his axe.

Matt knew he could not ignore this violent scene. It simply was not in his nature. But he did not have time to unpack his rifle either. So, he quickly laid his bike on its side, and started running towards the cabin. Then he yelled, "Hey, stop that! *Arrete ca!*"

The young man wheeled around, and staggered towards Matt. He looked to be completely deranged. Matt slowed to a walking pace. Then he said calmly, "Listen, buddy, I know this is none of my business, but I can't let you hurt somebody. Why don't we just…"

Matt's words were cut-off when the man charged him and swung his axe at his helmeted-head. Matt stepped aside quickly and pushed the man to the ground. As the man was trying to get up, Matt kicked him savagely and professionally in the head. The man slumped to the ground, and lay still.

Matt felt for a pulse on the man's neck, and confirmed he was still alive but unconscious.

The door of the shack opened a crack and a young woman rushed out of the door. She was wearing a blue flannel nightgown. She stopped after only a few paces. She looked terrified. She stared with horror at Matt, and then at the man lying on the ground. Then she asked with a waver in her voice, "*Est-ce qu'il mort*? Does he die?"

"I don't think so, Madame," Matt replied calmly. "Probably out of it for a few minutes, though. Are you all right?"

The woman breathed deeply for a few moments, while staring at the man on the ground. Then she seemed to be gradually calming down. Matt figured she was probably in her late twenties. She was fairly tall, and muscular. She was not beautiful, but she had a pleasant, healthy-looking face, and thick, short, nicely-trimmed and dark brown hair.

Then the woman mumbled, "He was trying to kill me. If you had not come along, and helped me, he would have." Then the woman looked hard at Matt's face, and said, "I don't know you, do I?"

"No Madame, just passing through, heading north."

"Heading north, I see. Listen, would you help me one more time, sir? Please help me put him on the bed and tie him down. I've just got to get away from him. His drinking buddy will be coming over again this evening. He will be mad as hell when he wakes up, that's for sure, but he won't die."

Matt shrugged, and said. "Okay."

It was really hard going. The unconscious man was heavy-set, and uncooperative dead weight. But they finally laid him out on the bed in the cabin, on his back, spread-eagled. Then Matt secured his wrists and ankles to the four steel bedposts with rope. The man was starting to come around, and the woman whispered, "You better get outside now. I need a few minutes. But I've been preparing for this. Please wait for me."

Matt went outside and waited. He had no idea what he was getting himself into, but then again, the woman would probably need some more help. Suddenly there was yelling again inside of the cabin. But it was only the man tied to the bed that was doing the yelling.

The woman came out of the cabin door, and closed it behind her. She was wearing a bicycle helmet, a backpack, and clothes for travelling outdoors. She waved at Matt, and said, "Please, just a moment more, Monsieur."

Then she walked over to the shed. A moment later, she wheeled a fat bike out of the shed. It was very similar to Matt's bike, with a saddle-bag on each side of the rear wheel. There was also a long leather bag securely strapped to the handlebar rack. Matt figured the bag probably contained some kind of firearm.

The woman pushed the bike over to stand next to Matt. She pointed at Matt's bike and asked, "Is that yours?"

"Yes, Madame."

"Please call me Suzanne. I am Suzanne Groseilliers. And you are…?"

"I am Mathieu Adams, Suzanne. Please call me Matt."

"I told him I was leaving him last night. I told him I was going back to Baie-Comeau. I told him that again just now, but he's still stinking drunk, and it may not have registered.

"I can't go south, he'll find me, and God knows what he'll do to me. He was nice enough when sober, but he turned into Mister Hyde after only two drinks, a classic alcoholic. And then he just couldn't stop drinking. I'm really glad I never knew him long enough to think about marrying him.

"Listen, Matt, can I ride with you, at least for today? I could use some company, and the trail going north is really rough. I need to figure out what I should do next, and I need some time to think it through."

"*Bien sur*, of course, Suzanne. Let's go."

40

There were only two operational military airports in the US state of Quebec, Dorval in Montreal and Lesage in Quebec City. The era of commercial flying had tapered out and died from prolonged fuel shortages more than a hundred years before. And the era of fixed-wing and helicopter bush flying was relegated to the interesting literary world of fables and legends.

President Frank Palermo had offered Commandant Lamar Petrie two choices. He could fly from Cleveland to either Montreal or Quebec City on a military, LNG-powered, turboprop transport plane. That offer was conditional, of course. Firstly, it assumed the ground crews could get the plane to work again. And secondly, it assumed they could find enough fuel for it.

Sidney Lefebvre had not done the Air Force any favours. It was mostly non-functional now through lack of funding.

Petrie had selected Quebec City simply because it was closer to Baie-Comeau. He was told that he would have to work with the local VPF detachment to figure out a way to get the rest of the way to Baie-Comeau, and wherever else he needed to go after that. The president had given him a flashy, laminated, signed letter that he could show to people. It ordered everyone to help him complete his 'special assignment'. It also said people could recoup their losses by declaring them government donations on their personal or business income tax forms. But of course, for that standing order to be of any use, people would have to have something of value to offer Petrie. And things of value were few and far between in the impoverished country.

Petrie arrived in Quebec City early in the evening on Monday, May 8. The main VPF office was located in the ancient Chateau Frontenac hotel in old Quebec. The once thriving tourist industry in Quebec City was definitely a thing of the past. Like everywhere else Petrie had visited, the place was largely de-populated, and it had returned to a rural region of small family farms, and clusters of small villages.

Petrie had been told there were a few rooms in the Chateau that were kept free for the use of visiting VPF officers. A horse drawn carriage took Petrie from the airport to the hotel. The duty sergeant at the front desk escorted him to a tiny, basic room and told him the room was solely for his personal use during his stay. Then Petrie bought some prepared sandwiches in the VPF canteen to tide him over until breakfast.

The next morning, Petrie had a reasonably good breakfast of bacon, eggs and toast in the canteen. Then he showed up exactly at nine o'clock for his scheduled interview with VPF Commandant Gilbert Bourassa.

Bourassa was a bonhomie-kind of fellow who seemed to find pleasure in everything. He looked carefully at Petrie's letter of introduction from President Palermo, chuckled and said, "Let me guess, you cannot tell me anything about this 'special assignment' of yours, right?"

"No, Commandant, other than to tell you that I am to locate, interrogate and possibly arrest a suspect. I can also tell you that the suspect's name is Mathieu Adams, who goes by the name of Matt. We believe he took a maritime route to travel to Baie-Comeau. That's where I hope to pick up his trail."

"Well, there's not much in Baie-Comeau, and if he thinks you're on to him, he won't stay there very long, that's for sure," laughed Bourassa. Then he said with a big smile, "So, what do you know about the Quebec wilderness?"

"I don't know much about any true wilderness. I grew up in Cleveland, Ohio, and rose up through the ranks to be the Cleveland Commandant. Perhaps you have heard of our detachment? We have become renowned for our efficiency. Our motto is, 'Nothing slips through the cracks'."

Bourassa laughed heartily, and boomed, "No, but that's a good one! Ours is, 'We always get our man.' The Royal Canadian Mounted Police used that one too, at least in the movies. And the locals still informally refer to us as '*La Surete du Quebec*'. That means the safety of Quebec. We have a proud tradition, too."

"Ah, all right. Two proud detachments then. Very good."

"Right, well here's the thing I wanted to stress with you. The Quebec wilderness is mind-boggling in its expanse. It is full of dangers. Our climate is warmer than it was in the past, but it is still colder and harsher than Ohio's. Unless you have well-honed survival skills, it will kill you dead in short order. And tracking a man in the boreal forest is only for a top expert.

"I think the best thing I can do is temporarily assign such an expert to you. This senior officer can function as your adjutant, if you like. He will be under your command, of course. The man I have in mind will offer you advice proactively. You don't have to act on his advice, of course. But I respectfully submit, that the more times you blow him off, the more likely it will be that you will fail. And failure might include your death in a very remote place.

"Now, do you accept my offer?"

"Ah, yes, I think that would be fine."

"Very good, *tres bien*!" Bourassa boomed with a laugh. "The officer is waiting outside my office for you right now. His name is Sergeant Maurice du Maurier. I hope you will enjoy his company for a while."

"Yes, thanks, me too."

"Okay, that's it then. When you are in the field, please utilize this bureau, and me personally, to keep you connected with the rest of the VPF. You might not have any other way to do that, unfortunately. Sergeant du Maurier will tell you more about that. So, a*u revoir*, and good hunting, Commandant Petrie!"

"Thank you. Good-bye, Commandant Bourassa."

Sergeant Maurice du Maurier was standing just outside Commandant Bourassa's office door. He stepped right into Petrie's path, and offered him his hand. Petrie unconsciously shook it, and guessed, "Sergeant du Maurier, I presume?"

"Yes, Commandant Petrie. Can I buy you a cup of coffee in our canteen? And then perhaps I can have a little chat with you?"

"Sure, thanks, Sergeant, lead on."

Du Maurier was a rather short man. But Petrie could tell he was very fit and wiry, too. He had short, black, perfectly-trimmed hair. His face was either tanned, or weather-worn, or maybe both. He looked to be about fifty, but he could have been younger than that. Petrie guessed from his appearance that du Maurer had spent a lot of time outdoors, and in harsh conditions.

They found that they both preferred their coffee black. They were about to find that they did not resemble each other in most other respects.

After they each had taken a few sips of stale, reheated coffee, du Maurier said quietly, "I presume that you are here to track down someone. Is that right, sir?"

"Yes, Sergeant, a fellow named Mathieu Adams. He goes by the name of Matt. I have a letter from the president that empowers me in my mission, somewhat."

Petrie pulled the laminated letter out of his valise, and let du Maurier have a look at it.

After a few moments, du Maurier handed the letter back to Petrie, and said, "Okay, that might prove to be useful at some point, sir. In my opinion, however, it would be best to treat that letter as a last resort.

"In my experience, people in modern-day Quebec are not that much interested in, or impressed by, anything to do with big government. They are family and small-community oriented. The VPF is respected, however. So, I think our photo ID cards and our brand will be enough to induce people to help us.

"Now, can you share a physical description of the suspect with me, sir?"

"Yes, I have an image of him that I can show to you, Sergeant." Petrie reached into his valise again, pulled out another laminated piece of paper, and handed it to du Maurier.

Du Maurier studied the copied image intently. Then he said, "I'll guess mid-thirties, sir. Large man. Looks like the collar of a uniform in the image. Eyepatch and scarring around the covered-up eye. He may be a veteran who saw combat? He's expressionless. By first impressions, I'd guess he's as tough as nails."

Petrie was impressed, but he replied flippantly, "In the ball park, Sergeant, possibly. Now, I have to be very careful how much I tell you about him. Direct orders from higher up. You probably know how that works?"

"Yes, sir, intimately. And you think this Matt Adams fellow is in Quebec?"

"We think he arrived in Baie-Comeau on a grain-carrying lake freighter on April 28."

"I know you might not want to tell me this, sir. But do you think he knows Quebec, especially her wilderness?

"Yes, he knows both Quebec and wilderness, probably very well."

"Okay, so I take it then that you'll want to pick up his trail in Baie-Comeau, sir?"

"Right. The trail might be pretty cold by now, of course. But we have no updates on his whereabouts."

"Can we send out an all-points bulletin, to VPF detachments, and government depots where there is no permanent VPF presence? Say, work with the image you have, or better yet, send out the original, with his name, and what he's wanted for, sir?"

"Ah, maybe, okay, with some restrictions, Sergeant. The most we can say is that he is wanted for questioning, by me, personally. We should not suggest that he is dangerous, even though he might be. But people should be advised to notify the nearest VPF detachment if they think they have seen him."

"Okay, we can have that faxed by radio-telephone all over Quebec, sir. There is a message relay system in place. It will take longer to get to some places than others. Places around the coast are typically better connected than in the interior. And the satellite communication system is virtually non-existent in Quebec. That also applies to the GPS system. We'll have to use maps, and a compass."

"Okay, understood, Sergeant."

"Commandant, I think the best way to get to Baie-Comeau will be to use the Saint Lawrence River and the coastal ferry service. Our ferry boat will stop in Riviere-Du-Loup and Rimouski en-route to Baie-Comeau. We're probably talking about three days travel from here, weather and vessel seaworthiness permitting.

"Ferry boats travel all the way east to Blanc-Sablon and then they cross the Strait of Belle Isle to St. Barbe in Newfoundland. Then they turn around and work their way back to Montreal. The trip from here to St. Barbe takes about ten days, plus or minus a lot, depending on many factors. But usually eight and sometimes nine little boats are working the Saint Lawrence River and Gulf of Saint Lawrence circuit at a given time. So we may be able to get on one of those boats here in Quebec City in a few days' time."

"There is no other way, Sergeant?"

"No, not really, sir. Route 138 is a disaster, and we have no vehicles anyway, only an armoured personnel carrier, for crowd control. Sometimes we have a food riot, you see. That heavy, slow vehicle is an LNG hog, and really not an option for us.

"But, there might be one other way, Commandant. Can you ride a horse?"

"Heavens no!"

"Well, even if you could, we would still have to stop a lot and let them rest and graze on road-side grass. It would take about as long to get there, probably. And if you're not used to riding, it would be physically tougher, sir."

"Okay, so the boat is really the best option then?"

"Yes, Commandant. Would you like to get started now?"

"Okay, sure, Sergeant. Now, first we'll put together and send out the all-points bulletin. And then we'll see when a ferry boat might arrive back here."

41

The trail to the north of Relais-Gabriel really was as rough as Suzanne Groseilliers had predicted.

The black flies and mosquitoes were thick in many places. The weather had been sunny and dry recently, but there were still muddy puddles and patches of boggy ground along the trail itself. Matt and Suzanne took turns leading, which involved trying to pick a path that would avoid as much as possible the boggy sections, and the especially rocky sections. It was much faster than walking, but it was physically demanding. But Suzanne proved to be as fit as Matt, and they stayed hard at it until noontime.

They were working without a map or a GPS, but Matt did have a compass. And it was obvious that they were still on the once fairly well maintained Route 389. There were still broken-up sections of asphalt pavement and hard gravel road in places, albeit full of deep potholes and cracks.

They really did not have a chance to talk much until they stopped for lunch. Suzanne offered Matt a thick moose and cheddar cheese sandwich. Matt was very pleased to accept the gift. It was delicious.

Between mouthfuls, they got a little better acquainted. Matt found out that Suzanne had been a school teacher in Baie-Comeau. She said she was pretty good at it, and really liked the job. But as funds dried up, the other three teachers were fired in turn. She ended up trying to teach one class of eighty kids from Grade 1 to Grade 11. It was way too much for anybody, so she quit. The teachers they had fired did not want the impossibly over-loaded job either, so they closed the school.

Then Suzanne had met a seemingly nice guy named Leonard Lagrange. He had just arrived from Montreal, and he had some money. He told her that he wanted to get into market gardening, and then turn some land into a proper farm. So, he leased some land on the northern edge of Relais-Gabriel. Lagrange had thought that it would be easier to buy US government land if one first leased it, and developed it into something resembling a farm.

After a few platonic dates, Leonard had asked Suzanne if she would be his business partner, and she had accepted.

Suzanne said she was not naïve. She knew that a man and a woman living in a virtual wilderness could not remain simply business partners. Either something more would develop, or Suzanne would leave.

But she said it had started out okay. Leonard was gentlemanly and friendly enough, and after a few weeks, they started to sleep together. Neither party really loved the other, however. It was just a form of evening entertainment. And then Leonard's hard drinking had started, or more likely re-started. And, well, Matt had thankfully appeared at the climax of the conflict. And now she was running away, somewhere.

Matt had been listening intently, and nodding sympathetically. He was an introvert, and could never have opened up to a stranger like Suzanne had just done with him. But Suzanne was obviously in a desperate situation. And his heart went out to her.

He finished his sandwich, and asked, "So, you might be experiencing a bit of post-traumatic stress, Suzanne. I have some direct experience with that, unfortunately. I don't think you should be on your own for a while. You can tell me as much or as little as you want, but you have to keep talking about it. I know that. I didn't do enough of it myself. I'm not shy, but I do internalize things, perhaps overly so.

"And look, I'm not coming on to you. But I must admit, I *have* been a bit lonely. And to be frank, I'm running away myself."

Matt paused for a long moment. He could tell he had Suzanne thinking hard now, about many more things. Then he said quietly, "I think it's best to get moving again, Suzanne, and put some more distance between us and Leonard."

Then Matt stared even harder at Suzanne, and after another long moment he said quietly, "And put more distance between me and the VPF.

"You better know that right now about me, Suzanne. I'm not sure, but I strongly suspect they're hot on my trail. But I hope they're still a long way behind. I tried to make it difficult for them. I'm pretty good at that. I was a soldier once, and a good one."

"Yes, I figured it might be something like that," Suzanne replied quietly with a knowing nod of her head. "Thanks for telling me, Matt. Will you tell me what you did, or rather what they *think* you did?"

"Maybe in time, Suzanne, if we ride together for a while, and we get to know each other better."

After another moment, Matt added, "The other thing you should know right now is that I'm not stopping until I get to Kuujjuaq, at the very the end of the road, or rather the Sept-Isles railroad. It runs through New Emeril about forty miles east of Labrador City, and then north to Schefferville and ultimately it ends in Kuujjuaq."

"Wow, Kuujjuaq!" Suzanne gasped. "Right on the Arctic Ocean. Why so far?"

"Because all hell is breaking loose down south, Suzanne. And I want to start up again, and settle down, in a place where I can weather the storm. It sounds like Leonard and I sort of share the same dream, that is, to start up a farm. But you can rest easy. I'm not an alcoholic. A couple of beers just makes me sleepy and happy. Not that there's any beer anywhere nearby.

"Now, we really better get going again, Suzanne. We'll talk some more after supper, I promise."

They rode on together. About three hours later, Suzanne was leading, and she stopped suddenly. She pulled her side-by-side, double-barrel, 12-gauge shotgun out of its pouch, and shot a ruffed grouse off an overhanging tree limb. Grouse are relatively stupid birds, and the camouflaged creature had just dumbly stared back at her until she had pulled the trigger.

And as she went to put her gun back in its pouch, a good-sized snowshoe hare bounded across the trail. Suzanne reacted immediately and deftly shot that animal, too.

Matt was impressed with the moving hare shot. And now they had some fresh meat for dinner.

About an hour before sunset, they stopped by a stream and set up a camp. Matt put together a wider-than-normal lean-to, and Suzanne got a fire going, and then their dinner on the go.

She cleaned the hare and the grouse, and chopped them up into pieces. She had some stacked pans in her saddle-bag. She put a little cooking oil in the largest pan, and braised the meat. Then she pulled two potatoes, two carrots and an onion out of one her saddlebags, trimmed them, chopped them up and put them in the pan with the meat. Then she added some water. She had some dried red pepper, and Matt had some sea salt, so she added that, too. She put a lid on the pan, and simmered everything until it became a very tasty, chunky stew.

They lay beside each other that night in their separate sleeping bags under a shared, covering blanket.

And they watched the fire, and they talked and they talked until they fell asleep.

By the time they got to Fermont, they were in love with each other. And they were scrubbing each other down with soap in the evenings in a stream or a pond. And they loved to make each other laugh.

And they made love under the stars. It turned out they both had brought along some protection.

Late one night, Matt got up his nerve and asked Suzanne if she would travel all the way to Kuujjuaq with him. She gladly accepted.

They reached Fermont on May 11. So, they were averaging about forty miles per day.

There was a general store in Fermont where they stocked up on food supplies. The store received its goods from Labrador City, and neighbouring Wabush. The ancient road from Labrador City to the ocean port of Cartwright on the Labrador coast was just a trail now, too. But dog sled operators moved supplies along it under contract in the wintertime.

Suzanne did not have much money, so Matt paid for the food. Matt also wanted to buy six boxes of number six shot for Suzanne's shotgun. The shopkeeper told him he could not help him with that, but he thought the store and outfitter in New Emeril might carry those kinds of shells.

Matt remembered that they would cross the state border just north of Fermont. But when they got there they found there were no signs to mark the border.

Somewhere old Quebec Route 389 just became old Newfoundland and Labrador Route 500. But the trail proved to be as rough as ever.

Matt did not want to be seen passing through the village of Labrador City. He figured there would be people in the village that might observe and remember their passing. So, they skirted around the northern edge of the place. It was definitely not a 'city' any more, rather a collection of huts in a few places.

They got to the general store in New Emeril just after noontime on Saturday, May 13. They entered the store, and replenished their food supplies once again. Matt had to show his veterans card to buy the shells they wanted for Suzanne's shotgun. The female store owner dutifully entered the transaction into her ledger. She did not ask them where they were headed, and they did not offer that information to her.

They left Route 500 at New Emeril, and started to follow the old abandoned railway track that led to Schefferville. An older couple living in a cabin on the north-east corner of the intersection watched them leave the road and head off north beside the old railway tracks.

There was a narrow trail on the eastern side of the railway tracks. The elevated gravel bed of the old railroad provided a bit of a shield from the prevailing westerly wind. Animals like caribou used the trail, and a few human hunters.

The track from Schefferville to Kuujjuaq had been laid to carry ore from a number of different kinds of mines to a new port on the Arctic Ocean. For many years, the mines in the Labrador City and Fermont region had been sending ore south via a private railway to Port Cartier, about forty miles west of Sept-Isles on the Saint Lawrence River. A spur line connected the Port Cartier railroad to the Schefferville railroad just south of New Emeril. For a while re-vamped mines sent iron ore either north or south, depending on world market demand, and pricing.

The port in Kuujjuaq made economic sense for the first time when the Arctic ice disappeared. Ships could safely travel directly over the North Pole en-route to ports in northern Russia and Europe. And the regional climate got a lot warmer and a bit wetter when Hudson Bay to the west stop freezing over in the wintertime.

Then everything shut down. But the railway tracks going north and south from New Emeril were still there, for the most part.

42

Veterans Police Force Commandant Lamar Petrie and his temporary adjutant, Sergeant Maurice du Maurier, arrived in Baie-Comeau, Quebec early in the morning on Friday, May 13.

Petrie used the signed letter from the US president to insist that the little ferry boat remain at the dock in Baie-Comeau until he formally released it back into service. The ferry boat captain and his twelve passengers were not at all pleased by the indefinite delay. But du Maurier took the captain aside, and convinced him he would be in big trouble if he did not obey Commandant Petrie's order. The captain then reluctantly told his passengers they could get off the ferry if they wanted to; it was their choice, and matters were simply out of his hands.

Actually, delays like this were not uncommon in the coastal ferry boat service. But usually the delays were caused by high winds, or mechanical failures.

Du Maurier rented a couple of bicycles for their use. Their first stop was the multi-purpose, three-employee US government depot in Baie-Comeau. There was no permanent VPF presence in the town. The nearest VPF detachment was in Sept-Isles, about a hundred and five miles away to the east. And there was only one permanently-assigned VPF officer in Sept-Isles.

Visiting VPF officers could make use of a depot's services, and a spare office. Town and village depots helped with mail delivery and other government business. They were also message relay stations. Depots all had a tall communication tower. In this part of the country, the government used radio-telephones to pass and direct information and messages. And the VPF had full access to this functional but inefficient communication system.

The Baie-Comeau depot chief said she was unaware of the return of a Monsieur Mathieu Adams to the town. But she said there was a family named Adams living just north of the village. Furthermore, Monsieur Claude Adams came to the depot monthly to collect his mail, or to pay his taxes. She thought Claude might be related to Mathieu somehow. She noted that the deceased Phillipe Adams had been a well-known and well-respected resident of the town his whole life.

Petrie and du Maurier talked privately, agreed they had a potential lead, and decided to check it out. They approached the depot chief again, and asked her for directions to the Adams' residence. With that information in hand, they sent a brief faxed report to Commandant Bourassa in Quebec City. They also asked Bourassa to forward any pertinent information to them via the Baie-Comeau depot chief.

At about one o'clock in the afternoon, Petrie and du Maurier knocked on the front door of Claude Adams' bungalow.

A small boy opened the door and then looked up with fear at the two imposing VPF officers. Both men were wearing mud-spattered, official, dark-green coveralls, and dark-green lightweight helmets. The colourful VPF emblem was emblazoned on their breast pockets. Their senior ranks were identified with shoulder flashing. Both officers were also quite visibly wearing their holstered, large-capacity, automatic handguns.

The child yelled, "Papa!" and then ran back into the house, leaving the door wide open.

Claude Adams soon appeared at the door, and stared for a moment at the two officers. Then he said calmly, "Yes, how can I help you?"

"We're with the VPF," replied Petrie sternly. "We're looking for a Mister Claude Adams. Does he live here?"

"Yes, I'm Claude Adams. Can you prove who you are?"

The two officers reached into their breast pockets, pulled out thin wallets, flipped them open and let Claude look at their photo ID cards. Claude looked at their faces closely, and their documents. Then he nodded, and said quietly, "I think I know why you're here. Could we talk in my shed out back? I don't think my family needs to hear our conversation."

Petrie took a moment to consider the proposal, and then he snapped, "All right, show us the way, Mister Adams."

Claude led them to the door of his shed, and then led them inside. He closed the door and lit a kerosene lantern with a wooden match. Then he asked, "You're here to talk to me about my cousin Matt, aren't you?"

Du Maurier and Petrie both recoiled with obvious surprise. Du Maurier recovered first, and asked pleasantly, "Yes, that's right, Mister Adams. Have you seen him recently?"

"Yes, very early in the morning on Tuesday, ah, May 2. He just showed up at the house. He didn't knock on the door like you guys just did. Instead, he stirred up my chickens at about two o'clock in the morning and waited for me to check out the commotion. He frankly surprised the hell out of me. But I talked to him for half an hour or so in this very same shed. I had not seen him for, gosh, maybe twelve years?"

"What did he want?" asked Petrie bluntly.

"Well, basically he just wanted to buy a bike from me, and an old hatchet for camping in the woods. He said he was in some kind of a bind, and wanted to start a new life somewhere. He said he got on to a lake freighter in Detroit, and worked on it as a seaman until it got to Baie-Comeau. He thought you people might be after him, but he didn't explain why, other than to say he did something for the country. He said he was headed for Montreal."

"Montreal, are you sure?" snapped Petrie.

"Yes sir, that's what he told me."

"And did you sell him a bike, Mister Adams?" asked du Maurier politely, with a smile.

"Yes, for ten bucks."

"Can you describe the bike for us?"

"Ah, yes, it was a black La Rue fat bike, about two years' old, with saddlebags and a handlebar rack."

"That's a lot of bike for only ten bucks, Mister Adams," observed du Maurier.

"Well, he *is* my first cousin, and we were very good friends growing up. And I figured he probably was not able to collect his veteran's pension being in transit and all, and that he was probably pinching his dimes."

"Did you sell him anything else?" snapped Petrie.

"No, but I gave him back his rifle. He had left it with his parents when he went off to join the Army, and I got it for safekeeping after they both died. Before you ask, it was a Fleming 270 bolt-action with five-round clip and no scope. It was also unloaded, as I didn't have any ammunition to offer him. I just have a twelve-gauge shotgun. Oh, before I forget, I also gave him a bicycle helmet, a black one."

"Did he say anything else that might help us to locate him?" asked du Maurier. "We cannot discuss the reasons for our interest in him, but all VPF matters are serious."

"All he said was that he figured you guys would want to talk to me, and he told me to tell you exactly what happened during the brief time he was here."

"He said that, really?" Petrie asked with obvious disbelief.

"Yes sir, I swear it."

"Can you describe what he looked like, Claude?" asked du Maurier pleasantly. He was playing the good guy role well, but it was also his natural disposition.

"Full, dark brown beard, longish, dark brown hair, some scarring around his left eye. Looked healthy and strong, as always. Maybe a bit dirty, and he kind of smelled a bit. He was dressed properly for the woods, you know, stout waterproof boots, coveralls, layers of clothing, green rain poncho over top."

"No eyepatch?" asked Petrie.

"No, sir. He said he lost his left eye in the war though. I suppose that means he might have had an artificial left eye? It was not obvious to me, but I'm no expert."

"Anything else you can tell us right now?" asked du Maurier. "For instance, did he mention anybody else? Our job is just to track him down, Mister Adams, and bring him to justice. We do not intend to harm him in any way, unless he resists arrest."

"No, he didn't talk about anybody else. He said he did not want anyone else to know he visited me. So, my wife and kids did not know he was here, and they still don't. We apologized to each other for not writing back-and-forth while he was in the Army, and the war."

"Did you see him leave?" asked du Maurier. Petrie was now busy scribbling into a notepad.

"Yes, he went back down the lane, to the south, back to Route 138. He said he left his backpack near the intersection there, in a lean-to shelter."

"So, he'll be wearing his backpack, too, probably," observed du Maurier. He waited a couple of minutes for Petrie to stop writing. Then he gave Petrie a questioning look. Petrie just shrugged back at him. The temporary boss looked a bit annoyed for some reason, but then he often looked like that. Du Maurier wondered if Petrie wanted to project a cynical, mean-spirited image to unnerve citizens, and put them at a psychological disadvantage.

Du Maurier assumed they were finished with the interview, so he turned back to Claude, and said with a smile, "Thank you very much, Mister Adams. You have been most helpful to us.

"That's all for now, but if Mathieu Adams gets in touch with you again, even by mail, please let us know. You can leave a sealed letter for us at the government depot in Baie-Comeau. Address the envelope to the VPF, care of Commandant Petrie."

"And don't tell anyone we were here today, Adams," added Petrie with a bit of a snarl. "Come on, Sergeant du Maurier, we're done here."

43

When Commandant Petrie and Sergeant du Maurier got back to Baie-Comeau, they returned their rented bicycles, and then made their way on foot to the ferry dock. Petrie wanted to order the ferry captain to take them all the way to Montreal, at least as far as the first lock in the Saint Lawrence Seaway.

But before Petrie could deliver his unusual and no doubt upsetting official government edict, the ferry captain told them the Baie-Comeau depot chief urgently wanted to talk to them about something. So, the two officers walked back to the government depot to check out his assertion.

The depot chief was visibly relieved to see them again. She first handed them a relayed radio-telephone message from Commandant Bourassa in Quebec City.

In the faxed text message, Bourassa told them there had been a recent ledger sheet forwarded to the VPF firearms control branch that would certainly be of interest to them. A shopkeeper's ledger entry indicated that Mathieu Adams had purchased 27 calibre rifle ammunition in Relais-Gabriel on May 7. The shopkeeper had also noted that the purchaser had a full beard and no eye patch, but he otherwise resembled the image on his veteran's card. She also had noted that he was headed north on Route 389 in the direction of Fermont.

The depot chief then told them there had also been a local incident that might be of interest to them. She said that a guy named Leonard Lagrange had been in to see her that afternoon. The man had been living in Relais-Gabriel, but was about to leave for good, and get on the ferry to Rimouski to the southwest on the other side of the river. Lagrange said he was thinking about formally reporting a theft to the VPF, but he had not quite made up his mind yet whether he should follow through on that action. He had added crudely that it was always a hassle to deal with the VPF.

Lagrange then said his ex-girlfriend, Suzanne Groseilliers, had stolen a bicycle from him, among other things, on May 7.

The depot chief said she knew Suzanne, and it did not sound like something she would do. She had been a respected schoolteacher in Baie-Comeau until funding for the school had dried up.

But Lagrange had gone on to claim that Suzanne and a big bearded guy he didn't know had beaten him up, and tied him to his bed, leaving him to die of thirst and starvation. The depot chief said Lagrange was a known drunk, and he had a criminal record. So, she had asked him if he was sure he had not hallucinated the whole ordeal after getting really drunk again. Lagrange initially had admitted that was a 'remote possibility', but then he had cursed the depot chief for making such a rude suggestion. Then he had said angrily that Suzanne was, 'just a damn winter woman anyway that had ripped him off for a few small items', and that he had just decided to, 'drop the whole freaking matter and move on.'

The depot chief added that the ferry to Rimouski had left an hour ago, presumably with Leonard Lagrange aboard. Then she further added, 'and good riddance to the nasty man'.

Petrie and du Maurier thanked the depot chief for the new information, and then they went into the spare office in the depot for a private discussion.

This time du Maurier appeared to be angry. He yelled, "I read that Claude Adams guy all wrong, Commandant! I thought he was a straight-shooter, but the bastard clearly lied to us."

"Take it easy, Maurice," Petrie replied calmly, and informally for the first time. "He may not have lied to us. I think we'll find out eventually that everything else he said will check out completely. I bet Matt Adams *did* tell him he was headed for Montreal. Our quarry has a long history of using misdirection effectively. For your information, and just for your information, he was a sniper in the Army, and a really good one. He is a master of concealment, and knows how to evade an enemy."

Du Maurier took a long moment to consider the implications of what Petrie had just told him. He recognized that their quarry was obviously someone who could fight back with lethal force. So, his arrest might not be routine. As he came to grips with this new development, he appeared to calm down a bit.

So Petrie asked him, "So, do you know this Route 389 very well, Sergeant?"

"I've been up and down it once, Commandant, as far as Labrador City. It's a rough trail, and a hard old slog. Two fit people with wilderness survival skills could probably manage it okay on fat bikes, however."

"So Matt Adams is most likely headed to a place named Fermont?"

"Yes sir, there are just ghost towns between Relais-Gabriel and Fermont. They must be headed to Fermont, at least initially."

"And he might be travelling there with an ex-school teaching woman named Suzanne… Suzanne…"

"Groseilliers, yes Commandant, sounds like it."

"So, I don't think I'm up to a fat bike *triathlon leg* through the boreal forest. Are you, Sergeant?"

"No, not when there might be another way, Commandant. There's nothing much in Fermont. So the suspect is probably headed at least as far as Labrador City.

"I suggest we get back on the ferry boat, and take it to Sept-Isles, which is a little over a hundred miles to the east. Then in Sept-Isles we can hire the two local guys the VPF employs periodically to operate a little steam-powered railway cart.

"Two years ago, I went all the way up to New Emeril on it with them, to help the now retired Sept-

Isles VPF constable arrest and haul back a notorious wife beater and rapist. The cowardly felon had run off to Wabush, just southeast of Labrador City. Our two helpers waited for us while we completed the capture. We rented bikes at the general store in New Emeril, and rode off to the west. When we finally corned the guy, we bought a bike for his use in Wabush. When we all got back to New Emeril, we pretty well ended up just giving the bike we bought to the owner of the general store.

"In addition to helping with occasional VPF work, the two railway cart guys in Sept-Isles usually spend their summers on government contract trying to fix the old railway tracks just enough to make it passable for their lightweight, homemade cart. But when you travel with them, you have to let them stop a lot, to chop up deadfall for firewood, and fetch water for the boiler. And sometimes you have to let them drain their boiler completely, offload their cart and help them manhandle their cart past an especially decrepit section of track. They also set up the camp for you in the evenings on longer journeys. They use a canvas tent. For longer journeys, they pull another lightweight cart along behind their 'locomotive'. They load it with your gear, their camping gear, and food. You can drink the water along the way from any stream, as long as you catch it where it's moving.

"But if you're up to the idea, I think we could average about fifty miles a day using their services. It's about two hundred and twenty miles from Sept-Isles, Quebec to New Emeril, Newfoundland and Labrador, using the abandoned railroad. Quebec Route 389 becomes Route 500 at the Labrador border. The railway crosses Route 500 at New Emeril. There is an old railway spur that runs from just south of New Emeril to Wabush and Labrador City. It's been dismantled a bit though. Lab City and Wabush blacksmiths have pilfered it for scrap iron.

"But I think we should first investigate if anyone in New Emeril has seen our two suspects before we even think about heading west towards Labrador City, on rented bikes or whatever. After all, they could just as well be heading east on Route 500, to Cartwright, or beyond."

"Okay, so say a day to get to Sept-Isles, then say five days to get to a place in the sticks called New Emeril. Then what again?"

Sergeant du Maurier suspected that the Commandant was experiencing a bit of information overload. So he explained patiently, "Then we ask around and see if anyone in New Emeril has noticed a big bearded guy, and a former school teacher that a guy referred to as a 'winter woman', riding fat bikes stuffed with camping gear. And then we go from there."

"Okay, Sergeant, I get that part. But where could they be heading again? No, before you answer that question. Tell me, what's a 'winter woman'?"

"It's a crude expression that only a crude man would use, sir. A winter woman is a large person, and she keeps your bed warm during long, cold winter nights. You pretend you've got a sore whatever, and she ends up doing most of the chores. Then after she helps you plant the seed crops in the spring, you kick her out of your house. Then you party and drink with your buddies until harvest time. Then you go looking for another winter woman."

"Yes, that sounds pretty crude, all right. So, back on point, Sergeant. Where could they be heading?"

"If they stay on the road or trail, they'll be on the old Labrador Highway. It used to go east from Labrador City all the way to Cartwright Junction, just south of Cartwright, a harbour on the Labrador coast. And another road went south from Cartwright Junction, and eventually hooked back to Blanc-Sablon on the Quebec coast."

"Okay, and if they left the road?"

"They could probably ride beside the old railway track to travel one hundred forty miles north, to Schefferville, Quebec, or beyond."

"Is there something beyond Schefferville?"

"Kuujjuaq, Quebec, a village near the Arctic Ocean, is another two hundred and sixty miles to the north. The old railway ends there. There used to be a port there, for bulk ore-carriers, and a dredged channel in the Koksoak River. It's about thirty miles from

Kuujjuaq to Ungava Bay using the river. Ungava Bay becomes the Arctic Ocean further to the north."

"Geez, I hope they don't drag us that far north!"

"Me too, Commandant."

"Okay, let's go forward with your excellent suggestion though, Sergeant. Now, we better write up another little report for Commandant Bourassa, and tell him where we're heading next. Then we'll go tell the ferry captain to take us to Sept-Isles."

"He won't be too upset to hear that order, Commandant. That's where he's heading next, anyway."

44

Matt Adams and Suzanne Groseilliers arrived in the ghost town of Schefferville in the late afternoon of Thursday, May 18.

The abandoned railroad that they had followed had been built beside rivers and lakes, presumably to take advantage of more level ground, and easier routes through hills and ridges. But for Matt and Suzanne, it had meant that they did not have to travel very far to top up their water bottles.

The nights were feeling increasingly more threatening. They held each other close, but they had also taken turns listening to the eerie, natural sounds around them. Matt was startled awake one night, and wondered where Suzanne had gone. Then he heard the roar of her shotgun. She had fired a load of buckshot over the head of a prowling bear. Thankfully, the animal had reacted the right way, and quickly run away.

As he had fallen asleep in her arms again, he again realized, quite happily, that he had found a truly remarkable woman.

About two dozen First Nation Cree families had made the ruins of Schefferville their home. They had simply reclaimed what had always been their land when the railway and the mines had shut down. And they had never forgotten how to live successfully in the remote northern wilderness.

Matt asked an older Cree man who was walking in the village if there was a store of sorts nearby. He motioned for them to follow him. He led them for a hundred yards or so to a cabin, pointed at it without saying a word, smiled at them, and left them on their own.

The family inside the cabin was preparing an evening meal. They were visibly displeased by the interruption. But a jovial teenaged boy led them to a shed out back of the cabin. The shed was fairly well stocked with basic foodstuffs. The boy said it all came in to the village during the winter by dogsled from the south.

Matt asked if anything came down from the north, from Kuujjuaq. The boy answered that they did not trade much with coastal Inuit people. They preferred trading with inland Innu and Cree people. And if they really had to, they would occasionally trade with white people.

Matt also asked if there was still a government depot in the village. The boy said there was not, but he added that there was still a government tower with a bent aerial at the top. Then he told them there was no electrical power in the village. So no one could operate a radio-telephone, even if they had one. Wood was their only fuel, for heating and cooking.

Matt and Suzanne picked out the stuff they needed. To vary their diet, they made sure to include salted and dried fish, nuts, dried fruit, dried mushrooms and wild berry preserves. Then the boy went back into the cabin, and returned with an elderly woman. The boy explained that they would have to negotiate the fee with his grandmother. Matt suggested a price, and the gnarly-looking lady suggested a little more. Matt agreed, and asked her if she would accept cash. She said she would prefer to trade in goods, but Matt said they had nothing to offer, since they were travelling light. She then asked where they were headed. Matt told her Kuujjuaq, and that seemed to anger her for some reason. But the boy said something forcefully to her in a dialect of Cree, and the woman finally agreed to accept the cash.

Matt and Suzanne then continued on their arduous journey north. The land had progressively changed from a mixed forest around Baie-Comeau, to a boreal forest. Suzanne told Matt that a geography textbook she referenced to teach school claimed the forest around Baie-Comeau had been boreal until a century or more ago. She thought that as they went further north, the land should eventually change into a semi-barrens with stunted black spruce, white spruce and tamarack trees. Matt agreed with her, and told her he remembered that the Cree used to refer to the northern region as something like 'the land of the little sticks'.

But it was still very much a tall, thick, boreal forest that surrounded them. And the temperature was still quite warm, staying above freezing at night. Occasional rainfall made it miserable at times. But they both had good waterproof gear.

Matt and Suzanne thought they could tell that climate change was progressively changing the land, and the composition of the wildlife. They thought that the mixed forest must be moving north, and in turn, the boreal forest must also be moving north. And further, they concluded that the fauna must be changing with the flora.

Still, somewhere ahead of them was the Arctic, with its historically treeless tundra, and maybe some permafrost in a few places. But Matt was still hopeful that the region around Kuujjuaq could now be farmed to some degree, or at least provide a warm and wet enough climate to support a healthy vegetable garden.

They set up a camp just beyond the northern edge of the Cree village. The next day they rode north another forty miles or so. The railway tracks they were following looked a bit newer, but they were still rusty and not perfectly straight and level. The bridges were still sound, or at least sound enough to withstand their weight, and the weight of their bikes. Still, Matt insisted that they cross over bridges separately. That way, if something bad happened, the other party might be able to attempt a rescue.

They set up another camp, and went through their established evening routine. The land was still plentiful with wildlife. They shot mostly grouse and hare for fresh meat. Both species seemed to be in a high-population cycle. That made some sense, because they were not seeing many natural small animal predators like hawks, foxes, coyotes or lynx. But they were hearing wolves at night, and they had seen a few more black bears. Thankfully, those animals paid them little or no attention. It helped that Matt and Suzanne were very careful with their food waste, and burned everything completely. They also kept a fire going through the night. And, they still kept their rifle and shotgun close beside them in the lean-to shelter that they built every evening.

In the middle of the night, Matt woke up with a yell. He had the bad dream again, the first time in a very long while.

Suzanne woke up with alarm, and shouted, "What is it, Matt! Is a bear nearby?"

Matt was breathing heavily, and sweating in the chill air. After a moment, he looked sadly at Suzanne and said, "Just a dream, Suzanne. Sorry I woke you. I thought they had gone away. But I guess they might be starting up again."

"It's recurring?"

"Yes, mostly. The faces of people change. Sometimes the situations change a bit, too. But the basic plot remains the same."

"It might do you some good to tell me about the dream, Matt."

So Matt stepped her through the basic plot. And then he told her about the three-legged wolf he had shot as a teenager.

When he had finished, Suzanne said tenderly, "Lay back down again, Matt. You'll get chilled. Pull the blanket up, too."

They lay on their backs in silence for a while, then Suzanne asked, "So, you were a sniper in the war for a while, Matt?"

"Yes."

"You killed some men?

"A lot of men. It was my duty. They were all soldiers."

"But you still feel guilty. That's pretty normal, Matt."

They lay in silence again for a while. Then Matt said, "This dream was different than all the others. And I'm now going to tell you why I'm running away, Suzanne. You're my best friend, and I love you. And I know I can trust you."

He rolled over on his side, and stroked her hair, and her bare shoulder. Then he said bluntly, "The face of the guy I shot in this dream was that of Ernie Wolf."

"The president?" Suzanne gasped. "That's pretty weird."

"Yes, the president. And he was a sadistic, fascist bastard. And a psychotic creep that was going to blow up the *Second Chance* spaceship. And Mexico City, too."

"How do you know that?"

"Because the patriotic people that asked me to kill him told me so. And they were connected to benevolent oligarchs that knew everything about Cousin Ernie."

"Then you're telling me that you *actually shot and killed* Ernie Wolf?" Suzanne yelled incredulously. "How could you do a thing like that?"

"Because he was going to ruin what was left of America, and…"

"No, no, I mean how could you manage to do that, with high security around him all of the time?"

Matt then told Suzanne the whole story. He left nothing out.

When he was finished, she lay still for a long while. Then she asked, "How long was the shot again?"

"Eleven-hundred and seventy yards."

"And you did a long shot like that before?"

"Yes, some at twice that distance, actually. Not many soldiers in the world can come up to that standard, Suzanne. Canadian soldiers were once the best at it, long ago. It's both a science and an art."

"Wow. Thanks so much for telling me, Matt. Now we can deal with it *together*, until it's just a vague memory."

Matt looked lovingly at her, and stroked her hair again. Then he said softly, "I didn't tell you until now, until after we've travelled so far together, because I was afraid of how you would react. I don't want to lose you, Suzanne."

"That'll never happen."

"So, does this change anything between us?"

"I don't know. Shut up, and let's find out. Get to work, soldier boy."

45

Commandant Lamar Petrie and Sergeant Maurice du Maurier arrived in Sept-Isles, Quebec in the middle of the morning on Monday, May 15. It turned out that the ferry boat had recurring problems with its two LNG-powered engines. Those problems had delayed their departure from Baie-Comeau by eight hours, and the boat had only be able to cruise at about five knots on one engine.

Petrie and du Maurier went straight to the government depot in the town. In the depot, they had a brief discussion with VPF Constable Serge Tremblay. Petrie explained to Tremblay in a very nebulous way what they were looking to do. But Tremblay did not ask many questions. Instead, he immediately left the depot to track down the two local men that the VPF sometimes hired to take officers north on the old railway tracks.

Tremblay did not say so, but he was eager to return to his usually stress-free, one-man routine in the town. So, he had an ulterior motive for expediting the departure of the two senior VPF officers. He was very much like a small-town sheriff in the old Wild West, only without many bandits or aboriginal uprisings to deal with.

Tremblay returned to the depot with the two local men, Beaumont "Beau" Charpentier and Theodore "Theo" Boucher. Du Maurier outlined what the job would entail to the two burly young men. Beau and Theo said they were eager for some income. But since it sounded like they might be gone a long time, they said they first had to check with their wives. Petrie asked them to come back to the Sept-Isles government depot with their answer by no later than three o'clock that afternoon.

Beau and Theo arrived back at the depot at exactly three o'clock. They said their wives had tentatively agreed to let them take the job, as long as they only went as far as Fermont before returning. Then they said they could possibly go a bit further, and stay away a short while longer, but they would have to charge more per day.

Du Maurier had warned Petrie this would likely happen. By prior arrangement, du Maurier led the two men into the vacant waiting area in the depot, and 'talked turkey' with them. After some protracted, heated discussion, du Maurier left them snarling at each other in the little waiting room, and found Petrie in a spare office, waiting impatiently to hear the results of his negotiation.

Du Maurier told Petrie, "We eventually settled on ten bucks a day, each. I think that's pretty fair, but I left them stewing about it. They said they would put together a list of the stuff we'll have to buy for the trip to New Emeril. And they said we'll have to stock up again in the store in New Emeril.

"They're actually two good men, Commandant. I suggest we use their services, and offer them a bonus of twenty bucks each when they safely bring us back here. How does all of this sound to you, sir?"

"It's nominally acceptable, I guess, Sergeant," Petrie grumbled.

Du Maurier then relayed the slightly improved proposal to Beau and Theo. They suddenly seemed to be a lot happier, and shook hands vigorously with 'their buddy Maurice' to close the deal. Then du Maurier gave them some cash for supplies, and sent them away to get everything ready for a departure at sunrise the next day.

Petrie and du Maurier then checked into a nearby bed and breakfast. Du Maurier also arranged for the owner of the rundown establishment to cook up a moose and jigs dinner for the two VPF officers, complete with a bottle of Niagara red wine. He knew it would likely be a good long while before they could again experience something approaching civilized luxury.

46

It was still dark when Commandant Petrie and Sergeant du Maurier had their bacon, egg and toast breakfast early the next morning. Then du Maurier led the way through the still sleeping village of Sept-Isles. They quietly made their way to the end of a spur line that in turn connected to the old railway tracks that ran far off to the north.

Their hired helpers, Beau and Theo, were waiting for them in the emerging light of the new day. They were both smiling, and obviously in good spirits. They were busy chopping up the wood they would need for the first leg of the upcoming journey. Du Maurier and Petrie were pleased to see that they did not appear to be drunk or hung over.

While Beau and Theo were finishing up their preparations, Petrie and du Maurier had a close look at their rail-travelling contraption.

They had pinned two carts together. Both carts were about twelve feet long. The carts were resting on the rusty tracks, and looked ready to go. The carts were mostly made out of pieces of hardwood that had been bolted together. The axles were steel. The wheels on the carts looked to be old steel rims from a truck, beefed up with a welded steel band where the load of the cart would be transferred to the rail.

Du Maurier told Petrie that there would obviously be a lot of slop as the carts rolled along with an articulating pin in the middle of the 'train'. And he suggested there would probably be a fair amount of jolting and wobbling around. But then du Maurier said he was confident that Beau and Theo had devised a practical way to deal with uneven, decrepit tracks. It just meant that the ride would be physically strenuous, and not restful.

When the wood boxes on the front cart were completely filled, Beau and Theo took the two officer's packs, and tied them down beside their own baggage on the bed of the second or trailing cart. They tied down a waxed-canvas tarpaulin over the baggage and food that was stacked on the trailing cart. Then they offered Petrie and du Maurier the two forward-looking seats at the very front of the trailing cart.

Beau and Theo hopped up on to the first cart. Their forward-looking seats would be at the very back of the first cart. The firebox was right in front of them. There was a bin of firewood on each side of the firebox. The removable floor under the firebox was steel mesh. The boiler was directly over the firebox. And the little, single-acting steam engine with its flywheel and mechanical clutch was in front of the boiler. Bicycle chains running through the cart floor connected the drive shaft of the steam engine to a spur gear welded to the front axle.

Du Maurier remembered that the carts, and everything attached to the carts, could be disassembled. The firebox and the boiler could be emptied and refilled. And all of that would have to be done should they encounter an impassable section of track. Du Maurier suspected that he and Petrie were in for some heavy lugging at times. He had only hinted at that possibility with the Commandant. But he could think of no other way to continue their pursuit of Matt Adams with Petrie's almost total lack of wilderness knowledge and experience.

The boiler was soon steaming and hissing away, and venting live steam periodically through a relief valve. Beau and Theo took their seats, and looked back at Petrie and du Maurier to confirm they were ready. Petrie gave them a 'wagon-ho' sign with his right arm. Then Beau turned some valves and directed live steam to the steam engine. When the engine was chugging steadily, he slowly worked a lever to engage the clutch.

And then they were off.

47

Commandant Petrie and Sergeant du Maurier reached the southern outskirts of New Emeril just after noontime on Tuesday, May 23. They were both filthy from head to toe, and completely exhausted from the physically demanding trip. It turned out they had to help disassemble, manhandle and then re-assemble the two carts four times to get past impassable sections of track. And one of those impassable sections had been over a hundred yards in length.

But du Maurier was both surprised and pleased that Petrie was pulling his weight, and actually seemed to be enjoying the rugged, wilderness experience. He had proven to be made of sterner stuff than he looked.

It was sunny and warm, with just a light breeze. Beau and Theo started to set up their four-man canvas tent by the side of the track. Some local kids ran down the tracks from the village, and sat down on nearby tree stumps to watch the unusual activity. Petrie and du Maurier waved at them in a friendly manner. Then they started to walk to the north beside the tracks to check out the local general store.

After a couple of hundred yards, they saw the store ahead of them on their left. It was at the intersection of the north-running railway tracks, and an east-west running dirt and gravel road. The store was marked with a crude sign.

The middle-aged, female shopkeeper remembered du Maurier. But she was startled by the sudden reappearance of the VPF in the village, and the disheveled appearance of the two officers. But she listened respectfully and carefully as du Maurier described the two people they were pursuing. She said that she definitely remembered them. Then she listed out in great detail what they had purchased from the store on May 13, and showed the two officers the ledger entry she had made when she sold shotgun shells to Mathieu Adams. Petrie asked her if the couple had said where they were going. She looked embarrassed and said 'no', and then she asked, 'but maybe I should have asked them?'

Du Maurier then asked the shopkeeper if she had watched the couple after they left the store to see where they were heading. She admitted, rather sheepishly, that she had not.

Then Petrie told the shopkeeper that their two VPF helpers would be visiting the store shortly to buy some supplies. She replied that would not be a problem. She added that if the store was closed, they should just bang more loudly on the front door, and yell like crazy. She said she lived in the back, and would open up again for them.

When they were outside of the store again, Petrie said quietly, "She appeared to be a good, honest person, who had not suspected that a strange, travelling couple were fugitives. Do you agree with my assessment, Sergeant?"

"Yes, Commandant, certainly."

"So, what do we do now, Sergeant?"

"Well, Commandant, this is the intersection with Newfoundland and Labrador Route 500. There's a cabin further up the tracks, do you see it? It's on the right, on the other side of the intersecting road. People living there might have seen Adams and Groseilliers pass the railway intersection to stay on Route 500 to head further east. Or, perhaps they saw them turn off the road to follow the tracks north to Schefferville."

"Okay, then let's go check out that possibility, Sergeant."

The cabin had a front porch. An elderly couple were sitting on the front porch on rocking chairs. The couple remained sitting and rocking away as the two VPF officers approached, and walked up the stairs to their porch.

Du Maurier said politely in greeting, "*Bon jour, Monsieur et Madame. Comment allez-vous?*"

"It's okay, we speak English, if you would rather speak that way," mumbled the old woman.

The old man yelled, "Eh?" He was holding a hearing horn up to his right ear. "What do they want, Eloise?"

"I don't know yet, Herbert, they haven't said yet!" yelled the old woman back at the old man.

"Well, ask them all ready, old woman!" yelled the old man.

Then the old woman asked the two officers quietly, "What do you two young fellows want?"

Du Maurier replied loudly, "We are sorry to bother you people. But we are wondering if you remember seeing a big, possibly bearded man, and his woman traveling companion. They were probably riding bicycles at the time, and may have passed by your cabin on Saturday, May 13. They would be wearing backpacks, probably, and have saddlebags on their bikes. They would also be dressed for all kinds of weather."

"Yes, we saw them, me and Herbert, from the porch you're standing on," replied the old woman while nodding emphatically. "They came up the road from Labrador City, and turned to follow the tracks north. Thought it was strange at the time. No one does that."

"Eh?" yelled the old man.

"Be quiet!" yelled the old woman. Then she added quietly to the two officers, "But Herbert won't remember. He's got a touch of dementia to go with his deafness."

"I'm truly sorry to hear that, Madame, I mean about Herbert," du Maurier replied with compassion. Then he added more cheerfully, "Okay, that's actually all we needed today, Madame, thank you very much. And oh, could you tell us your last names, for our records?"

"Sure, it's Pelletier, both of us, no secret about that," replied the old woman proudly. "Been married for sixty-two years!"

"Right, Herbert and Eloise Pelletier, thank you again," replied du Maurier with a smile. "Please enjoy the rest of your day. Good-bye now."

"Eh?"

"Shut up, old man!"

Petrie and du Maurier then retraced their steps by walking south beside the tracks. Beau and Theo had finished setting up their camp for the night. Their two helpers were both pleased to hear that they were in a good spot to top up on their supplies. They grabbed some empty wooden boxes and walked north to visit the store.

When Beau and Theo were out of hearing range, Petrie said, "So, Adams and Groseilliers are heading for Schefferville, Sergeant. And that means we'll have to keep using our two Sept-Isles helpers and their rinky-dink steam locomotive to continue the pursuit."

"Yes, Commandant. On the plus side, we won't have to figure out a way to travel east or west, by using roads, or trails."

"Right, Sergeant. Now, how do we handle Beau and Theo?"

"I think we should bump up their completion bonus to fifty dollars each, Commandant, to keep taking us north. But we should also tell them we may have to go all the way to Kuujjuaq.

"Then they'll probably tell us to get stuffed, Commandant. If so, I think you should show them your letter from the president.

"Then if they still flatly refuse, well, then we'll both take out our hand guns, and tell them they can go to jail, or be shot, or they can take us as far as Kuujjuaq. I suspect they'll eventually agree with our point of view, sir."

"Yes, very good plan, Sergeant, as always."

48

As it turned out, Commandant Petrie and Sergeant du Maurier did not have to draw their guns on their two helpers from Sept-Isles. Petrie did not even have to show them his letter from the president. He just reiterated that their mission was viewed as critically important by the president, and that it was everyone's duty to see it through to the end, no matter how difficult the job might prove to be. And he told them that he had just bumped their round-trip completion bonus to one hundred dollars per man.

But their relationship with Beau and Theo changed as they travelled further north of New Emeril.

The further north they went, the more anxious Beau and Theo appeared to be. They looked worried all the time about what might be going on in their wilderness surroundings. And the two men began taking turns keeping watch at night while tightly holding on to their loaded, single-barrel shotgun.

And their friendly banter and joke-telling completely disappeared.

Du Maurier picked up on the change, and shared his concerns with Petrie. Petrie replied, "Well, now that you mention it, they have seemed rather subdued lately.

Is there something we can do about that, to keep up their morale?"

"Yes, Commandant. I think we should both take a turn on guard duty at night with them. They admitted to me just now that they have never been north of New Emeril. So, they might have some good reasons to be concerned. The land is getting wilder all of the time. If we share all the workload with them, even the night watchman duty, we'll all be better rested to be able to complete this pursuit, or apprehension, or investigation, whatever it is."

"Okay, Sergeant, that's another good suggestion. Let's go tell them."

They finally reached the southern outskirts of the little Cree community nestled within the ruins of old Schefferville in the late afternoon on Tuesday, May 23.

They were all dead tired. On the trip from New Emeril, they had to disassemble, manhandle and then re-assemble the two carts two times to get past impassable sections of track. And one of those impassable sections had been about two hundred yards in length.

But the carts were holding up well. They were well designed, and well made. But the four men were running a bit short on a few supplies.

Beau and Theo began to set up their camp beside the tracks. Petrie and du Maurier walked ahead to the north into the village. Two brave and curious teenage girls walked right up to them and asked them who they were. The two officers showed them their ID cards, and du Maurier asked the girls if there was a store in the village. The girls then led them to the same cabin that Matt Adams and Suzanne Groseilliers had visited on Thursday, May 18.

A teenage boy was the only person in the cabin. Everyone else had not yet returned from a fishing trip. The two officers stood just outside the cabin door, and showed the obviously frightened boy their ID cards. The boy just glanced at their cards. He could not keep his eyes off of their holstered automatic hand guns.

Then du Maurier described the two people they were pursuing. The boy said he remembered them very well, having passed through the town five days before, heading north. He told them that they had bought some stuff from the store, mostly food items, using cash. Then he added that they had said they were going to Kuujjuaq.

Du Maurier then asked the boy if they could have a quick look at the stuff available in the store. The boy led them to the neighbouring shed. While they were looking around, an old woman stormed into the shed. She yelled something at the boy. Du Maurier recognized the language as Cree, but he only knew a few words. The boy yelled something back, and pointed at Petrie's holstered hand gun.

The woman then turned her attention to the two officers. Then she growled angrily, "We don't serve your kind here. So get out."

Du Maurier replied calmly, "And what kind would that be, Madame?"

"The white, thieving, government kind."

"Well, we are white, and we are government, that is true. But we are not thieves. We pay cash."

"Your cash isn't any good here. And I won't trade with you."

"You will be civil with us, Madame, and sell us the bit of stuff we need to continue our mission of keeping the peace. Or, I assure you, we will use appropriate force with you. And you will be arrested when we come back through here again, heading south."

The woman looked like she was about to lunge at du Maurier. But the boy grabbed her by the arm, and yelled something angrily in Cree at her. Then she looked completely exasperated, stared hard at the two officers for a long moment, and then mumbled something to the boy. Then she turned and stomped out of the shed.

A few moments after she had left, the boy took a deep breath, smiled and said, "She said to deal with you myself. She's never let me do that before. And she said to be quick about it."

"Did she treat the two people we are looking for the same way?" asked Petrie.

"No, but she was pretty short with them. You see, she hates white people. And Inuit people. And bad dogs. And pesky bears. I think she has had a lot of bad experiences."

Du Maurier smiled, and said quietly, "Okay, well, hard times do make people hit out impulsively, especially at strangers. But it's dangerous and foolish to hit out at VPF officers. Please keep telling her that.

"Now, we *will* be quick about it. We'll need a box to hold the stuff we'll buy from you, and we'll pay for that box, too. And rest assured, young man, that we'll pay a fair price."

The boy looked happier suddenly, and went to fetch an empty wooden box from the neighbouring cabin.

49

Matt Adams and Suzanne Groseilliers finally arrived in Kuujjuaq in the middle of the morning on Thursday, May 25.

They were both physically fatigued, but surprisingly healthy. They had many black fly and mosquito bites, and a few bruises and scratches. But they had bathed regularly, and they were in good spirits. Matt had a thick brown beard, but Suzanne had trimmed it for him regularly with a pair of scissors. She had also neatly trimmed his brown hair, and had successfully coached him through the trimming of her own thick, dark brown hair

Matt thought he had read once that Kuujjuaq had for centuries been at the very edge of the tundra. He was very pleased to see that Kuujjuaq was now completely surrounded by a thick, heavily-undergrown, boreal forest. There seemed to be vibrant, new growth everywhere.

He could also see that they could not easily travel any further to the north even if they had wanted to, unless they travelled by canoe down the Koksoak River to the sea. And only narrow, boggy trails led off to the east and west of the village.

Matt and Suzanne had talked at length during the last leg of their journey about what to do next. Ultimately, they had both agreed to 'make a stand' in Kuujjuaq. If the VPF somehow found out where they were, well, they would just have to deal with that at the time.

But there would be no more running away. And Matt was not going to resist capture.

Matt had told Suzanne that he was simply not going to kill another person, ever. He told her that he had, 'done more than enough killing in that damn, stupid and pointless war with Central America.' And he told her again that he had killed Ernie Wolf to give Americans the opportunity to move away from fascism and racism, for a little while anyway. And he stressed he also did it to save the *Second Chance* project, but also maybe just for a little while.

Matt helped Suzanne set up their evening camp at the southwest edge of the village. When she told him that she could handle the rest of the well-practised ordeal, he rode his bike north on what looked to be an old concrete road. He decided to head towards a tall tower in the northeast. As he got closer, he could see that the tower was in the midst of a few cabins.

There were a few people walking about. They looked to be Inuit-Metis. Most people gave him a wide berth, with their eyes averted, but some people smiled and waved at him. So, he waved back and smiled at those people.

There was a well-made, tidy-looking cabin right next to the tower. An old sign above the front door of the cabin read 'US Depot Kuujjuaq'. There was a straight, intact aerial on top of the tower. And there were solar cells on the roof of the cabin that looked to be in pretty fair shape.

Matt knocked on the door of the cabin. The door was opened by a rather short, older man, with a nicely-trimmed grey beard. The man greeted him with a smile, but his smile quickly changed into a frown, and then a look of concern or worry on his wrinkly face. Matt immediately wondered if the man had recognized him, somehow.

After a long moment, the man said quietly, "I think you should come inside, sir. I think I know who you are. But let's not say, or do, anything rash. Come, come in, yes that's great. And sit over there, yes, and I'll go back behind my official looking desk."

When they were seated facing each other across the old wooden desk in the cabin, the man flipped through some documents stacked high on the desk, apparently found the one he wanted, and handed it to Matt. Then he asked, "Is that you, sir?"

The document looked like an old Wild West wanted poster. There was a prominent black-and-white image of his face in the centre of the document. It looked like a rather crude copy of a digital photograph that was taken of him in El Paso the day he had accepted the spy job in Akron. He was wearing an eyepatch in the image. But there was a close enough resemblance otherwise.

The caption below the image simply read, *'Mathieu 'Matt' Adams. Wanted for questioning by Commandant Petrie of the Cleveland, Ohio VPF. If you see this man, please notify your nearest VPF detachment.'*

Matt handed the document back to the older man on the other side of the desk. Then he took a deep, slow breath and said clearly, "Yes, I am Mathieu Adams."

The man nodded slowly, and then he looked steadily into Matt's eyes for a long moment. Then he said calmly, "I am not a VPF officer, Mister Adams. I guess I'm what you might call a government depot chief. But there are no people to boss around in this job. I'm a one-man show here, and the chief of nothing, really. But I *am* the elected mayor of the two hundred or so mostly Metis and Inuit people that still live in Kuujjuaq. My name is Sammy Gadbois. You can call me Sam."

"Now, are you a fugitive, Mister Mathieu Adams?"

"Please call me Matt, Sam, just Matt. It looks like I may be considered a fugitive by the VPF, but the all-points bulletin you just showed me is not clear about that. I do not have a criminal record, and I have never been charged with anything."

"Are you dangerous, Matt? I am unarmed."

"No, Sam, my dangerous days are over with."

Then Matt decided to trust Sam Gadbois, and give him a sense of who he was as a person. He smiled, and said, "I grew up in Baie-Comeau, Sam, and worked as a seaman for a couple of years, on the Great Lakes. I'm also a US Army veteran, who just wants to start a new life somewhere. Actually, right here, if I can.

"I have a lady friend with me, Suzanne Groseilliers. We'll get married when we can. I met her in Relais-Gabriel. We rode our bikes all the way from there. The last long bit was along the old railway from New Emeril. We just arrived here. Suzanne is finishing up a lean-to shelter for us on the southwest edge of the concrete road, or whatever it is, or was."

"It's an old runway, for airplanes, Matt. This used to be the Kuujjuaq Airport. The Americans actually built the first airbase here in the Second World War, when this place was called Fort Chimo. And they built a US Army base here too, I guess to protect the airbase. Then they gave it all to Canada after the war. And now, it's all American again, since Canada was assimilated by the US.

"Our airport shut down a long time ago, with other airports. And this place has been in steady decline since the port and the railway closed. Young people move away if they can. Many people have returned to ancient Inuit or Cree ways."

The man looked at Matt for another long moment. Then he looked sad, and said, "Matt, I have to tell the VPF that you're here. It's my job."

"I know, Sam. You have to do what you have to do. How will you contact them?"

"By radio-telephone, Matt. The message will be relayed along coastal depots. They are all solar-powered, like this one is, with batteries. But it will take a good long while to get to, let's see, Quebec City, I guess. The government is tied into the hard-wired telephone grid from there. So, you probably will have a bit of time before the VPF arrives all the way up here in Kuujjuaq.

"I don't know how they will get here, actually. They might come the same way you just did. Or they might come by boat, I suppose. The Navy and the Coast Guard used to come here, years ago, occasionally. But those armed forces are now not what they used to be, not by a long stretch.

"The last time the VPF, or before that the FBI or the Department of Homeland Security, sent an officer or an agent here was when they trained me to do this job. And that guy was dropped off at the mouth of the Koksoak River by a Coast Guard cutter. He finished the journey here in a freight canoe. You see, the dredged channel in the river silted-up long ago. And huge spring floods once again change the character of the river every year. It's really only navigable by canoe.

"Now, what were you hoping to do here, Matt, with Suzanne?"

"Well, we both grew up in the bush. So, we can hunt and fish and look after ourselves all right. And I can trap and cure furs and leather. But what we really want to do is build a farm, by maybe starting with some market gardening. And Suzanne is a pretty good school teacher."

"Now, we could really use a school teacher. We haven't had one for years, but we still have a school house, of sorts. A re-opened school might induce young families to stick around, too. But I'm not sure we could pay Suzanne much, though.

"Your farm idea is quite ambitious, Matt. The soil is weak and acidic, or even non-existent here, in many places. But the climate has really changed, for the better thankfully, even quite a noticeable bit during my lifetime. So, maybe you could make that happen, with a lot of hard work and perseverance?

"But I may be able to suggest an alternative for you, or something you could possibly work at in parallel. This would be something that could give you a bit of income, maybe, and an angle on some land.

"We have one blacksmith here, a man named Peter Tagoona. He's a crusty old man, not like me, a nice old man." He laughed at his own little joke, and then he added, "Peter needs to train somebody to take over his business. None of our young people want anything to do with him. But I bet you're tough enough to stand up to him, and to learn his craft. You certainly look to have the physical strength to learn how to be a blacksmith.

"Peter has his forge about half a mile away from here, closer to the river and the old port facilities. He also owns a whole bunch of land near his forge, in what used to be Aqpik Park. It's all just wilderness now. Peter has never done anything with it. It's on our side of the river, opposite Grande île Elbow. I bet if you could get along well enough with Peter, he might rent you a good chunk of that land. Or, maybe in time, even sell some of it to you.

"So, if you're interested, I can take you around to Peter's shop tomorrow morning, at say nine o'clock?"

"That would be great, Sam. Thank you very much."

"Okay, it's a deal." Then Sam scratched his chin while thinking, and said, "You know, Matt, there is a family named Adams here. Their ancestors have been here a long time. Is there any chance you could be related to them?"

"I think it could only be a very distant relationship, Sam, if it were so."

"Okay, I just thought I would ask. Now, you better leave me alone again, Matt, so I can send a message out about you.

"And, Matt, I hope you are not in any serious trouble. I think you and Suzanne will be most welcome here. I, for one, would like you to stay, and try to make a serious go of it."

"Thanks again, Sam. See you tomorrow morning."

50

Sam Gadbois and Matt Adams arrived together at Peter Tagoona's blacksmith shop at nine o'clock in the morning on Friday, May 26. There was a lot of white and black smoke coming out of a stone chimney that extended high up over the centre of the cabin's rusty, sheet-metal, gable roof. There were vents along the peak of the roof, and it looked like turbulent air was flowing out of them.

The front door of the large cabin was wide open, as were all of the windows, and a back door. So, Sam and Matt simply walked into the place without knocking.

It was very warm inside. There was a forging oven blazing away in the centre of the place, with anvils and metal tools of all descriptions arranged in bunches nearby, and a steel tub full of water. It was unclear to Matt what the blacksmith was currently trying to make. There were bits of rusty metal of various shapes and sizes stacked up around the cabin, and a whole lot more bits of steel or iron out back. An old man, presumably the blacksmith, was shovelling what looked to be lumps of charcoal into the firebox of the oven.

Sam and Matt waited patiently until the old man noticed their presence. When he finally looked over at them, he threw two more shovel loads of black lumps into the oven, and closed the firebox door. Then he motioned for Sam and Matt to follow him outside through the back door.

They stood beside a pile of charcoal. The old man nodded respectfully at Sam, and looked long and hard at Matt, up and down. Then he growled, "Morning, Sam. Can't say that I know your large friend here. He's got lots of scars. Is he a scrapper?"

"This is Mathieu Adams, Peter," replied Sam pleasantly. "He goes by the name of Matt. He's a war veteran. He's almost thirty-five years old, but that means he's mature and very serious about life. He has just arrived in Kuujjuaq, with his wife or partner, Suzanne Groseilliers. They want to live here. Matt could really use a job, Peter, and we were wondering if you would consider taking him on as an apprentice."

Peter sniffed a few times, then he spat on the ground. Then he once again looked hard at Matt, up and down a few times. And then he growled, "Well, he looks strong enough. But looks can be deceiving. The proof is in the pudding, as they say. Just have to start him out on something tough but necessary to find out, I suppose."

Peter sniffed and spat again. Then he asked gruffly, "Know anything about blacksmithing, Matt?"

"No, sir."

"How about making charcoal?"

"A little. I helped my dad make some once, in Baie-Comeau, where I grew up."

"Well that's something, I guess. I have to use charcoal, no coal around here. And I have to make it all myself. Nobody else uses the stuff. And I'm pretty picky about quality, with everything I do. That's how I've stayed in business so long. My charcoal has to be made just a certain way so I can in turn blacksmith just a certain way, which happens to be the right way.

"I don't cast anything. Everything I make is all forged, with a hammer on an anvil. It's hard, hot work, and you better like to sweat. I make it strong with quenching and tempering. That's an art, and it takes years of practice to get it all right. You'll have to have patience, and put up with a lot of guff from me if you want to be a proper blacksmith.

"There's still lots of scrap steel down at the old dock, from old cranes and such. Some day my local supply will run out, but then there will be all of those otherwise useless rail tracks to use. I have a two-wheeled cart you pull by hand to gather the steel and charcoal I need. With my arthritis, I've had to pay a big moron of a man to do that for me lately. It's simple work, but he still screws it up. So, that would be one of your jobs, if I take you on.

"Pay will be half minimum wage until I see what you can do. Then minimum wage. Then, well, if you really take to the trade, I'll consider making you a partner, I suppose. I'd like to retire someday, maybe in a year or two.

"So, what do you say, Matt? Interested?"

"Yes, sir, very much so."

"Got a place to stay?"

"We built a lean-to at the southwest edge of town, near the end of the old runway."

"Too far away. There's a clearing upwind of the charcoal piles. Stream right beside it. You can set up a proper camp there. I'll let you build a cabin there, too, if you make the grade up to minimum wage. Won't charge you no rent."

"Okay, thanks very much, sir."

"Okay, too. Call me Peter. Want to get started?"

"Yes, Peter."

"Okay, follow me further out back. I'll get you started on a new charcoal pile, and leave you to it to see how you handle it. Thanks for bringing him around, Sam."

Sam slapped Matt on his back, and whispered, "Good luck!"

Matt shook Sam's hand, smiled and whispered, "Thanks!" And then he ran to catch up with Peter.

51

Commandant Petrie and Sergeant du Maurier finally arrived in the village of Kuujjuaq around mid-morning on Wednesday, May 31.

They asked Beau and Theo to stop 'the train' about hundred yards from a cabin that was adjacent to a tall tower. Village people seemed completely disinterested in their noisy, smoky arrival, and stayed well away from them.

Du Maurier told Petrie that the local people may have just been frightened by the amazing arrival of loud, ancient technology in their isolated village. Du Maurier speculated that no local people had ever imagined that a machine could deliver a couple of armed police officers to their village at the edge of the Arctic Circle. Du Maurier also told Petrie that he suspected the cabin next to the tall tower might still be a working government depot.

The final leg of their trip was delayed five times when Beau and Theo said they had to make critical repairs to the structure of the two carts, or to the boiler, or to the firebox, or to the steam engine. They had continually complained that the extremely long trip, and the lack of time allowed for routine maintenance, had caused the myriad of problems they claimed to be experiencing.

Both Petrie and du Maurier strongly suspected their two helpers were just working a ploy to add a few more paid days to their final tab. Du Maurier fearlessly predicted they would experience nothing but clear sailing on the homeward leg when Beau and Theo started thinking earnestly, and perhaps more lustfully, about getting home. Petrie agreed with his prediction.

The abandoned railroad from Schefferville to Kuujjuaq had appeared to be newer, and the intentionally-designed slop in the wheels of the carts had compensated effectively for the bits of uneven wobble in the tracks. In fact, on the last leg of their journey, they did not have to take the carts apart even once to haul them in pieces past unacceptably bad sections of track.

Petrie and du Maurier left Beau and Theo to set up their evening camp. The two officers were wearing their grimy, mud-spattered and now tattered VPF coveralls, and their side arms. They walked over to the cabin beside the tall tower, and knocked on the door.

The door was opened by a rather short, older man, with a nicely trimmed grey beard. The man greeted them with a smile, but his smile quickly changed into a look of utter disbelief.

After a long moment, the man seemed to recover a bit, and he said quietly, "I am the government depot chief here, Sam Gadbois. I think both of you gentleman should come inside now, so we can talk privately. Come, come in, yes that's great. And sit over there, yes, and I'll go back behind my official looking desk."

They sat down on hard wooden chairs on opposite sides of the cluttered old desk inside the cabin. Sam flipped through some documents stacked on his desk, apparently found the one he wanted, and handed it to Petrie. Then he asked, "Are you the Commandant Petrie that is mentioned in this all-points bulletin?"

Petrie glanced at the document quickly, and then replied with suppressed excitement, "Yes, why?"

"Because the man you want to talk with, Commandant, arrived here last week, on Thursday, May 25, with a lady friend. I first talked with Matt on that very day, in this office."

"I am Sergeant Maurice du Maurier, Sam. Where is he now, this Mathieu Adams fellow?"

"He's still here, in Kuujjuaq, Sergeant. I helped him get a job as an apprentice blacksmith. And I helped his girlfriend, Suzanne Groseilliers, get a probationary teaching job."

Then Sam looked quickly at both officers, and said with unrestrained amazement, "But first tell me, please, how did you get here so fast? I only sent the alert notice out by the coastal radio-telephone relay network six days ago!"

"We have been travelling in the bush for over two weeks, Sam," replied Petrie, trying hard to restrain his pride in what they had accomplished. "We had no way to know about your alert. I have been on Adams' trail since May 5. Sergeant du Maurier joined me on May 8, in Quebec City."

"Still, you have done remarkably well to get here so fast."

"Thank you, but we are just doing our jobs, Depot Chief," replied Petrie in a cavalier manner. But he was a vain man, and the praise made him glow warmly inside.

"Did you tell Matt Adams that you recognized him, Sam?" asked du Maurier immediately. He was not impressed by the way his temporary boss dealt with strangers, even obviously decent, honest strangers.

"Yes, I showed him the all-points bulletin, Sergeant, and Commandant."

"Did he threaten you in any way, Sam?" asked du Maurier with genuine concern. "How did he react?"

"No, he said he was, quote, 'no longer a dangerous man.' He said he grew up in Baie-Comeau, and worked as a seaman for a while. He also said he was a US Army veteran, who just wanted to start a new life somewhere. Actually, he said he wanted to live right here, in Kuujjuaq.

"He told me he was going to marry Suzanne Groseilliers. He said he met her in Relais-Gabriel. He said they rode their bikes all the way from there. The last leg of their trip was along the old railway from New Emeril. They built a lean-to shelter on the southwest edge of the concrete road you've probably seen. But they've just re-located their camp to a clearing behind Peter Tagoona's blacksmith shop. I can take you there, if you would like."

"No, Sam, I think you should stay here tonight, and draw us a little map right now of how to get there, and what the lay of the land looks like," replied du Maurier. Then he wondered if he had over-stepped his authority, and asked, "Right, Commandant?"

"Yes, ah, that's right. They have a shotgun and a rifle, we believe. And we don't know how they will react when we show up to talk to them."

"They both struck me as decent, hard-working people, for what that's worth," offered Sam quietly. "I hope Matt Adams has not done anything really bad…?"

"We can't talk about that, it's a state secret," snapped Petrie. "But we will employ standard approach and arrest procedures, the same tactics we use to apprehend armed criminals. Better to use caution and even excessive force initially and apologise later, if necessary.

"You see, Mathieu Adams was awarded a dozen medals, including the Congressional Medal of Honour, and three Purple Hearts. He cannot be treated lightly."

"The Medal of Honour!" exclaimed du Maurier with genuine awe.

"And three Purple Hearts," added Gadbois quietly, who was happily dumbfounded. His already favourable opinion of Matt Adams just shot through the roof.

"Yes, a rather unsung hero of the last war, it seems," replied Petrie briskly. "But we must keep that information to ourselves, all of us. Now, please work on that map for us, Sam."

52

It was early in the evening on Wednesday, May 31. Matt Adams had just washed himself clean of charcoal soot down at the little stream beside the clearing. Suzanne was just putting the finishing touches on a moose stew.

They had built a wide lean-to shelter, with additional vertical front and side walls on it to block the wind a bit more. And they had staked out where they were going to build a cabin someday in the clearing. And there were slabs of moose meat hanging at the edge of the clearing from a high tree limb. Matt had shot the cow animal with his rifle two days before, then skinned and quartered it.

Suddenly, they both heard the sharp snap of a branch breaking in the woods nearby. They leapt to their feet, and Suzanne moved quickly to grab her shotgun.

"Freeze!" they heard from within the trees nearby on their right. Then they heard another male voice yell, "Don't even flinch!" from somewhere in the trees on their left.

A man suddenly appeared from their right side. He was pointing an automatic hand gun at Suzanne's head, while sighting along the top of the weapon with his arms fully extended.

Another man approached slowly and carefully from their left side. He was pointing an identical weapon in the same manner at Matt's head.

"We're with the VPF!" yelled the man on the right. "Move away from that gun, Madame. Okay, now lay face down on the ground, arms and legs spread wide. That's it. Now, lay still."

"You too, Mister!" yelled the officer on the left.

When Matt and Suzanne were both lying flat out on the ground, the two VPF officers approached them quickly, pulled their arms to their backs, and placed hand cuffs on their wrists. The officer tending to Matt yelled, "Check the lean-to out, Sergeant! They should have a rifle as well as a shotgun with them."

A moment later the other officer yelled, "Got the guns, Commandant! The site is secure."

"Right, search the woman, Sergeant, I'll search the man."

Matt and Suzanne were helped to their feet, and then methodically searched from head to toe.

"She's clean, Commandant!"

"He is too, Sergeant. Okay, sit her down again by the lean-to, while I have a private chat with this fellow. You first, buddy, start walking in the direction of the blacksmith shop. Watch your step."

When they reached the edge of the clearing, the officer with Matt said, "Okay, that's far enough. Sit on that stump right there, sir. Here, I'll give you a hand.

That's great. Now I'll sit over here, on this stump. And we'll have a nice little chat.

"I'm..."

"Let me guess, Veterans Police Force Commandant Petrie, from Cleveland, Ohio."

"How did you know that?"

"Depot Chief Sam Gadbois showed me my 'wanted poster'."

"So you admit that you are Mathieu Adams?"

"Yes."

"And the woman is Suzanne Groseilliers?"

"Yes. Who is the other officer with you, Commandant?"

"Sergeant Maurice du Maurier, from the Quebec City detachment."

"You've both come a very long way, then. I can't believe you found me so fast."

Petrie smiled for the first time, and said proudly, "Well, we have our efficient, professional ways, Mathieu."

"Please call me Matt. How did you do it?"

"On May 5, I was commissioned by President Frank Palermo to track you down. I took an Air Force transport plane to Quebec City, where I recruited Sergeant du Maurier. We rode on a ferry boat to Baie-Comeau. We talked to your cousin Claude there. Then we rode a ferry boat to Sept-Isles. Then we rode a steam-powered railway cart right to Kuujjuaq. We arrived here this afternoon. And Depot Chief Sam Gadbois told us exactly where to find you."

"Impressive. Is Claude all right?"

"Yes, he's fine. He's a straight-shooter. You didn't make it easy for us, however."

"Frank Palermo is president now? I thought he was a secretary of state."

"He was. He took over when President Wolf was killed.

"Now, Mathieu, President Palermo has directed me to ask you a few questions. What we ultimately do with you, and with Suzanne, depends upon how you answer these questions.

"First question, did you kill President Ernie Wolf?"

"Yes."

Petrie looked completely stunned by the immediate, direct answer. Then he mumbled, "Why?"

"To keep him from blowing up Mexico City, and the *Second Chance* spaceship. And because he was a fascist bastard set on destroying what is left of our once-great country."

"Ah, okay. Next question then, who paid you to do it?"

"No one paid me, I volunteered. A social club in Akron, Ohio suggested the idea to me."

"Right, we know about that club. They are tied into a benevolent oligarch network. President Palermo is now part of that organization.

"Next question, what were you intending to do next, before we captured you?"

"Live here. Make a life here, with Suzanne. Me as an apprentice blacksmith. Her as a schoolteacher. She just got a job with the village at half pay to see how it works out. And some day, we were going to build a farm right here, and raise some kids."

"You weren't going to run further away?"

"No, this is the end of the line for me, and Suzanne. We planned to live here and die here, one way or another."

Petrie paused for a long moment to consider Matt's blunt, non-evasive answers. Then he said quietly, "President Palermo wants to run the country like a business. That sort of means like a mafia family, only not in a truly criminal sense, except for some invisible and well-earned corruption, I suppose. He calls himself 'Don Palermo', you know, like the Godfather of the United States.

"The fascist organization is being dismantled. The president has made peace with all of the oligarchs, and has become one himself. He won't be blowing up Mexico City, or anywhere else for that matter. And he won't be blowing up the *Second Chance*. In fact, the US is now a joint venture partner in that massive project again.

"Don Palermo instructed me to tell you that he appreciates what you did, on a personal level. Ernie Wolf's assassination set the stage for him to assume the presidency, and put America back on track again. But no one must ever find out how it actually came about, who was behind it, and how it was done.

"So, next question, will you keep it a secret, forever?"

"Yes."

"Okay, last question then. Don Palermo would like you to be his friend. Will you be his friend?"

"Yes."

Petrie suddenly appeared to have had a great weight lifted from his shoulders. He straightened up, smiled and said, "That's great, Matt.

"With that successfully out of the way, President and Don Palermo further instructed me to tell you that he may never call upon you to help him, as his friend. But if that day should ever come, he knows you will not refuse to come immediately to his aid.

"Now, Matt, you also need to agree to stay right here, in Kuujjuaq, where Sam Gadbois can keep a close eye on you for us. If we ever hear from Sam that you have disappeared, well, Don Palermo will be very angry. And, rest assured Matt, when Don Palermo is angry, people die.

"So, one additional question, do you promise to stay right here?"

"Yes, until the day I die."

"Then that's it then, Matt.

"Oh, and I'll ask Sam Gadbois to help you fill out the right forms to get your veteran's pension started again. I can't promise you when cash will get all of the way up here. But maybe once a year by boat?

"Here, let me help you to stand up now, Matt. That's great, now let's go re-join the others."

When they got back to the lean-to, Petrie said pleasantly, "Okay stand her up, Sergeant, and be gentle about it. Okay, that's great. Now, take the cuffs off her, while I take the cuffs off Mister Adams here."

"What the…?"

"Just do it, Sergeant! That's an order."

Sergeant du Maurier could not believe what he had just been ordered to do. After all the intense effort to track down and apprehend this fugitive couple, it suddenly looked like they were going to be released!

But Maurice du Maurier was a good cop, who obeyed orders. So he took the handcuffs off Suzanne, while Petrie took the handcuffs off Matt.

Suzanne was crying now, from a mixture of fear and confusion. Matt swept her into his arms and whispered into her ear, "It's all right, baby. It's all over. And we're free. Free at last. As long as we stay here."

Petrie overheard what Matt said to Suzanne, and he confirmed with a smile, "Yes, you are both free, as long as you stay here.

"Orders from the president, Sergeant du Maurier. You did your duty, to the letter, and rest assured, the VPF will thank you for it. Now, come along, and we'll leave this fine young couple to enjoy the rest of their evening together."

Du Maurier's mouth was agape with confusion. Then after a long moment, he just shook his head a few times, shrugged, laughed awkwardly, and mumbled, "Man, a career in in the VPF is *full* of surprises."

"And we're both now going to have long careers in the VPF, Sergeant. Good evening folks."

Du Maurier managed to add politely with a smile, "*Bonne soiree, Madame et Monsieur.*"

53

Commandant Lamar Petrie and Sergeant Maurice du Maurier arrived back in Quebec City safe and sound on June 21, 2484. The logistics had worked a lot more smoothly on their return trip than on their outward-bound trip. But of course, they knew exactly where they were heading on their return adventure.

They discussed their trip at length with Commandant Bourassa. But all Petrie would say about the culmination of the pursuit was that, 'the suspect cooperated fully, and satisfactorily answered all of the questions that the president had instructed me to ask him.'

Bourassa was visibly angered by the complete redaction of that part of the investigation, but he was politically astute enough not to press the matter. He was even more angered when Petrie then asked if he could speak privately with the president over the telephone in Bourassa's own office. But once again, Bourassa decided to appease the arrogant visitor from Cleveland. He now just wanted to get him quickly and completely out of his hair.

Two hours later, the call was finally placed by Bourassa's staff, and Petrie found himself all alone in

Bourassa's office with the telephone receiver in his hand.

"This is President Palermo. Who am I talking to?

"This is Commandant Petrie, of the Cleveland VPF calling, Mister President."

"What, you're not still in Cleveland, I hope?"

"No, Mister President. I've just returned to Quebec City, where I made my base for the pursuit of Mathieu Adams."

"Oh right. Lamar isn't it?"

"Yes, Mister President."

"Look, Lamar, I've been rather busy lately. I still haven't got everything squared away yet. Sorry if I sound a little muddled."

"I understand, Mister President."

"So, did you locate this Adams fellow?"

"Yes, we found him in Kuujjuaq, Quebec, pretty well as far north as you can go in that state using summertime trails."

"Really? Never heard of it."

"Not many Americans have, Mister President."

"And you asked him all of my questions?"

"Yes, Mister President. He openly admitted to killing Ernie Wolf. He said he was trying to keep him from blowing up Mexico City and the *Second Chance*. And he said he wanted to give you a chance to save America from fascism."

"Good, good."

"He also said he's not a mercenary. He said he volunteered after the idea was suggested to him by the benevolent oligarch front in Akron."

"Okay..."

"He said he went to Kuujjuaq to start a new life. He said he never intended to go any further. He promised to stay right there for the rest of his life, and he knows that our man there will immediately alert us if he disappears from the scene."

"Good, good. What's he going to do there?"

"Our depot chief helped him get hired as an apprentice blacksmith. He met a woman while he was running away, a Miss Suzanne Groseilliers. She got hired as a probationary school teacher in the village. He said they're going to try to build a farm, too, and raise a family. I asked the depot chief to help him get his veterans pension started again."

"All right, so far. More tax payers, always good. Did you ask him if he'll be my friend?"

"Yes I did, Mister President. He said 'yes' without any hesitation. Then I told him you may call on his services some day. And that if he refused, or ran away from you, you would be very angry with him. I'm sure he understood the implications of you being angry with him. He seemed like a tough, smart, politically aware kind of fellow, for what my observations about human nature are worth to you."

"And he promised to keep everything secret, forever?"

"Yes, Mister President."

"All good, really good. Now, who did you involve in this operation, I mean people that may have some insight as to what it was all about?"

"Well, only two people really, but they would still have to make some educated guesses. I'm thinking specifically about VPF Commandant Gilbert Bourassa here in Quebec City, and the man he assigned to help me in the field, VPF Sergeant Maurice du Maurier. They both helped me out a lot, actually."

"Okay, well, I'll promote them both, and tell them about it in a personal letter. Then I'll tell them in the same letter to keep their mouths shut, forever.

"I've got the same issues with you now, Lamar. I don't believe you're my enemy, but I'm going to keep you really close to me anyway. Now, I'm still looking for someone to take over the leadership of the VPF. I used to do that job, if you remember. And I think I want a secretary of state, but only one. Any of those jobs interest you?"

"Er, ah, yes, Mister President. Those both would be fantastic promotions."

"Okay, then get your butt down to Washington right away. I know you're recently divorced, and don't need to be anywhere else. So, look me up in the White House. We'll talk. But I've got to run now. Later, Petrie."

Then the President abruptly hung up.

Petrie was reeling from all of the great news, and the imminent positive changes in his life.

Then he wondered with horror, *'how in the hell am I going to get to Washington, D.C.?'*

Then he starting wondering if the very astute Sergeant du Maurier would have some ideas about that. After a long pensive moment, he decided he would try him on, but also tell him about his pending promotion to lieutenant. Petrie thought du Maurier might need some additional coddling to agree to help the visiting Cleveland Commandant out *yet again*. The man had been subjected to a humiliating information black-out, and a lot of physical abuse, in the last month.

Then he reluctantly concluded that Maurice du Maurier had probably earned a lot more respect from the VPF, and from himself. Petrie was not a man noted for self-criticism, so the conclusion was remarkable.

Epilogue

President and Don Frank Palermo never called upon Mathieu Adams to perform a personal service for him, or for the United States.

The descendants of Mathieu and Suzanne Adams survived the horrible sacking of Kuujjuaq in 2794 by a marauding group of mutant bandits that attacked from the south. And much later, in the year 5144, descendants of Mathieu and Suzanne helped fend off a truly alien invasion. And then they went on to found the town of Notawa, the nucleus of a re-emergent, democratic America.